Hearts Afire

Helena's heart turned over at the sadness in his voice—the privations Major Brett Stanford must have endured were unimaginable.

"But at least you have lived," she said. It was a simple statement, quietly made, but he suddenly understood the frustration she must have been battling her entire life. What would he have done in her position? Gone mad, very likely. He rose, still holding her hand, pulled her up to face him, and replied, "You too are living now."

The look in his eyes made her heart pound. His touch made her skin tingle. Brett's other hand slowly traced the curve of her cheek and then gently cupped her chin. His lips touched hers gently, caressingly, then firmly as his arms slid around her waist and pulled her to him.

Helena's entire body seemed to burst into flame—like the blaze they had just witnessed. Yet, as unnerving as it was, it was also more exhilarating than anything she had ever experienced. He was right: she was alive, at last. . . .

A Foreign Affair

Evelyn Richardson

A SIGNET BOOK

> *For Bob, a man who brightened
> life for so many of us*

SIGNET
Published by New American Library, a division of
Penguin Putnam Inc., 375 Hudson Street,
New York, New York 10014, U.S.A.
Penguin Books Ltd, 80 Strand,
London WC2R 0RL, England
Penguin Books Australia Ltd, 250 Camberwell Road,
Camberwell, Victoria 3124, Australia
Penguin Books Canada Ltd, 10 Alcorn Avenue,
Toronto, Ontario, Canada M4V 3B2
Penguin Books (N.Z.) Ltd, Cnr Rosedale and Airborne Roads,
Albany, Auckland 1310, New Zealand

Penguin Books Ltd, Registered Offices:
Harmondsworth, Middlesex, England

First published by Signet, an imprint of New American Library,
a division of Penguin Putnam Inc.

First Printing, March 2003
10 9 8 7 6 5 4 3 2 1

PUBLISHER'S NOTE
This is a work of fiction. Names, characters, places, and incidents either are
the product of the author's imagination or are used fictitiously, and any resem-
blance to actual persons, living or dead, business establishments, events, or
locales is entirely coincidental.

Chapter One

The slanting rays of early morning sun filtered down between the high fronts of closely packed buildings as horse and rider picked their way through the narrow cobbled streets. Its golden light warmed the white stuccoed facades and threw into high relief the delicate baroque curves that distinguished the ornate Viennese architecture from the more stately classical lines found in Paris and London.

But neither horse nor rider had any thoughts to spare for architecture or ornament this morning. In fact, both of them were intent on escaping all the material relics of humanity as they made their way across the bridge over the Danube, and headed toward the liberating expanses of the Prater's meadows and parklands.

When they reached the entrance, the rider urged her mount to a brisker pace, and the animal, eager to gain the enormous park beyond, pricked up its ears and snorted eagerly.

Free of the confines of the city, Helena drew a deep breath, drinking in the tangy scent of autumn and the peaceful vista of trees and grass softened by the early morning haze. Of course, Vienna was small compared to Paris and London. Her mother's French maid was forever sneering at its cramped, twisting streets and unimpressive palaces, comparing it most unfavorably to her native Paris. Helena herself, drawing from dim childhood recollections of London, could agree with her mother when she labeled the Austrian capital *provincial* and called it hardly worthy of the great international Congress that was now being held in its crowded confines. Still, to someone who had spent the better part of her life roaming the countryside of Hohenbachern, with its rolling green hills dotted by rustic villages unchanged since the Middle Ages, Vienna seemed crowded and noisy by comparison, and their rooms, after the light, airy chambers of the Schloss von Hohenbachern, were dark and stuffy.

It was only these morning escapes to the solitude of the Prater, with its wide meadows and broad expanses of grass and trees, that kept Helena from losing her mind entirely. But she had promised her mother, and a promise was a promise even when it meant leaving the freedom and informality of life in Hohenbachern far behind.

When sovereigns, diplomats, and ministers from all over Europe had begun gathering in Vienna to reestablish order after years of war and upheaval, Helena had agreed to accompany her mother to the Austrian capital while her stepfather, the Prince von Hohenbachern, remained with his army on the Saxon border.

Flitting from one ball to another, dancing and flirting until dawn, the Princess von Hohenbachern was in her element, but her daughter, accustomed to the simple rural life at the schloss and the ebullient companionship of her young stepsisters, Sophie and Augusta, was overwhelmed and alienated by the atmosphere of frenzied gaiety, the hordes of foreign visitors crowding the capital, and the streets choked with horses, private equipages, and the three hundred extra coaches provided by the emperor for the comfort and convenience of his guests.

Helena and Nimrod reached the park's central tree-lined alley and, giving in to the pent-up energy that threatened to consume both of them, broke into a gallop. Oblivious to the few other riders who had ventured forth at such an early hour, they thundered to the end of the alley and were wheeling around when Helena's attention was caught by the sight of another horse and rider off to her right. "Whoa, Nimrod." She pulled hard on the reins. "I must have a closer look at this."

Halted in the midst of his liberating gallop, Nimrod snorted and tossed his head in disapproval at the rude interruption, but he obeyed his mistress' command well enough and halted at the edge of the dew-laden pasture.

Not a hundred yards in front of them, a magnificent black horse rose on its hind legs, pawing the air in front of it like the valiant steed of some ancient Teutonic knight, the Teutonic knights that had filled the stories Helena's nurse, Ursula, had told her every night before putting her to bed.

The sight of such a powerful animal balancing delicately on massive haunches was so astounding that it was some minutes before Helena was even aware of the rider on its back, and she held her breath in awe while he remained erect and unmoving as the horse, still on its hind legs, drew in its forelegs and slowly, deliberately pirouetted before dropping gracefully back to the ground.

It was only while the animal rested after its superlative effort and its rider leaned forward to pat his horse's neck that he appeared to be a separate human being rather than an integral part of the animal itself, like one of the centaurs of old. And it was only then that Helena noticed that the rider wore the bright red tunic of a British cavalry officer and not, as she had expected, the more sober uniform of one of the members of the Spanish riding school.

She watched in fascination as, pausing only to catch their breaths, man and horse proceeded through all the movements of the *haute école,* from *piaffe* to the higher stepping *passage,* to the leap of the *capriole* when, airborne for a moment, they were transformed in the observer's imagination from the centaur, Chiron, to the mythical flying horse Pegasus.

Helena had always considered herself to be a more than competent horsewoman. Certainly the cavalry officers who were her stepfather's frequent guests at the schloss had always been loud in their praise of her equestrian abilities, even when she had first arrived in

Hohenbachern with her mother at the tender age of ten. But her abilities paled in comparison to this man's.

Slowly, carefully, so as not to distract the horse and rider, and praying that the mist obscured them to some degree, she urged Nimrod forward to get a better look.

The rider's communication with his mount seemed nothing short of supernatural. He barely appeared to use the reins or even his heels, yet the horse responded to what must have been commands of some sort or another, for surely it could not perform such complicated maneuvers without some guidance from its master.

Helena remained rooted to the spot, transfixed by admiration for the horseman's skill until finally Nimrod, deprived of his promised exercise, began to fidget ever so slightly. "Be still, Nimrod," she admonished him, fearful that any movement on their part would break the concentration of the magnificent pair in front of them and ruin the magic of the moment. Then slowly and carefully she turned her horse around and keeping to the grass at the edge to muffle the sound of his hooves, she walked him slowly back down the alley.

Once out of earshot, however, Helena gave Nimrod his head and they flew back along the alley, kicking up clods of dirt behind them. When they reached the other end and slowed to a trot, it somehow seemed clumsy and awkward after the grace and skill of the other horse and rider. They wheeled and galloped back toward the horse and rider, stopping just out of earshot to turn and begin the gallop back down the alley.

Back and forth they rode until at last Helena saw the horse and rider make their own way toward the alley and, pulling Nimrod into the obscuring shade of the trees, she watched as they trotted slowly back toward the city.

Hidden from view and no longer distracted by the superb mount or the incredible feats of horsemanship, Helena was at last free to observe the rider himself. Almost as magnificent as the animal he rode, he sat erect, yet easily in the saddle. Such naturalness on the part of a man so tall and broad-shouldered could only mean that he had spent the better part of his life on the back of a horse. And what a horse it was, at least sixteen hands high, powerful, broad-chested, and black as night. In fact, from the little Helena could see of the rider's dark hair and aquiline profile as they passed her, it appeared that man and horse were not so very different from one another.

She finished her ride in a thoughtful mood suddenly dissatisfied with her own equestrian abilities. After such a display of horsemanship, every motion of hers seemed crude and clumsy in comparison with the smoothness, strength, and skill of the man who had just left the park.

Inspired by what she had seen, Helena remained in the Prater longer than usual trying her best to emulate the seemingly effortless communication between man and beast that she had just observed until at last, utterly exhausted by the exercise and the concentration it required, she turned back toward the city and the palace on the Bräunerstrasse, where she and her mother had been fortunate enough to get an entire floor to themselves. The rooms were elegantly decorated and well proportioned, and though they seemed a trifle cramped and overdecorated after the simple spacious salons of the Schloss von Hohenbachern, Helena knew they were lucky to find anything at all. They had only been able to find suitable quarters through the influence of her stepfather's childhood friend, Princess Elizabeth von Furstenberg, whose palace was just around the corner on the Graben.

The heavy wooden doors swung open as they arrived, and Helena handed Nimrod over to the stable boy, who had appeared the moment they entered the cobbled courtyard. Slowly she climbed the curving stone staircase to their quarters. Not for the first time, Helena blessed the Princess von Furstenberg for procuring them rooms on the first floor. Not only did they have larger windows and more light, their occupants faced much less of a climb than their neighbors who were crowded into the small dark rooms on the floors above them. After her strenuous morning, she was doubly glad of this.

Pulling off her hat and gloves, she headed straight for her own bedchamber, eager to shed her tight-fitting habit, but as she passed her mother's door, the princess' maid, Marie, beckoned to her. "Mademoiselle, Madame la Princesse is having her morning chocolate and she is waiting to speak to you.

Helena stifled a sigh of annoyance. "Very good, Marie. I shall go see her." Usually her mother, worn out by the gaiety of a previous evening, did not even rise until noon, which allowed her daughter plenty of time to ride, refresh herself, and dedicate a few uninterrupted hours to reading the *London Times,* and the Viennese papers.

Helena found her mother draped against piles of pillows, a cup of chocolate in one hand and a looking glass in the other. Tilting her head from side to side, the princess surveyed herself critically in the early morning light.

"No new wrinkles, I hope, Mama." Helena sat down on a blue damask settee at the foot of the ornate gilt bed.

Pushing back her lace-edged nightcap to check for signs of gray at her temples, the princess laid down the glass. "No, thank goodness, but one cannot be too careful, and morning light is the most revealing. It is better to discover one's own flaws first than to have them pointed out by somebody else later. Fortunately for all of us, social events occur in the more forgiving light of late afternoon and evening."

"I doubt that most women have your fortitude, Mama."

The princess shrugged. "It is merely a matter of practicality. Being a beauty is a serious business. One cannot simply leave it all to nature."

"Naturally not." Helena's eyes twinkled as she surveyed the array of vials and bottles on her mother's dressing table. No, the Princess von Hohenbachern left *nothing* to chance. Her lengthy toilettes were nothing if not thorough. "But tell me, Mama, how was the ball at the Hofburg last evening?" Helena knew her duty. A beauty's existence was sadly diminished if she had no one with whom to share her latest triumphs.

"A sad crush." The princess wrinkled her delicate nose. "In his anxiousness to offend no one, the emperor invited anyone and everyone. A person might as well have been consorting with the crowds in the streets, for that matter. There were petty secretaries rubbing elbows with princes of the blood and members of Europe's most ancient families all mixed together with *parvenus* of the lowest sort."

She shook her head at the folly of it and then brightened. "But I did meet a truly delightful member of the British delegation, a most charming man, and not at all what you would expect from *that* crowd. He possessed all the sophistication so notably lacking in that silly boy Stewart, and none of the reserve one finds so awkward in Castlereagh. Really, it is such a pity that the British could not find someone more sophisticated than Castlereagh to represent them at the Congress. He is simply no match for the likes of Talleyrand and Metternich— delightful gentlemen both of them. But *this* Englishman will do well, very well indeed. The Princess Bagration and the Duchess of Sagan think so at any rate; they were both vying for this attention as if he were the only man in the room, and making fools of themselves in the process." The princess could not hide a tiny triumphant smirk as she recalled the scene. "Naturally, he was charming to both of them, but it was clear where his interest lay. He danced both the waltz and the polonaise with me, and he hinted that he would be calling soon. No other woman at the Congress has been distinguished by such marked attention. I shall be the envy of them all."

"No other woman at the Congress has been distinguished by such marked attention? But, Mama, I thought you only met him last evening."

"Met him, yes. Julie Zichy introduced us last evening, but it is certainly not the first time I have laid eyes on him; everyone knows Major Lord Brett Stanford. He is a much sought after gentleman, and indeed, he dances divinely—so graceful, and such a fine figure of a man— but then, cavalry officers always do."

"He is a cavalry officer?" The image of one very skilled and athletic cavalry officer flashed before Helena's eyes. If her mother's cavalry officer were anything like the rider whose equestrian prowess she had witnessed in the Prater an hour ago, small wonder that all of Vienna, or at least its female contingent, was well aware of his presence.

"Yes, and quite a hero as well, if half of the stories

one hears are true. He was with Wellington in the Peninsula and then accompanied him to Paris."

"And what is this cavalry officer doing in Vienna besides inciting competition among its already highly competitive female population? I suppose he has something to offer beyond excellent dancing skills and flirtation."

"Really, Helena, you need not sound so scornful. These *dancing skills* and *flirtations,* as you call them, can have far-reaching consequences—not that *I* waste my time dabbling in politics, but others do. A few approving glances or encouraging smiles directed at the right person at the right time can be just as effective, if not more so, than all those everlastingly dull political discussions you attend at the Princess von Furstenberg's. And they are certainly far more amusing. As to what he is doing here, Julie Zichy says that Wellington made him his aide in Paris because he can write French as well as speak it, something that the rest of the British seem unable to do. And now, his skills are needed here. Can you credit it that not one other person among all those people attached to the British delegation can write in the language? Certainly, the man speaks it quite charmingly, and with all the courtesy of a Prince de Ligne or a Talleyrand. One wonders where he learned." The dreamy look that stole into the princess' eyes suggested that the French phrases over which the gentleman had such command were not only well spoken, but highly complimentary.

The princess paused to tilt her head back as Marie gently smoothed the miracle jelly her mistress had recently discovered on the princess' smooth white neck and shoulders. Composed of various herbs, moss, and honey, it was reputed to rejuvenate everything it touched; however, Helena, who watched idly as the maid applied the precious concoction, was not at all sure that the results were worth the extra hour a day this regime demanded. Her mother's skin was as flawless as it had always been, though nothing her daughter could say would ever convince the princess that even someone endowed with natural beauty should not be ever vigilant. "But, Mama, those discussions are at least interesting."

"I said *amusing,* love, not *interesting.* I am sure all the discussions at the princess' are very interesting, else you would not be there, but the rest of them are dull dogs indeed—von Schulenberg, Gartner, Gagern, and the others. If you do not have care, my dear, you will become as dull as they are."

"But I already am."

The princess waved away the maid's hand to look at her daughter, an expression of mingled exasperation and resignation in her soft blue eyes. But it was perfectly clear from the twinkle in Helena's own eyes that she did not consider the possibility to be the disaster that her mother did. "You need not give up so easily, love. If you just put your mind to it, you could be quite pretty."

"Really, Mama. Surely you do not believe that I would swallow such a plumper, even from you."

"Well, intriguing, then," the princess temporized. She should have known her daughter would cavil, for she had never been able to get away with telling anything but the absolute truth to Helena. Even at the tender age of four, her unnervingly clear-eyed daughter had been remarkably acute, and she had only grown more so in the intervening years. "You, I am sad to say, had the misfortune to inherit the Devereux features, which are handsome enough, but . . ."

"But not stunningly beautiful like the Chevenels. I know, Mama. My nose is too long and my . . ."

"Your nose is just right for your face, which is aquiline and delightfully refined. And if you did not drag your hair back in such an unbecoming knot, but allowed some curls to escape so as to soften the effect and call attention to the fineness of your eyes—but never mind, I can see that you are longing to be off to your musty old library and your boring newspapers. And I must continue with my toilette if I am to continue to hold the interest of the gallant major. I expect he will attend the reception this evening, where, if all goes well, I shall be universally acknowledged as his premier interest."

"I wish you luck, Mama, though I have always thought you far prettier than either the Princess Bagration or the Duchess of Sagan."

"Thank you, my dear. So do I." The princess winked impishly as her daughter rose to leave.

Chapter Two

But the Princess von Hohenbachern and her daughter were not the only ones who considered the princess' attractions superior to those of the many other beauties gracing the capital. Charles Stewart, standing with Castlereagh and other members of the British delegation at Metternich's customary Monday reception, surveyed the hordes of dignitaries and their wives with a dispassionate eye as they crowded into the Austrian chancellor's impressive quarters on the Ballhausplatz. Stewart, who had not the least interest in conversing with his half brother, or any of the other members of the British delegation, only had eyes for the female members of the assembly. After carefully scrutinizing all corners of the room, he leaned toward the fellow cavalry officer standing next to him.

"Damned fine-looking women, eh, Stanford? Have you ever seen so many beauties all in one place? But as usual, you have chosen the pick of the crop. The von Hohenbachern woman outshines 'em all; but, by God, they are something to behold. Old Capo d'Istria tells me that the tsar has even given names to them: Julie Zichy is the *Celestial Beauty,* Rosine Esterhazy the *Astonishing Beauty,* Caroline Scecheny the *Coquettish Beauty,* and of course everyone calls the Princess Bagration the *Naked Angel.* But to my way of thinking, the Princess von Hohenbachern is the choicest armful. She seems to think the same about you, lucky dog. Saw you dancing with her at the Hofburg the other evening, and she could not take her eyes off you."

"It is the uniform. No woman can resist a cavalry officer, and no one knows that better than you, sir."

"What? Oh, I should know, eh. Very witty, Stanford." Stewart clapped Brett on the shoulder approvingly. "You are a clever fellow. Women like a clever fellow too. You'll go far with 'em all. Mark my words."

He was not sure that he agreed entirely with Charles Stewart's prediction that he would go far with them all, but Major Lord Brett Stanford felt reasonably certain that he had made a most favorable impression on the lovely Louisa, Princess von Hohenbachern, and if he was not entirely mistaken, she was even now sending a most encouraging smile in his direction. "Well, I certainly shall try my best to entertain, sir. And at the moment I do believe that the Princess von Hohenbachern appears in dire need of amusing. If you will excuse me, sir . . ."

"Certainly. Go to her, lad." Stewart gave him another hearty buffet on the shoulder before turning to the Earl of Clancarty, standing on his other side. "Stanford was always a great one with the ladies. No matter where we were in the Peninsula, stinking village or provincial capital, from Lisbon to Madrid and every outpost in between, he always had a bevy of beauties clustering around him—got a silver tongue, that man, and he makes as fine a figure in the ballroom as he does on a horse. They simply cannot resist him, but they never attach his interest for very long either. Wherever he goes, he leaves a trail of disappointed hearts behind."

Meanwhile, the scourge of Peninsular ballrooms was attracting coquettish smiles and alluring glances from more than one admiring female as he made his way to the corner of the room where the Princess von Hohenbachern was seated with Julie Zichy and watching his progress with a good deal of satisfaction. The princess would have enjoyed the major for his looks and conversation alone, but the fact that any attention he paid to her made her the envy of nearly every female at the Austrian chancellor's reception only served to make him all the more attractive to her.

"Why, Major, how delightful to see you again. We

are fortunate indeed to be honored by your company. Members of the British delegation are always in much demand, especially those who speak French as charmingly as you do."

"You are too kind, Princess. But how do you know that I have not sought you out simply because you speak my native tongue?" Brett quirked a teasing dark eyebrow.

"Of course I do not, naughty man." But there was no doubt in the princess' mind as he bowed over her hand, holding it far longer than politeness required, that he was there because he found the Princess von Hohenbachern as attractive and intriguing as she found Major Lord Brett Stanford.

"What I do not understand, Princess von Hohenbachern, is why we members of the British delegation were not told that we had such a beautiful advocate amongst the confusing mass of sovereigns attending the Congress."

"Oh," the princess shrugged elegant white shoulders in a manner that had never failed to drive men to distraction, "I have not the least interest in political affairs, nor does the Prince von Hohenbachern. My husband is just a simple soldier who follows orders, and I"—she smiled a slow provocative smile—"am here because it is so very boring in the country, especially when he is off with his troops. And it is so very gay here in Vienna at the moment."

"Surely you must have *some* interest in the momentous affairs being decided here at the Congress," Brett probed. No one he had yet encountered, from the rulers who had traveled to Vienna from all over Europe to the doorkeepers at the palaces lining the Herrengasse, to innkeepers of the city's crowded hostelries or the strolling musicians who thronged the streets, was without some opinion at least as to how the map of Europe should be redrawn after the depredations of Napoleon.

Smiling, the princess shook her head. "Absolutely none."

Brett heaved an inward sigh of relief. When Wellington had called him into the library at the British embassy in Paris before Brett left for Vienna, he had particularly instructed his aide to keep an eye on the ladies. "Now, Stanford, I am ostensibly sending you to help out Castlereagh because you are so proficient at French, but I am also sending you because in the Peninsula you proved yourself to be an excellent observer. You are accustomed to assessing a situation quickly and reporting it accurately. I need to know what is going on in Vienna, and I need to hear it from someone I can rely on. And a good portion of what goes on does so in the salons of some of Europe's most influential and attractive women—the Princess Bagration, the Duchess of Sagan, the Countess Edmond de Talleyrand-Périgord. They have the ears of the most powerful men on the Continent, for it is in their company that these men discuss the issues of the moment.

"These women are very powerful in their own right, and they are more than willing to use their, ah, *charms* to sway some susceptible man to accomplish their own political ends. There are other women who, though not so obviously political, have equally powerful connections among the rulers and diplomats gathered in the city that they do not hesitate to use. All of them can be a fount of information to an attractive man who expresses an interest in such things.

"I expect you to express such an interest, Stanford. And the more attention you pay to the ladies, the less attention anyone will pay to you. I have it on the best authority that the Viennese consider Charles Stewart, who spends his entire time flirting, to be something of a joke, even if he is Castlereagh's half brother. You and I are rough soldiers to whom this all seems like so much tiresome intrigue. We have done our parts to win peace in Europe. It is now up to the diplomatic fellows to see that it remains that way. But I do need a good observer to be my eyes and ears there."

The duke did not miss the moment of hesitation before his aide had responded. *Very good, sir.* Wellington smiled sympathetically at Brett. "It may seem at present to lack all the excitement and the challenge we overcame in the Peninsula, but console yourself, lad, with the thought that there are some very lovely ladies attending the Congress—and the place is overrun with spies and informers of every description. I think that you will find in the long run that Vienna offers enough excitement even for a fire-eater like you."

The duke had been entirely correct. Vienna was a hot-bed of intrigue. The Austrians alone had increased their budget for informers fivefold, and spent lavishly for reports from chambermaids, scullions, toll keepers, and guards to such a degree that the members of the British delegation had all been instructed to burn the contents of their wastepaper baskets every evening without fail. In Vienna there was no such thing as an innocent question or a friendly remark, whether it came from the host who welcomed diners to Vienna's popular restaurant the Kaiserin von Oesterreich or the Danish countess sitting next to someone at a state dinner.

With the duke's instructions in the forefront of his mind, Brett had kept himself constantly on the alert, making note of every word that was uttered, every frown, every nod, every smile that gave a clue as to the speaker's particular interest in the political game being played out in the Austrian capital. And while he was listening to everything everyone else said, he was also trying to exert an equal amount of effort to guard his own words and expressions so as to reveal nothing to those who watched him with the same intensity as he watched them.

It was all very exhausting, and he had soon found himself in desperate need of distraction and diversion. Then his eye had fallen on the Princess von Hohenbach-ern one evening at a ball in the Hofburg. It was natural that he should notice her, for she was an outstandingly beautiful woman, even among a host of beautiful women, but beyond that, there was an air of lightheartedness and gaiety that captured his attention as she waltzed around the palace's ballroom in the arms of one partner after another. She was enjoying herself, truly enjoying herself, purely and simply enjoying herself and nothing more. Her eyes never sought out those of some delegate or another at the other side of the room as so many other women's did. She never seemed to pause and reflect on what had been said. Her partners were not noticeably attached to any particular delegation; sometimes they were French, sometimes Austrian, or German, or Russian or English. In fact, the only distinguishing characteristic among them was that they all danced extremely well and appeared to concentrate all their attention solely upon her.

After observing her closely for some time, Brett had begun to hope that the Princess von Hohenbachern was interested in nothing more than the pleasures to be found in the delightful give and take between an attractive man and an attractive woman who had the wit and sophistication to appreciate this repartee to the fullest. It was only when he had finally assured himself of this that he had asked Julie Zichy to introduce them, and he had been pleased to discover that the princess was as charming and delightful as he had hoped.

Brett had left the Hofburg, as dawn was breaking, in a very optimistic frame of mind, indeed. Not only had he discovered someone exquisitely beautiful who could enter into a flirtation in the spirit in which it was meant and who appeared to have no political connections or ambitions, but astoundingly enough, she had turned out to be a fellow countrywoman as well.

Having established all this, he now hastened to seek her out again at the earliest opportunity, and he smiled down at her with a good deal of satisfaction. "Then you are a most unusual lady indeed, for everyone in Vienna, even the lowliest chambermaid, appears to be utterly obsessed with politics."

The princess wrinkled her dainty nose. "People talk of nothing else; I am quite *ennuyée* with it all. Surely now that Napoleon has been safely dispatched, we can get back to enjoying ourselves and forget the unpleasant events of the last decade. Do you not think so, my lord?"

Brett smiled into the enormous cornflower-blue eyes. "I certainly hope so." His gaze traveled down to the parted lips, lingered for one delicious moment, then slid down the long slender column of her neck to the elegant white shoulders and back to the eyes, leaving no doubt in his partner's mind that he, for one, was quite ready to take her suggestion. "As someone who helped to dispatch the man, I assure you, I am more than ready to enjoy the fruits of my labor."

"Ah, then we must make sure that you have adequate

companionship. Nothing is very enjoyable if one is alone."

"Very true. And everything is more enjoyable when it is shared with a beautiful and charming woman."

A shiver of anticipation ran down the princess' spine. Ah, but the man was handsome with those high cheekbones, strong nose, and intensely blue eyes, eyes made to appear even more blue by the deeply tanned face. The way he looked at a woman made her feel utterly irresistible, made her feel as though he would do anything to win her. It had been a long time, a very long time, since the princess had flirted with such a man, and it made her feel ten years younger. Vienna was turning out to be better than she had dared hope. "A beautiful woman is nothing without a man to appreciate her," she murmured throatily.

"My feelings precisely. I am glad we are in such agreement, Princess. But the beautiful woman in this case is always surrounded by crowds of admirers—too much distraction for the true connoisseur. A true connoisseur of feminine charm and beauty needs peace and quiet to appreciate it properly, something like a carriage ride in the Prater tomorrow afternoon, perhaps, where there is nothing to keep him from concentrating entirely on the object of his admiration."

"Oh." One white hand flew to her throat. The man was not only divinely handsome, he was masterful as well, enough to make any woman's pulses beat faster, even a woman who had been the constant object of masculine attention and admiration from the moment of her come-out. "Oh yes. I shall look forward to it."

"And so shall I." A bow, the quick pressure of warm lips on the back or her hand, and he was gone, leaving her to look forward to the next day with breathless anticipation. Seated in a barouche next to the handsomest man in Vienna, who, being a cavalry officer was undoubtedly an excellent whip, she would be the envy of every female who saw her. It would serve to secure her reputation as one of the leading beauties of the Congress. No woman could have asked for anything more. The princess smiled happily to herself as she considered the delights that tomorrow offered.

Chapter Three

The princess rose earlier than usual the next morning and remained closeted with her maid for an inordinate amount of time, even for her. Orders were given that no one, not even her daughter, was allowed to interrupt her toilette as she prepared for the promised drive in the Prater.

Thus excused from her customary late morning chat with her mother, Helena hurriedly disposed of her habit after her ride and hastened to the library to take advantage of the extra free time. However, as she entered the cozy, book-lined room, a room she had come to look upon as her own private sanctuary, she was astounded to discover that it was already occupied. A tall dark-haired gentleman in a scarlet coat was there before her, perusing the shelves with a good deal of interest. His back was to her, and he was so intent upon examining the collection, her carefully chosen collection lovingly wrapped and carefully transported from the Schloss von Hohenbachern to Vienna, that he remained entirely oblivious of her presence as she entered the room.

It was not until she quickly exited and reentered, coughing politely, that he turned around. It was a simple enough movement, but executed with an athletic grace that struck a responsive chord in her memory—a memory of a horse and a rider who had moved as one, a certain morning in the Prater. A cavalry officer, her mother's cavalry officer, was the superb horseman who had caught her attention that morning and enraptured her with his prowess.

"Oh!" Helena dropped the copy of *Wiener Zeitung* she was clutching.

The officer bent quickly to retrieve it and handed it back to her, all in one fluid movement accompanied by a devastatingly attractive smile. *"Bonjour, mademoiselle."* Bright blue eyes swept over her, taking in every detail from head to toe with a look so intense that she was left feeling as though he had learned all there was to know about her in a single glance. *"Où se trouve ta maîtresse? J'attends la Princesse von Hohenbachern."*

Ta maîtresse! Helena looked down at her plain lavender-striped morning dress, which was utterly devoid of ornamentation except for the simple flounce around the hem. He was entirely correct; she did look like a fashionable lady's maid, she supposed. She glanced back at the major, who was looking at her expectantly. Her mother's description was all too accurate. Not only was he devastatingly handsome, his French, the little that she had heard of it, was exquisitely pronounced. "But of course, sir, I shall go fetch her this instant."

Helena could not help chuckling at his astonished expression upon being addressed in his native tongue. He recovered instantly, and executing a ruefully gallant bow, he apologized. "Ah, mademoiselle, forgive me. I had no idea you were British. Ordinarily it is only Frenchwomen who possess such a decided air of fashion."

"Why, thank you, sir." Helena curtsied with what she hoped was a properly maidlike and respectful air. "If you will excuse me now, sir, I shall get the princess."

"Thank you. Such a lovely day should not be wasted, though we have been exceedingly fortunate in the weather thus far. It has been exceptionally fine, don't you think?" He flashed her a singularly attractive smile that made her feel as though he actually cared what she herself thought about the weather in Vienna at that moment.

"Yes sir. I shall not be a minute, sir." Helena hurried out of the library, but as she closed the door behind her, she leaned against it struggling to gather her wits about her. Small wonder that her mother had chosen this man to be her latest flirt; he had charm by the barrelful—a charm that extended even to maids.

Left alone, Brett went back to examining the shelves: *Letters from Albion to a Friend on the Continent, An Inquiry Into the Nature and Causes of the Wealth of Nations, Advice to Young Ladies on the Improvement of the Mind.* Then there were titles by authors he recognized as German political theorists: Karl Freiherr von Stein's *Nassauer Denkschrift* and Gentz' *Fragmente aus der neuesten Geshchichte des politischen Gleichgewichts in Europa.* Brett let out a low whistle of surprise. These were not the books he would have expected to find lining the walls of a fashionable lady's library, especially a lady who professed to a profound disinterest in politics. Could he have been entirely mistaken in his view of the Princess von Hohenbachern as a delightfully and totally frivolous individual?

Certainly her maid was a sprightly creature. There had been an alertness about her, a knowing twinkle in her large hazel eyes, and a countenance that wore an unusually thoughtful expression for a woman of her station. In Brett's considerable experience, the maids usually resembled the mistresses; coquettish mistresses had coquettish maids while proper young ladies guarded their virtue and reputation with dragons of equally rigid propriety. Yet, the divinely lovely and coquettish princess was attended by someone who more nearly resembled a governess than a fashionable lady's maid.

It was an intriguing consideration, most intriguing, but it was also trouble. Was the Princess von Hohenbachern another one of Vienna's clever political ladies after all? Brett certainly hoped not, for he had been looking forward to giving himself up totally to lighthearted dalliance with a skilled coquette and indulging in the luxury of admiring a beautiful face without having to wonder what was going on in the mind behind it. Was he going to have to be on his guard with the Princess von Hohenbachern as well as everyone else? Was she also someone whose every word he should be remembering so that he could later transcribe it into one of the *flying dispatches* that were sent almost weekly to Paris for Wellington's perusal? Surely not. Surely his instincts about women, sharpened by years of experience, instincts which had never been wrong before, were not going to fail him now.

"Major." The princess, looking exquisite in a carriage dress of deep blue Gros de Naples and matching bonnet that enhanced the blue of her eyes, appeared minutes after her maid had left.

Eyeing her appreciatively, Brett relaxed at least a little. No woman who presented such a picture of perfection, as though she had just stepped out of the pages of *La Belle Assemblée* could have the time for anything but her toilette. Brett was well enough versed in the details of feminine dress to know that such a high degree of finish did not just happen. It took hours of preparation and attention to the smallest detail on the part of both mistress and maid. Once again, he wondered about the maid whose own costume and coiffure had been neat, but plain to the point of being nondescript. While such an unobtrusive appearance was highly desirable in a servant, it did strike him as odd that the personal attendant of someone as elegantly *à la mode* as the princess would not at least have some interest in such things herself.

However, there was little time for conjecture in the captivating presence of the Princess von Hohenbachern. She exclaimed over the carriage he had managed to procure for the drive, vowing that the equipage was vastly superior to any of the other vehicles making their way along the Jagerzeile toward the entrance to the Prater. And certainly no one else drove as well as the major. "But then, there is no better whip than an Englishman, and no one who handles his cattle as well as a cavalry officer. I count myself fortunate indeed in my escort, Major." The princess smiled up at Brett, allowing him to appreciate the full effect of the enchanting dimple in the corner of her mouth, and pressed against him just enough to make him aware of her voluptuous figure, yet not so much as to distract him from his driving.

It was another glorious autumn day, and the princess was delighted to observe that the Prater was full of carriages, none of which carried as handsome a pair as the Princess von Hohenbachern and Major Lord Brett Stanford. "You have made me the envy of all the ladies present, sir. I am indeed fortunate."

"That is most gracious of you, Princess, but I would venture to contradict you by asserting that it is the elegance of your person and your exquisite taste that inspire the envious glances cast in our direction, not my equipage."

"You are too kind, my lord. Such a rustic as I cannot begin to compare with the rest of the fashionable crowd that has descended upon the city."

"You, a rustic? I think not."

"Oh, but it is quite true." The princess sighed gently. "Since arriving in Europe I have spent my days immured in the country with only the servants for company. These dreadful wars have made it impossible to travel, and the prince has been off fighting for much of the time. He came to England directly after the Peace of Amiens was signed, and our courtship was a most whirlwind affair. We returned to the Continent soon after meeting one another, and no sooner had we returned than war broke out again. I have been a virtual widow since, living the quietest of lives in Hohenbachern and always in fear that I would wake up one morning to find the war on our very doorstep."

She pressed one gloved hand to her brow and was silent for a moment while she allowed him to imagine the loneliness of her pathetic existence. Then, brightening, she flashed Brett a dazzling smile. "So you can well understand, my dear major, why I am so delighted to be alive and well and in Vienna as we celebrate the peace that has finally descended on our poor countries. You must forgive me if I appear rather giddy with the relief of it all, but the strain of these past years has been considerable. And now all I wish to do is wipe away unpleasant memories by enjoying myself to the fullest. I thank you sincerely for your efforts to help me do so. It is such a lovely day; let us make the most of it."

And make the most of it they did. The princess was an amusing conversationalist who seemed to possess an endless fund of titillating gossip about anyone and everyone. There was no member of the august assemblage

gathered in Vienna too staid or too respectable not to
have some scandalous tidbit that she could relate about
them with her enchanting laugh and slyly infectious
smile.

"So you see, Major, we are all very gay here. In my
heedless youth, I sought this giddy sort of life to such
an extent that I was the despair of my parents. My first
husband was a most wild young man, a member of the
Prince Regent's set, though, of course, he was only the
Prince of Wales at the time, and we moved with a very
fast crowd indeed. But our activities then absolutely pale
in comparison to those now to be found here in Vienna.
Why, it is so frantic that it makes even my head spin."
She smiled ruefully, but, the sparkle in her eyes was a
very clear indication that she considered herself more
than equal to such a challenge.

"And the prince, your husband, does he not long to
share in all this gaiety with you?"

"Good heavens, no! He is far too serious for such
diversions. I am afraid he considers his wife to be a sadly
frivolous creature."

"But an exquisitely beautiful one. Such beauty should
not be hidden away in a country schloss, but displayed
in an arena worthy of it where it can be appreciated by
the rest of the world."

The appreciative gleam in the blue eyes smiling down
at her and the warmth in Brett's voice made the princess
shiver with delightful anticipation. Heavens, but the man
had a deliciously seductive way about him. "You flatter
me, Major. But the sad truth is that I *am* a sadly frivolous creature. I must have music and clever conversation
and lights and gaiety surrounding me, for what is the
purpose of life if one cannot enjoy it to its fullest?"

"What indeed?"

"There has, however, been little enough to enjoy as
of late with that Corsican monster making war all over
Europe. The terrors I have been through, the worry . . .
well"—she waved her hand dismissively—"that is all in
the past now and best forgotten. At least there is peace
on the Continent to a certain degree, but who knows if it
will endure? Even now the prince is off with his regiments
on the Polish border, ready to defend us should discussions

here not go well. Oh, these terrible times! I vow, I simply detest politics. But"—she brightened as she bestowed another dazzling smile on her companion—"I shall not repine. For the moment I am indeed fortunate to be so charmingly distracted, for which I thank you very much indeed."

Chapter Four

The day was so fine and the society so congenial that the drive lasted a good deal longer than either Brett or the princess had anticipated, and both parties returned to their respective lodgings more than satisfied with the outing and looking forward with agreeable anticipation.

The princess had been extremely pleased to note that she was indeed the envy of many women forced to ride in inferior equipages driven by men of inferior looks and only moderate ability.

And for his part, Brett had established to his complete satisfaction that the Princess von Hohenbachern was a woman whose sole occupation in life was the pursuit of amusement, and the more lighthearted the amusement, the better.

However, the next social event Brett was called on to attend had nothing to do with amusement and everything to do with duty. He had just returned from his morning ride in the Prater the following day and was on his way to his quarters to change when he was forestalled by a messenger from Castlereagh himself informing him that the foreign secretary wished to see him immediately in his study.

Castlereagh looked up from a pile of documents as Brett entered, his handsome narrow face wearing a grave expression, but then, Brett could not ever recall a time when the foreign secretary did not look grave. Certainly, as a man who felt himself responsible for helping to ensure that peace continued in Europe, Castlereagh had a perfect right to look grave.

"Ah, Stanford. Good of you to come so quickly. Sit down, man, sit down." The foreign secretary indicated a chair on the opposite side of his massive mahogany desk. "Now, Wellington has assured me, and I have also heard from others, that your command of the French language is excellent. You do not, by chance speak German, do you?"

Brett shook his head.

"Well, no matter. Most of the Germans, whenever anyone else is present, speak French anyway, rather badly, but at least comprehensibly. The thing is this. Our role here, as I see it, is to maintain the balance of power in Europe so that no one nation gains ascendancy over the others. We may have peace now, but it is an uneasy peace and war could break out again at any moment. The Prussians, for example, have territorial ambitions of their own. We all have witnessed their abominable imprisonment of the Saxon king, whose former support of Napoleon they are using as an excuse to take over his territory. I tell you, the Prussians are not entirely to be trusted. Besides that, members of our own Parliament, who rarely if ever concern themselves with European affairs, are now suddenly expressing a great deal of agitation over the fate of Saxony, which looks as though it will be annexed by Prussia unless we are able to stop it.

"The key question in all of this is where do the rest of the German sovereigns stand on the issue of Saxony and the future of the German states in general? My people tell me that these other German sovereigns spend endless hours discussing their future. Most of these dispossessed rulers lost their lands to Bonaparte, and now they look to the Treaty of Paris to reinstate them. This treaty insures that the German states will retain their independence, but they will be united by a federal tie. I need to know to whom they will look for leadership once their powers are reinstated and they form this federal tie. Will it be Austria or will it be Prussia? They are all minor players on their own, but together they are strong enough to present a real threat, and if they are ruled by Prussia, then Prussia may feel strong enough to ignore the rest of us and support Russia in its claim to Poland, which would unbalance the entire system.

"Already armies are massing on the Polish Saxon border, preparing to fight if need be. However, if the German states allow themselves to be led by Austria, which has far fewer territorial ambitions than Prussia, we are safe." Lost in thought, the foreign secretary gazed abstractedly out the window over the red-tiled rooftops of the city.

"But surely you must have some plan for seeing to it that Prussia does take over in this manner?" Brett was reasonably certain that the foreign secretary had not called a junior officer into his study to discuss his views on British diplomacy.

"Perhaps, but it is all such an impenetrable mess and the alliances are constantly shifting. Everyone here is continually striving to discover what everyone else is thinking, and this thinking itself changes from moment to moment. I am weary of it already, and we have only just begun. At any rate, I am sending Clancarty to a soiree tonight at the Princess von Furstenberg's, where the German sovereigns meet on a regular basis. Of all the members of our delegation, Clancarty understands European politics the best. His recent service in the Netherlands has made him see how crucial it is that no one foreign power grows too strong. He will know what to listen for, what to say, which dissatisfied German princeling he should remind that England, with its own strong connections to Hanover, possesses a great sympathy for German concerns. But Clancarty is only one man. While he does the talking, I need someone else to observe the rest of the guests. Of course you will not be able to understand the conversations you overhear if they are in German, but my guess is that with foreigners present they will speak in French, if not out of courtesy to the foreigners, at least out of a wish to prove that they are not so provincial as the rest of us think they are. I do hope you and Clancarty cannot only discover something useful, but establish a certain amount of influence with them. We cannot ever again allow another nation like Russia or Prussia to grow so powerful that

it can establish a stranglehold on Europe the way Bonaparte did."

"No indeed, sir." Brett rose. "I shall do my best, sir."

"That is all any of us can do, Stanford." Castlereagh
sighed heavily. "Wellington assures me that, in addition
to your linguistic capabilities, you are a very sharp observer. You must not only pay attention at the Princess
von Furstenberg's soiree, but keep an eye out for anyone
who might be watching you. There are spies everywhere.
In the last eight years alone, the emperor has increased
the Austrian budget for its agents fivefold, and it now
seems that every chambermaid, every innkeeper, every
tollgate keeper is in the pay of Hager, who runs their
secret police, and they are sending him daily reports on
all of us. In addition to that, John King, our own agent,
tells me that he has been able to intercept reports from
any number of agents in the employ of other delegations
who are keeping track of us. There is Herr H, who appears to be connected to the Prussians; another agent,
who simply signs himself ***, who seems to be an aristo-
crat of some sort, possibly in Hager's pay; also 00, who
specializes in Hungarian affairs; and Nota and Chevalier
Freddi, who are experts in Russian and Italian matters.
So you see, Vienna is fairly seething with spies. But
there is no need for me to warn you of this. You are a
solider, you are accustomed to these things. I rely on
you to keep your wits about you. Good day, Major."

"Good day, sir." Slowly and thoughtfully Brett descended the stairs from the foreign secretary's rooftop
study to the street, where he joined the fashionable
throngs strolling along the Herrengasse. He was in no
mood either for company or for the solitude of his own
quarters, but he needed to think, to sort through the
complexity of the problems Castlereagh had just
sketched out for him, and walking along in the relative
anonymity of the crowd suited his mood exactly. He
knew so few people in Vienna that he was reasonably
assured that no encounter with an acquaintance would
interrupt his train of thought, and he had always found
that he thought more clearly when he was active. The
casual pace along the Herrengasse was perfect for his
questioning frame of mind, and the noises of the street,

the cries of street vendors, the steady clop. of horses'
hooves, the rumble of carriages all merged into an agreeable hum of activity that stimulated his thoughts.

Castlereagh had alluded to a confusing number of political possibilities, but the one thing he had remained
absolutely clear on was his determination to maintain
peace in Europe and keep it from suffering ever again
the expansionist ambitions of a single nation.

Brett agreed wholeheartedly with the foreign secretary. As a soldier in the Peninsula, he had seen more
than he ever cared to of the misery caused by imperial
France's hunger for territory. He would never forget the
hollow cheeks and haunted eyes of starving peasants in
Spain, the horror of villages plundered by French troops,
and the desolation of a land whose crops had been
stripped bare by a foraging army.

Brett had originally joined the cavalry fired by the
ideals of his youth, many of which had been strongly
influenced by his friendship with the son of General de
Broglie living in the neighboring émigré community at
Juniper Hall. As a boy he had thrilled to the saga of the
family's escape from France in an open boat across the
Channel. He had been present when the news of the
death of the king and queen of France had reduced the
household to shocked silence. He had seen the horror
in the faces of these former aristocrats, many of whom
had supported the democratic ideals of the revolution
only to have it turn on them later.

Then and there, Brett had vowed to help his friend
fight to rid France of the bloodthirsty tyrants who had
taken away their lands and killed so many people. Eventually, Brett had lost touch with the de Broglies when
he went to school, but he had never lost touch with his
determination to avenge the wrongs that had been done
to them and to so many people like them. At the first
opportunity afforded to him, he had joined the cavalry
and gone to fight in the Peninsula.

The harsh realities of war that he had witnessed during the Peninsular campaign, the deaths of comrades,
and the determination of the Spanish people to rid themselves of French tyranny had only strengthened his re-

solve to do his part in defeating Napoleon and bringing peace to Europe.

When peace had come at last, he had thought his job finished, but he had felt at a little bit of a loss as to what to do next. The idea of returning to guard duty at St. James' or some other equally tame existence did not appeal to his adventurous spirit, especially after his years of campaigning. Having seen Spain and Portugal, he now longed to see more of the world. Wellington's request that Brett accompany him to Paris as his aide, while it did not necessarily offer the same sort of adventure or intensity of purpose that championing a cause in battle did, had at least allowed Brett to postpone his return to England and the mediocrity of everyday existence.

Now it appeared that there was still work to be done. If Castlereagh was right, there were still those who sought to fill the void left by Napoleon, nations whose territorial ambitions were not yet completely clear, but who posed just as much a threat to the freedom of Europe's inhabitants and England's peace and prosperity as the French had. Keeping these territorial ambitions at bay might not require quite the same sort of physically heroic resistance as fighting the French, but it was just as critical to the future of Europe, and Brett resolved to do his part with the same determination and skill that had won him Wellington's attention in the first place.

Recalling Castlereagh's warning, he scanned the crowd around him as he strode along, but since he had not the slightest notion of those who had been present outside the British delegation when he had originally left it, he had no way of knowing if any of the individuals surrounding him now had trailed him. From now on he resolved to be more alert. Aside from Castlereagh's verbal admonition, Brett knew that the foreign secretary and others at the British delegation took the threat of foreign agents very seriously indeed—so seriously that Brett, along with everyone else, had been ordered to burn the contents of their wastepaper baskets every evening so that no chambermaid, valet, or anyone else could retrieve the scraps and hand them over to Hager's *Polizei.*

Brett continued his stroll, pausing in front of the massive doors of St. Stephen's cathedral, stopping occasionally to listen to the barrel organ player, one of the countless street musicians who strolled from house to house playing popular stage melodies. One of the things that appealed to Brett about the city was the music. It was everywhere, not only in the salons and concert halls, but in the streets, from the barrel organ players to strolling harpists, to the Tyrolean clock makers, who filled the air with their mountain harmonies as they made their way home from work in the evening.

As the Princess von Hohenbachern had pointed out, the entire city seemed so bent on merrymaking that it hardly seemed possible the entire map of Europe was being redrawn in the salons of its many palaces and foreign delegations, that the fates of hundreds of thousands of souls were being determined at its conference tables, and that agents of all nationalities and backgrounds stalked streets and haunted the alleyways seeking any scrap of information that could be sold to the highest bidder.

Brett shook his head in bemusement as he considered the evening before him. He felt helpless when confronted with the vagaries of politics. In battle, the objective was clear—to drive the enemy off this ridge or out of that fort which allowed him to dominate the countryside, or to chase him across a border and back into his own territory—and one planned one's approach accordingly. But politics was entirely different. How in God's name did one convince a group of quarrelsome, German princes jealous of their individual power and suspicious of everyone else, to act one way instead of another, to side with one nation instead of another? To a man accustomed to using his own and others' physical prowess and skill to solve problems, it seemed a virtually impossible task.

Chapter Five

The question still plagued Brett as he and the Earl of Clancarty entered the brilliantly lit apartments of the Princess Elizabeth von Furstenberg that evening. The damask-hung rooms were filled with German barons, dukes, and princes in elaborate uniforms of all kinds, the light from the crystal chandeliers catching the glitter of medals on their chests and making the gold embroidery on their high collars and heavy epaulets gleam. Here and there were scattered heavily jeweled females, but for the most part, the preponderance of the guests crowding the princess' salon were male.

Brett's gaze swept the room and then paused in astonishment. Among the richly costumed throng, there was one member whose simplicity of dress made the others with their ornate embroidery, heavy ruchings, and trimmings look gaudy and overdecorated. This young woman, her glossy brown hair pulled back into a simple knot, wearing a gown of white lace over a white satin slip, appeared as pure and graceful as a Greek statue among the buxom overdressed Germans.

But it was not so much the simplicity of her attire that caught his attention as it was the person herself. For there, conversing in the friendliest of fashions with two of the princess' most distinguished-looking guests, was none other than the Princess von Hohenbachern's maid!

"Ah, Milord Clancarty, we are indeed honored to have you join us this evening." The Princess von Furs-

tenberg hurried over to greet the new arrivals. "Do let
me make you known to the rest of my guests, most of
whom you have not likely met, as they have no official
presence here or on any of the committees with which
you might be familiar—hence the gathering at my humble abode. Over there is someone you may recognize,
however; Baron von Stein, who is such a proponent for
the creation of a new German Reich. There in the other
corner is someone you are less likely to know, our chief
advocate, Baron Hans Christoph von Gagern. Officially,
he is here representing both Duke Frederick William of
Nassau and Prince William of Orange Nassau, but he
also spends much of his time and energy advancing the
cause of those of us whose voices would otherwise remain unheard."

Taking the arms of both men, the princess led Brett
and the Earl of Clancarty to the corner where the baron
was conversing earnestly with the young lady who had
caught Brett's eye. As they approached, Brett decided
that he must have been mistaken in his first impression.
Not only would no servant be at such a gathering but
he had never encountered one who spoke with such confidence or with such an expression of eager intelligence
on her face. And he had never known any servant, not
even the most indispensable of batmen or valets, to hold
the attention of a gentleman, as this young woman appeared to be doing.

Who was she?

Brett had encountered very few women in his life,
much less young women, who did anything more than
gossip or flirt. And he had rarely seen a woman attend
a gathering where conversation was clearly confined to
topics of a most serious nature. She must be a very unusual young lady indeed to be included in such a select
company, not to mention involved in a discussion with
one of its most influential members.

"Milord Clancarty, Major Milord Brett Stanford, may
I present you to one of our most important advocates,
Baron von Gagern. And, I am sure you will be delighted
to make the acquaintance of one of your very own
countrymen, Miss Devereux."

"Lord Clancarty, Major." The young lady's curtsy of

acknowledgment might have been directed at the Earl of Clancarty, but the impish smile and the twinkle of amusement in the large hazel eyes were for Brett alone.

Blast! Brett felt his face turn hot. He had not found himself at such a disadvantage with a woman since his salad days, and she was clearly enjoying his discomfiture. He was just thankful that years of campaigning under the Peninsula's merciless sun had tanned his skin to such a degree that only the most acute of observers would be able to detect the flush he was powerless to keep from rising to his cheeks.

"I am most pleased to be introduced to you at last, Major." Miss Devereux's response was conventional enough, but the sly smile that accompanied it left him in no doubt that she was well aware of her advantage and the effect that it was having on him.

Brett bit his lip. Damn the woman! Not content with laughing at him secretly, she was now going to make him look like a fool in front of Clancarty.

"For I believe that you must be the one whose superb horsemanship has quite taken my breath away," she continued serenely, her eyes dancing with suppressed laughter.

"What?" She had succeeded in making him look like a fool all right, but not because he had so stupidly mistaken her for a servant. He now simply goggled at her blankly—something he tried to avoid at all costs—as he struggled to make sense of what she was saying, but he was at a complete loss. Major Lord Brett Stanford was a man known to be awake on all suits, and he was not about to lose this reputation because of a mere chit of a girl. Brett tried valiantly not to grind his teeth as he forced his lips into a polite smile.

"I believe it is you," the young lady continued, "is it not, who rides a most magnificent black horse that knows all the movements of the *haute école* as well as most horses know their way to the stables, a horse that performs them as easily as another horse would trot."

"I do own a black horse, yes." Brett was damned if he was going to give anything up to this vixen who appeared to delight at keeping him at a disadvantage.

"Then I am most pleased to make your acquaintance,

for I would most dearly love to hear how you have
worked such magic. I have never seen anything equal to
it, not even at the Spanish Riding School." The wicked
glint of amusement had disappeared to be replaced by
an expression of genuine interest and admiration.

Too bemused to frame a reply, Brett groped for a
response, any response to this self-possessed young
woman who, in a matter of minutes, had rendered him
tongue-tied: him, Major Lord Brett Stanford, the man
who could always be counted on to charm the starchiest
of dowagers or set at ease the most awkward of shy
young misses.

"Oh, Stanford is an old cavalry fellow and those cavalry fellows spend so much time in the saddle that they
practically are horses." Clancarty came to his rescue.
"Undoubtedly, he finds all these Congress goings-on
very dull stuff indeed after his time in the Peninsula.
But the warriors' days are over now, and it is up to us
diplomats to see that their duties are confined to the
parade ground, eh, Stanford? Von Gagern here I am
sure will agree with me." The Earl of Clancarty turned
to the baron and, taking his arm, pulled him a little
apart. "I am sure, Baron, that you can enlighten me a
great deal . . ." and in no time had immersed the two
of them in a deep discussion on Napoleon's former Con-
federation of the Rhine and the fate of its sovereigns
now that the emperor had been exiled to Elba.

"Vienna is a rather unusual place for a cavalry officer
to find himself. Are you with Sir Charles Stewart, then?
I hear that before he became ambassador he too was in
the cavalry."

Brett gave a start. He had been hoping that while he
was concentrating on the interchange between von Gagern and Clancarty, the disconcerting young woman
would have disappeared, but apparently he was not to
be so lucky. "Yes. Yes he was in the cavalry. And he
was also in the Peninsula, but I am not with him. I have
been assigned to the British delegation for the very simple reason that I can read and write French and no one
else can—most unglamorous, but necessary."

"A linguist in addition to being a superb horseman?
You are a man of many talents, Major."

"No. The French I learned quite by accident as a result of a boyhood friendship with a group of émigrés who settled nearby." Brett had no idea why he was offering such a disclaimer, but there was something about Miss Helena Devereux's ironic gaze that made him feel the need to prove himself. To be sure, she had expressed genuine admiration for his horsemanship, but her evident astonishment at his affinity for the French language made it very clear that she not only rated the intellectual abilities of cavalry officers rather low, but that she was a woman who prized intelligence above all other things. Certainly her presence in this crowd was a clear indication of her own mental capacities. The guests at the Princess von Furstenberg's soiree were obviously intent on serious discussion of a most thorny topic. But why had this young Englishwoman, intelligent though she might be, been included among the guests?

"I too owe my presence here to an accident of linguistic ability." The hazel eyes twinkled at his obvious discomfiture. She knew that she had read his thoughts and that once again she had gained the advantage over him. "My stepfather, who is a German, is a friend of the Prince Regent's. I was quite young when on a visit to England he met my mother, married her, and brought us back here to live. And, therefore, German comes to me almost as naturally as English and more naturally than French. The Princess von Furstenberg invited me here because she hoped that Lord Clancarty would accept her invitation to her soiree, and even though everyone here speaks French, she asked me to be here in case there should be any need for a translator. We are all very anxious for the English to understand our cause, and she wanted to insure that language, at least, would not pose a barrier to understanding."

Brett eyed her curiously. The teasing note in her voice had vanished entirely, and she now spoke with an urgency he had never before heard in the conversations of young ladies. "That is certainly most gracious of you to help out, Miss Devereux. Most young ladies would infinitely prefer waltzing at the Hofburg to listening to dull political conversations."

A look flashed into her eyes that he was at a loss to

interpret. It almost seemed to be anger or scorn, but her response was not so much angry as passionate. "When Mama and I first arrived on the Continent, our new home was a simple, tranquil country dotted with villages that were very little different than they had been at the dawn of the Holy Roman Empire. That peacefulness was soon destroyed, however, as the French marched in and the opposing armies fought back and forth across our lands, burning villages, destroying crops, and imposing new ways on people whose lives had remained unchanged for centuries. We can never go back to those simple times, but the least we can do is to make sure that our way of life is never threatened again, that we are never again forced to pay homage to a distant ruler or state that has no concept of our lives and our ways."

"And what is it that you are proposing to do to keep this from happening?"

Helena shot him a suspicious glance. People in general, and the English in particular, tended to consider the aspirations of a few small German states to be so paltry as to be laughable. At best they were condescending to any man who dared to advance their cause, much less an unsophisticated young woman, but this man was not laughing at her. His bright blue eyes, fixed so intently on her, betrayed nothing but the most sincere interest in what she had to say.

"Well," she began cautiously, "it is naturally assumed that the German states will form an alliance, but there is a vast difference between a federation of equals and a hegemony in which the interests of many are subordinated to the interests of one. We have all seen what happened in Saxony when the Prussians took it upon themselves to take it over and imprison the king as punishment for his support of Napoleon. How did they know that he had any choice in the matter? But whether he did or not, it was merely an excuse on their part to grab more territory for themselves."

Something in his face must have given her pause. A flush rose to her cheeks, her eyes flashed, and Brett could see her gloved hands clenching and unclenching at her sides. "It may seem nothing to you," she continued fiercely, "this disposition of *souls* as they call hand-ing bits of territory to one nation or the other, just so long as it is peaceful and quiet again in Europe. But there is a vast difference between being joined with Austria in a pact of mutual support and protection and being taken over by the rigid centralized administration of a militarist state like Prussia. Being annexed by the Prussians would be no better than the slavery we endured for the last decade under the French."

"But surely the most expedient measure, and the one most suitable to you all is to reestablish everything to its previous state and . . ." He paused uncomfortably. It was only one delicately raised eyebrow, but the incredulity that it expressed made him feel like the veriest fool. He was not accustomed to feeling foolish or naive, especially where women were concerned. "Will, will they not do this?" Brett wondered uncomfortably how the man who had been dressed down by the fiercest commanders without so much as batting an eyelash could stammer like this under the scornful gaze of a mere slip of a girl.

"It is not that simple." Shaking her head and sighing, Helena at last took pity on him. After all, what could an Englishman who had spent the past several years fighting in the wilds of Spain and Portugal be expected to know about European politics, especially German politics. "It is a matter of old rivalries and new threats to our way of life. France may have suffered a revolution, but its territories remained largely intact. Many of the German states, on the other hand, have been completely abolished during these wars, their hereditary rulers dispossessed, and their people left with no one to turn to for guidance and leadership. These people are not accustomed to change of any kind, and they are now lost and confused. It is clear to anyone who has spent even a short amount of time among the Prussians that they intend to restore order not by restoring former leaders, but by enforcing their own system on everyone else through martial law. These are simple, peaceable folk who want nothing more than to return to cultivating their lands and celebrating their ancient customs. This will not happen if the Allies allow Prussia to have its way.

"But many of the Allies are so afraid of Russia's gain-

ing too much power that they will do anything to stop
it, even if they have to give land to Prussia in return for
its support against Russia. To those not familiar with
German politics, one state seems very much like another
and Prussia is no different than Austria, so that to give
territory to Prussia in order to keep a buffer between
Russia and the rest of Europe seems the logical solution.
They do not understand the danger of this, but they
must be made to. It is difficult to do so, however, because none of our leaders is allowed to sit on the coun-
cils or to vote on the crucial issues. If Prussia is given
control of a German federation, soon there will be no
federation of German states at all; we will just be swallowed up by Prussia, and believe me, we will be no better off than we were under Napoleon. All our fighting,
dying, and suffering will have been for nothing. We cannot let that happen."

The passionate conviction in her voice made him
smile. She sounded so much like the young Brett Stanford telling his parents so many years ago why it was
imperative that they buy him a commission in the First
Hussars. He too had been determined to stop oppression
and change the course of history for the better.

"But I see that I bore you. If you will excuse . . ."

"No." Brett caught her wrist as she turned to leave.
"You mistake me entirely. I smile because it could be I
who uttered those words you just spoke. You believe as
strongly as I do that people should be protected from
tyrants. As I told you, I learned my French from the
émigrés who lived near me at Juniper Hill. But I also
learned from them what happens when change comes
too quickly, when people's lives are taken over by an all
powerful government. And I learned that a tyrant who
begins by trying to establish order in one place soon
progresses to trying to establish order over an ever ex-
panding territory. No, Miss Devereux, you misunder-
stand me entirely. I am not laughing at you. I heartily
agree with you. It was because I held beliefs like yours
that I joined the cavalry in the first place. And then,
having seen firsthand the misery caused by foreign rule
in Spain, putting a stop to it became the reason I continued to fight, to watch my friends die, to endure . . ."

Brett paused, struggling against the memories that threatened to overwhelm him, and drew a deep breath. "But now *I* am the one who is making *you* smile."

Helena was indeed smiling, for he truly did voice many of her own convictions, convictions that always caused her mother and her mother's friends to shake their heads and look askance at her. "Now it is *my* turn to apologize, Major. but we live in a sophisticated age where such enthusiasms are regarded with dismay, if not downright suspicion. It is considered bad *ton* by most of society if one is passionately devoted to anything, which is why I do my utmost to avoid most of society and why I am so often the object of ironic smiles and cynical remarks that imply I am not only naively idealistic, but also a fool for espousing any cause with passionate interest."

"Yet here you are in the midst of the largest fashionable gathering it has ever been my privilege to witness."

"Here?" Her gaze swept the room. "But these are quite simple people. They are not the Metternichs, the Talleyrands, the Tsar Alexanders of the world."

"No, I mean here in Vienna. The *crème de la crème* of all of Europe is here crammed into its palaces, its inns, and any accommodation that is to be found, no matter how humble or how uncomfortable. People are willing to endure any inconvenience simply in order to be here. It is the only place to see and be seen."

"Oh, Vienna, yes." She dismissed the assembled monarchs and ministers, potentates and plenipotentiaries with a scornful wave of her hand. "But here, at the Princess von Furstenberg's salons, we are not the bored sophisticates who are so jaded that the only thing left to amuse them is the redrawing of the map of Europe. For us, it is our very way of life that is at stake. Others may be here to enjoy the excitement of intrigue or to savor the heady sense of power that comes from negotiating the future of the Continent and changing history, but we are here to fight for our very existence."

Brett was silent for a moment, struck by her words. When he had first been given his assignment by Wellington he had been bitterly disappointed, for he had hoped to be one of the duke's *flying dispatch* riders carrying diplomatic pouches between Vienna and Paris. The role of observer and translator had seemed unbearably tame in comparison. And Vienna, with its frivolity and its political intrigue seemed almost a mockery of the fighting and suffering that had preceded it. Brett had asked himself a hundred times what he, the man who had led cavalry charges at Salamanca and Talavera, was doing in the ballrooms of the Austrian capital. But this young woman now made him feel as though perhaps the work at the Congress was a fitting conclusion to all the fighting after all, that someone, at least, was trying to see to it that after twenty years of war, Europe emerged a better place for its inhabitants as well as for its rulers. "Fighting for your existence? How?"

"We *must* convince the powers that be to keep Prussia at bay, to allow Austria to lead the German world, otherwise we will be swallowed up by Prussia, which aspires to become the Sparta of Europe. Believe me, the Prussians are greedy as well as militaristic. Austria, on the other hand, will let us be. The rest of the world *must* be made to see this. We *must* make it understand."

Once again, Brett heard the quiver of passion in her voice, and he suddenly found himself wanting to swear to her that he would do his utmost to see that her dreams would come true.

But it was not his place to do this, and Clancarty, having finished his discussion with Baron von Gagern, was now turning back to address the two of them. "Miss Devereux, the baron informs me that you are well acquainted with everyone in this room. I do hope I can prevail upon you to introduce me to some of the others. German politics and the multitude of states, principalities, and electorates quite make my head swim. They are so very confusing to us foreigners."

Helena warmed to the diplomat's ingenuous appeal. "I shall be delighted to do so, my lord." And recovering her poise, she smiled graciously and led the two of them toward a group of bemedaled gentlemen engaged in earnest conversation in the far corner of the room.

Chapter Six

As Brett and the Earl of Clancarty strolled back to the British delegation later that evening, it occurred to Brett that while he knew the name of the young woman who kept popping into his life in a most unnerving fashion, he still had no true notion of her identity. While her comments on his horsemanship had been flattering indeed, it bothered him that she had been able to observe him unawares. And when he had been introduced to her at the Princess von Furstenberg's soiree, she had known who he was but had given no clue as to her background. In every situation she had him at a disadvantage—an unusual state of affairs for him. It was a rare person indeed who could establish an advantage over Major Lord Brett Stanford, and while some might have succeeded at it once, no one had ever succeeded at it a second time.

This young woman had done it, not once, not twice, but three times. Not only had she observed him in the Prater and then later allowed him to think she was a maid, but she had thoroughly enjoyed his discomfiture at their formal introduction. And now he was leaving the Princess von Furstenberg's salon with no clearer idea of who she really was than when he arrived, except that he knew her name and that she was a passionate advocate for the sovereignty of the smaller German states. The Princess von Furstenberg had simply introduced her as Miss Devereux and the young lady had done nothing

further to elaborate on that except to say that her stepfather was German. Which stepfather? And from which
German state? And what was she doing running tame
in the Princess von Hohenbachern's library? Brett was
thoroughly annoyed with himself for not having discovered anything further about her. And it irritated him
even more to think she had deliberately kept it that way.

For he was certain that she had not been forthcoming
on purpose in order to maintain her advantage over him.
Usually young women were all too eager to tell Major
Lord Brett Stanford everything about themselves—their
parents, their friends, where they lived, what hours they
were to be found at home, and the next social events
they planned to attend. Not this young woman. This
young woman had been singularly reticent about any
details of her existence, though she had not had the
slightest qualms about giving him a piece of her mind.

Brett smiled to himself as he climbed the stairs to his
chamber. No, she had been most forthright, insistent,
one could even call it, about her political opinions and
the course of action needed to put them into effect. Most
young ladies did their utmost to keep their opinions to
themselves so as not to run the risk of offending an
attractive male—not this one. Not only did she not worry
about offending him, it almost appeared as though she
would enjoy it. Certainly she had been determined not
only to express her opinions, but to convince him of
their validity.

Wellington's words of warning concerning the political
machinations of the women to be found at the Congress
rang again in Brett's ears. Was Miss Devereux one of
those women the Duke had cautioned him against?
There had been nothing duplicitous or intriguing about
her manner. She had been forthright to the point of
bluntness about her politics and she certainly had not
tried to exert her feminine charms on him.

In fact, Brett reflected as he stripped off his coat and
poured himself a glass of brandy, he would have to say,
judging from his first encounter with her, that Miss Devereux depended on her intellect rather than any attractions she might possess to advance her cause. He rather
suspected, having observed the plainness of her dress

and the simplicity of her coiffure, that she scorned to use such standard feminine ploys. Not that she was unattractive. There was a liveliness in her face, a sparkle in her eyes, and a vitality about her that had drawn him to her immediately in a way that he was not usually drawn to women.

In her company he had felt oddly inspired in a way he had not since leaving the Peninsula. And then there had been that teasing twinkle, that ironic smile that were far more intimate than any fluttering lashes or seductive glances. She had been laughing at him, but at the same time she had been inviting him to share in her amusement, an amusement that no one else but the two of them could share. Yet all the while, she managed to convey the sense that she herself was under no illusions about herself or anyone else.

Brett found such a lack of affectation as intriguing as it was unusual and as delightful as it was novel. Thus it was that arriving the next night at Prince Trauttmansdorff's reception, he found himself scanning the crowd not only for the beautiful and alluring Princess von Hohenbachern, but for the lively intelligent face of Miss Devereux.

He had barely entered the brilliantly lit room, however, when he was accosted by a vision of loveliness. Jaded though he might be after years of flirting with the beauties of Portugal, Spain, and Paris, he felt his body's immediate response as he fought to keep his eyes from straying to the entrancing white bosom revealed by the Princess Bagration's daring décolletage. Not for nothing, he thought grimly as he schooled his features into a creditable semblance of bored indifference, was she called the *Naked Angel*.

"Oh, Major, I wonder if I might have a word with you." The seductive huskiness of her voice and the wealth of promise in her dark eyes left him feeling powerless to resist being drawn into what was sure to be a web of intrigue.

"But of course, Princess. You have only to speak and I am yours to command."

Any Englishwoman would immediately have detected the irony in the effusiveness of his response, but the

alluring Russian took it as her due. "Not here. Not now.
It is far too public. I shall send a message to you tomorrow. Until then, not a word." She held a finger to full
red lips and smiling invitingly slipped back into the
crowd as unobtrusively as she had appeared. But
throughout the rest of the evening, when a prickling sensation at the back of his neck told him he was being
watched, Brett would look up to find those dark eyes
looking at him, the red lips curving into a mysterious
smile. What did she want with him? He was less than a
minor player in these affairs, and all the world knew that
the tsar had made her half of the Palm Palace, which she
shared with the Duchess of Sagan, his de facto embassy
and much more. Why, if she had the ear of Alexander,
would she bother with a simple British major?

Free of the Princess Bagration, Brett again began to
survey the crowd in search of Miss Devereux, but he
looked for her in vain. After listening to her scornful
dismissal of the Congress' more frivolous aspects the
previous evening, he had not held any realistic expecta-
tion of encountering her at this reception. Still, there
had been something about her, a refreshing honesty, an
idealistic passion, that had made him hope, despite her
professed distaste for such social affairs, that she might
appear to enliven his evening.

Instead, he had been accosted by the Princess Bagration, and though she was one of the women who had
been expressly mentioned by Wellington in his instructions before Brett left Paris, Brett could not suppress
the vague feeling of unease he always experienced in her
company, or of being put off by the naked desire he
read in her eyes every time she looked at him. He knew
it was unreasonable, for, after all, he himself had cast
admiring looks at hundreds of beautiful women, but all
the same, it made him acutely uncomfortable. And her
obvious intriguing only made it worse.

Not wishing to run the risk of further encounters with
her, Brett left the reception early. As he walked back
to his quarters, he consoled himself with the thought
that the Princess Bagration, who was as voracious as she
was shameless, would no doubt find some other hapless
young man whom she considered equally as attractive

and would soon forget the very existence of Major Lord Brett Stanford. He even allowed himself to hope that somehow her promise to contact him had merely been an impulse and nothing more, a flirtatious ploy on the lady's part to attract his attention at that particular moment, for whatever reason, and then forgotten as soon as the moment and the impulse had passed.

Unfortunately, the lady was as good as her word, and the very next day, a messenger appeared at the British delegation bearing a heavily scented missive inviting Brett to call on her at the Palm Palace later that very day.

Brett took the note, read it, and nodded carelessly to the liveried servant.

"The princess awaits your response, milord."

Clearly, a written response was expected, and just as clearly, Brett foresaw all the possible compromising conclusions that could be drawn by someone reading a note written in his hand to a woman who was rapidly becoming as notorious for her political scheming as she was for her many lovers. No matter how innocent his note might be, it would not look that way to anyone else. Brett nodded casually to the servant. "Very well. Take me to your mistress."

Undoubtedly there was very little that could shock those who were in the service of the *Naked Angel*, but Brett was certain that he caught a flash of alarm in the man's eyes before his face resumed its wooden expression. "But certainly, milord. If you will be so good as to follow me."

What, Brett wondered, for the hundredth time as he followed the man through the narrow streets to the Palm Palace, did the Princess Bagration want with him? Such persistence on her part seemed to preclude any possibility that it was simply physical attraction that drew her to him. His natural wariness, sharpened by years of campaigning, only reinforced his suspicions that what she required of him was something more than what Charles Stewart crudely referred to as *the Bagration's insatiable desires* where men were concerned.

Climbing the palace's left-handed staircase toward the princess' apartments, Brett turned the question over and over in his mind, but still could come up with no satisfactory explanation for the summons that left him in a position of frustrating uncertainty. Obviously, Brett had been unable to do any sort of research before his visit and was left to seethe with frustration over his lack of preparation while the servant went to inform his mistress that the response she awaited was actually there in person, pacing the parquet floor in her elegant anteroom.

Meanwhile, Brett cursed himself for a fool. Courageous though he might be, and accustomed as he was to leading his men into dangerous situations, it was as foreign to him as it was unacceptable to enter into any confrontation without reconnoitering thoroughly before engaging in any actions. He always took the time to prepare himself mentally so that he could anticipate the enemy's state of mind. In this case, the enemy had caught him off guard and he was going to have to deal with it without any time for reflection.

After nearly half an hour, the sharp hurried click of heels told him that his questions were soon to be answered. Brett stopped his pacing and turned, ready to follow the servant, when, to his great surprise, he recognized the round genial face of Alexander, tsar of all the Russias.

"Your Highness, I . . ."

"Good morning, Major." The tsar smiled at Brett in the friendliest of fashions. "It is refreshing to see a fellow military man among all these courtiers and diplomats. We military men are accustomed to action rather than these endless discussions which are as pointless as they are vexing. I trust you can encourage your fellow Englishmen to proceed with the forcefulness and dispatch that has characterized their conduct in the Peninsula."

"Of course, Your Highness. I shall do . . ."

"Very good. I count on you then." And the tsar disappeared out the door and down the stairs as rapidly as he had appeared, leaving Brett even more amazed and mystified than he had been before.

"Ah, Major, so good of you to come. I had not expected your presence so immediately, but then you English are always so punctilious."

Brett, who had been staring bemusedly after the tsar, jumped and turned around to see his hostess, still *en negligée,* her blond curls hanging loose around her shoulders, gliding across the room to greet him. Calling on all his training as a soldier, Brett drew one deep steadying breath and awaited developments.

"Come. Sit beside me." Princess Bagration sank onto a nearby sofa and patted the damask-covered seat close to her, far too close to her for her guest's comfort or peace of mind.

Reiterating to himself that he was there to serve his country, Brett gingerly took his place beside her, hoping against hope that she could not see how tight his collar felt or the beads of sweat that he could feel starting to gather on his forehead.

The princess was a beautiful and alluring woman, and the fact that she was obviously on intimate terms with the most powerful man in Europe only made her all that much more dangerous to a man who had no experience in the constantly shifting world of political intrigue and diplomatic alliances. No matter how demanding the conditions were on the Peninsula, no matter how dire the situation, he had always been sure of which side he was on and of its motives. Here he was sure of nothing except that it behooved him to exercise extreme caution.

"You have no notion what a relief it is to be able to relax and enjoy a frank conversation with a simple soldier." The princess ran a hand through the riot of golden curls that framed her softly rounded face. "I adore Alexander, but his enthusiasms can be utterly exhausting, and when he is at one and the same time a ruler and a friend, it can be very complicated indeed. Which is why I wish to speak with you. When I call you a simple soldier, I do not mean any disrespect. All that I mean is that you, like me, are merely a subject of one of the nations gathered here, not a ruler or a diplomatic representative. We are both forced to bow to the whims and the passions of those who are redrawing the map of Europe. It is a relief to know that an ill-judged or misspoken word between you and me will not decide the fate of nations, whereas an ill-judged or misspoken word between them, or between one of us and them . . ." She shrugged her shoulders with an air of resignation that, nonetheless, allowed the negligée to reveal even more of the smooth white skin than it had before.

While her words might echo his thoughts to an uncomfortable degree, they still did not answer his question. Why was he here? Brett remained silent, trying to look thoughtful as he fixed his gaze on the elaborate pattern on the parquet floor, on the ornately decorated porcelain stove in the corner, anywhere, but on the enchanting mouth, the slender neck, the sparkling eyes that smiled up at him seductively from underneath half-lowered lids.

The princess laid a hand on his arm. "Alexander is most concerned about Castlereagh's position in all these discussions. He is a passionate man himself, and he simply cannot fathom the impassivity of your foreign secretary. Ah, Castlereagh, such a beautiful face, like an angel, yet so unrevealing, so unemotional. It drives us Russians mad." She wagged a playful finger at Brett. "You English are all so cold. We can none of us tell what you are thinking."

"Perhaps we are not thinking anything at all, Princess. Perhaps we are simply lost in admiration of your beauty." This time he did allow himself to look at her, scrutinizing every detail, from the pulse at the base of her throat to the way she caught her full lower lip in her sharp white teeth. He had known enough women to have developed a sixth sense for when they were after something, not to mention a lively sense of self-preservation. And this woman was definitely after something.

"If you, dear Major, could perhaps convince Castlereagh to meet privately with Alexander, informally, someplace away from all the pomp and ceremony that surrounds them . . ." her voice trailed off suggestively.

And away from the prying eyes of interested parties, Brett added silently.

"Somewhere where they could become better acquainted without the inevitable pressure of people around them. Perhaps here." She laid a pleading hand on his shoulder. "I would be most happy to volunteer my apartments for the cause of better understanding between your country and mine."

"You overestimate my influence, Princess. As you so

correctly stated, I am but a simple soldier, here to act as secretary and messenger for my delegation. The foreign secretary does not know me from a score of other young men assigned to the delegation for the very same purpose."

"You are far too modest. Surely someone who was chosen by Wellington himself is not so unimportant, so lacking in influence as you claim to be."

Brett froze. How did the Princess Bagration know that he had come to Vienna at Wellington's behest? He had not told anyone that Wellington had expressly asked him. So how did she come by this knowledge? Was nothing secret in this city? "I do not know why you should think such a thing, Princess. Truly, I have not the slightest influence with either Wellington or Castlereagh, and I am very much afraid that you have wasted your time and your effort."

"Oh, not at all. I have enjoyed our conversation immensely. In fact, I am hoping that now you know your way to the Palm Palace, you will continue to call on me. I find the English fascinating, though stiff, very stiff. You, Major"—she let her hand drift slowly from his shoulder down his arm—"are not stiff. In fact, you seem delightfully human and approachable, which is why I chose you. Please think about what I have said, and if you cannot convince your oh-so-reserved foreign secretary to call on me and Alexander, perhaps you can visit me regularly and I can explain things to you and you can in turn explain them to him."

"Perhaps." He did his best to sound noncommittal.

"If you cannot get away from your duties, you might write me a note so that I do not think you find my company distasteful. I am very sensitive by nature, you know."

He was certainly not going to write anything, Brett resolved, no matter how innocent it seemed. Any correspondence could be portrayed in a compromising light given the right innuendo. "I beg your pardon, Princess, but my time and my life are not my own. If I do not haunt your doorstep, believe me, it is duty rather than inclination that keeps me away. And it is duty now that forces me to bid you adieu."

He rose, lifted the hand that still clasped his arm, bowed over it, and was gone before she could frame a response.

Pursing her full red lips in a moue of frustration, the princess also rose and returned to her boudoir to continue her much interrupted toilette while Brett, his mind seething with a turmoil of conflicting possibilities, hurried back to the British delegation where he spent the next several hours at his desk capturing his thoughts in reports to Wellington and Castlereagh before the impressions he had received during his visit to the Palm Palace began to fade.

Chapter Seven

Meanwhile, a few streets away in the library of one of the palaces on the Bräunerstrasse, someone else was examining her own impressions. Helena was curled up in a comfortably upholstered bergère reading the pamphlet *Saxony and Prussia* recommended to her by the Princess von Furstenberg. As she read, however, the old enmities and various political complexities that the pamphlet was trying to explain receded into the background and the memory of intensely blue eyes alight with interest in a dark angular face took their place.

Who would have thought that the sort of man who could win her mother's approval would also have been the type of man to admit to her daughter that it was *because I held beliefs much like yours that I joined the cavalry*? And who would have thought that someone who could dance and flirt as divinely as her mother claimed Major Lord Brett Stanford did would even care that Prussian territorial ambitions could be as destructive as Napoleon's wars had been.

Or at least he had seemed to care. He had certainly spoken eloquently enough about the depredations of the French army in the Peninsula, and seemed to sympathize with her concerns about the Prussians taking over the rest of the German states the way they wanted to take over Saxony.

But perhaps he had just been doing his best to charm her as he had charmed her mother. If the major was as

adept as her mother seemed to think, he would know
that the way to win Helena's approval was to be as
knowledgeable and interested in topics that were of concern to her just as he knew that dancing and flirting were
the way to win her mother's. Perhaps he was actually no
different from her mother's many other gallants who
were irresistibly fascinating to women because they focused all their energies on learning what was particularly
appealing to them. The fact that in Helena's case, her
interests were serious and political rather than frivolous
and social might make a man who discussed them appear
to have more substance than those who confined themselves to the social. But perhaps he was just more clever.
A truly clever man would be able to charm all types of
women while her mother's gallants only charmed women
who were bent on enjoying themselves, women like
her mother.

Helena had always scornfully dismissed her mother's
admirers as self-satisfied cicisbeos, for whom the game of
flirtation was far more compelling than the actual people
involved in it. For them, flirtation was more about
power, about establishing the superiority of their own
graceful appearance and captivating manners than it was
about using them to bring happiness and pleasure to
another person. Helena had considered this self-
absorption to be the height of vanity, and the men ruled
by it to be ridiculous rather than attractive. In the early
days she had pointed out this self-absorption, this emptiness to her mother as the cause for her mother's dissatisfaction with all of her romantic affairs, but the princess
had refused to listen and Helena had finally given up.

Now, however, Helena was forced to ask herself if
she had been so critical simply because she had not yet
encountered someone who was truly skilled at the game.
Giving vent to an unladylike snort of disgust, Helena
tossed the pamphlet across the room in a fit of frustration. Why was she even wasting a second thought on
any of this? It did not matter to her in the least whether
or not Major Lord Brett Stanford was genuinely interested in the problems of the German states or even the
future of Europe. No, it did not matter to her at all.

But, Helena admitted grimly to herself as she rose and

went to sit at her escritoire, what did matter was that she, who had no use for attractive men or flirtation, had on three separate occasions found herself irresistibly drawn to this one particular man. Was she no better than her mother after all? Was she only more intellectually discriminating? No! Helena had spent far too much of her life cultivating her own interests, creating an existence whose meaning and satisfaction came from something other than masculine attention and admiration to fall for a handsome face and charming matter at this stage in her life. Her mother's example had been too ever present for her daughter not to learn that one could not pin all one's hopes for happiness on a man.

Angrily she pulled out a sheet of paper, stabbed her pen into the inkwell, and began to write furiously.

Dear Sophie and Gussie,
It is some time since I last wrote to you, but Mama and I have been settling in to our apartments here in Vienna. The city is full of people and very crowded and noisy. Mama is very busy attending balls nearly every evening, but I miss the two of you and the quiet countryside around the schloss. Except for its superior bookstores and theater, Vienna has little to recommend it, though I am able to procure newspapers of all kinds and to talk with many of Papa's friends who visit the Princess von Furstenberg. While it is all very interesting, I do not enjoy it half so much as being at home. How are your lessons proceeding? I do hope that you are paying attention to all that Abbé Ferrand teaches you and that you do not tease Fraulein Hauptmann too much. Do take care of yourselves and write me.

Helena laid down her pen and gazed out the window across red-tiled rooftops to the spire of St. Michael's Church. The most difficult thing about her trip to Vienna was missing the girls.

From the moment Helena had arrived at Hohenbachern a lonely lost little girl of eight, Sophie and Gussie had been the brightest spots in her solitary existence. The instant she had entered the cheerful nursery on that

cold blustery day nearly thirteen years ago, she had
fallen in love with the chubby blond babies. Sophie had
been a little over six months old and Gussie only a year
older, but even at that young age, their outgoing natures
and unconditional love had warmed the heart of a lonely
little girl exhausted by weeks of travel and confused by
the considerable upheaval in her young life.

After that she was constantly to be found in the nursery playing with the babies, laughing at their antics, and
helping Ursula feed and care for them. They in turn
would often sit solemnly watching as the governess,
Fraulein Hauptmann, instilled her young charge with a
zeal and an appreciation for the educational principles
of the Fraulein's idol Rousseau.

Later, when it was time for Sophie and Gussie to
begin their own lessons, it was Helena who made them
mind the Fraulein and convinced the two lively little
girls to sit still long enough to absorb at least some of
the knowledge she was trying to instill in them. As time
went on, the Fraulein, worn out by years of teaching,
abdicated more and more of her responsibility to her
former student, and Helena, now studying under the
scholarly Abbé Ferrand, took over their education. She
truly enjoyed the task and seemed to have an uncanny
ability for making lessons, whether they were in history,
geography, or even mathematics, come alive for the girls.
Soon she was able to command their attention and keep
them seated at their desks in a way the Fraulein never
had.

This arrangement was not only helpful to the governess, but it was extremely rewarding to a young girl who
had never felt anything but superfluous to the existence
of the adults around her until she had arrived at Hohenbachern. At the schloss, life was different from her former life in England. The prince was a devoted father
who doted on his girls when he was not off with his
regiment, and since all of the social life in the tiny princi-
pality revolved around its prince, all the entertaining was
confined to the schloss and its environs, which meant
that Helena actually saw more of her mother than she
had in all the years they had lived in England.

The Prince von Hohenbachern had married Lady

Devereux to give his tiny daughters a mother, but it was her daughter who actually took on the responsibility for their upbringing, and she lavished them with all the love and attention she had longed for but never received. In return they adored her. Their protests, when she had left for Vienna, had been loud and long, but she had promised to write them and encouraged them to write her. Still, letters were no substitute for being there.

A lump rose in Helena's throat as she pictured them, their blond curls flying as they rode alongside their carriage as far as the village and then waved good-bye as it turned on to the main road to Munich.

"There you are. I have been looking for you this age, though I suppose I should have known I would find you here. What do you think of this new bonnet? It is quite in the French style, and I do think the ostrich feathers add a degree of elegance. Do you not agree? The Countess Edmond de Talleyrand-Périgord was wearing one like it at the *fête* last week, and I vowed I would not rest until I could have one made up for me." The Princess von Hohenbachern paused in front of a convenient-looking glass to admire the charming picture she made and then sank gracefully into the bergère chair her daughter had just vacated. "I shall be all the rage in the Prater this afternoon, for I do think I appear to more advantage in it than the countess. Her complexion is too dark and her nose to long to do it justice."

"It is vastly becoming, Mama." And indeed, the bonnet was a perfect frame for the princess' blond beauty. "But I am a poor judge of such things, you know, for I have not the least notion of what is *à la mode* or what has become hopelessly *passé*."

"It is not so much a question of whether or not something is the latest kick of fashion as it is whether or not it shows one's particular characteristics to their best advantage. As I say, I saw the bonnet on the countess and admired the design, but I selected it because it is perfect for me, and, I guarantee that when I wear it, it will become the kick of fashion, while on her, it just looked like a bonnet." The princess rose and walked over to the looking glass again, turning her head from side to side to assure herself that it was equally becoming from all angles. "I daresay that it will turn quite a few heads this afternoon."

"Are you just going for a drive, or . . ." Helena hated herself for asking the question. What did it matter to her if a certain English officer was expected to call that afternoon? But she could not stop herself from asking.

"Do you never pay attention to such things?" Helena's mother shook her head, a look of mingled exasperation and resignation wrinkling her smooth white brow. "Balls and routs may be too frivolous to attach your interest, but the celebration commemorating the battle of Leipzig?"

"Ah, er, yes, I suppose the Princess von Furstenberg did mention it, now that I think of it, but my attention was occupied with other things at the time." Helena flushed as she admitted to herself that she had been too preoccupied with her conversation with Major Lord Brett Stanford to pay much attention to anything or anyone else at the Princess von Furstenberg's soiree for the rest of the evening. "With all of Vienna attending the celebration, you will have ample opportunity to show off your bonnet, though surely there is someone special you hope to dazzle with it."

"You can be very clever when you put your mind to it, you know." The princess smiled conspiratorially at her daughter. "The Esterhazys have very kindly offered me a space in their landau—not that I do not expect that certain other people may join us, of course."

"Ah." There was a wealth of meaning in her daughter's reply.

"Yes, the major has been most attentive in spite of the Bagration's shameless attempts to capture his interest. She has been casting her eyes at him from the moment he arrived, and at the Trauttmansdorff's reception I saw her approach him in the most brazen manner."

"Then, if the celebration is such an important event, perhaps I should attend it as well. That is, of course, if the Esterhazys have room in their carriage." Knowing her mother, Helena felt reasonably certain that somehow the princess would have arranged it so that there would be an empty seat next to her in the carriage in case they should happen to encounter a certain handsome English major.

The princess could only stare at her daughter.

"Well." Helena hunched a self-conscious shoulder. "It is to honor the soldiers who fought against Napoleon, after all, and Papa is one of those soldiers. Since Papa cannot be here, then we should do our best to represent Hohenbachern for him."

"Then we must find something suitable for you to wear." Recovering from her astonishment, the princess immediately got down to business. "You simply cannot appear in that same old bonnet, and it is far too warm for your pelisse. I have another new straw-colored satin bonnet that I have not yet worn that you could wear. And if you were to drape the Vittoria cloak I just had made over your white muslin walking dress, it should add some distinction to your costume. I shall have Marie bring them to you immediately so you can try them on for effect." The princess hurried out of the room, leaving her daughter to wonder what on earth had possessed her to commit to attending what was bound to be one of the biggest crushes of the entire Congress.

In fact, Helena had no need to speculate on her reasons for attending the ceremony. Much to her chagrin, she knew perfectly well why she had volunteered to go. It was to see for herself if Major Lord Brett Stanford was just like her mother's many other gallants, only perhaps more clever. Or if he truly were different, she wanted to assure herself of it. But at the back of her mind, she knew that not even that was the true reason, for what did it matter to her if he was different or not? Why should she care? The answer was that she *wanted* him to be different. But why she wanted him to be different was a question that she refused to entertain.

Chapter Eight

So it was that Brett, scanning the crowd gathered in front of the high altar set up in the Prater, where all Vienna gathered to hear the archbishop give his blessing and lead them in prayers for continued peace, was surprised to see Miss Devereux occupying the very place he had expected to take next to the Princess von Hohenbachern in the Esterhazys' landau. Granted, when the princess had spoken of attending the celebration, she had only given him the faintest of hints that he might find the place next to her empty, but from what little Brett had seen of the Princess von Hohenbachern, he felt sure that she expected her admirers to treat even her vaguest hints with all the seriousness of a royal command. Surely she had intended for him to sit by her in the carriage in the space now occupied by the omnipresent Miss Devereux? But perhaps the Esterhazys were also acquainted with Miss Devereux and, thinking to please the princess had, unbeknown to her, invited a fellow countrywoman to share in the occasion. Or perhaps they had known that the princess was already on friendly terms with Miss Devereux, who, despite her clearly voiced distaste for all the social gatherings of the Congress, seemed to cross his path with disturbing regularity.

Brett was still puzzled by the unexplained relationship between the two Englishwomen, a relationship that neither one seemed terribly eager to elucidate. In fact, if the truth were told, he had begun to wonder if they were not purposely keeping it from him. Miss Devereux had been singularly unforthcoming about it, and when he had questioned the princess about it several evenings later, she had been just as unhelpful when he had introduced the topic in the middle of a waltz.

"I made an acquaintance of a friend of yours the other evening."

"Mmmm," the princess had murmured caressing his shoulder ever so discreetly. "I have a great many friends in Vienna."

"This is a young woman, someone who must be quite close to you, for I first encountered her in your library."

The princess' blue eyes had opened wide. "*My* library? Surely you do not think that *I* have a library, Major. I assure you, I have no interest in such things. It is not *my* library. As you know, our apartments are rented, and since I am not likely ever to use the library in them, I have given leave to all my acquaintances to make free of it; though most of my friends have far more enjoyable things to occupy their time, as do I, than to waste it buried in a library." She smiled wickedly at him.

"This was a Miss Devereux, a young Englishwoman who looks as though she spends a great deal of her time in libraries."

"Ah, Helena." The princess had sighed. "You are in the right of it. She does spend a great deal of her time in libraries—too much time, in fact. She is far too serious for her own good. But in spite of the fact that it would do her more good to be out enjoying herself, I do allow her to use the library."

"Then you *do* admit to knowing her. She is a friend of the family?"

"Yes, yes, that is it . . . a family friend. I have known her this age, since she was a child. But let us not talk of a serious, young woman when the music is so delightful and I am so fortunate to have such an excellent partner."

And that had been the extent of it. Since the princess had been dancing with him at the time, the vagueness of her response had not struck Brett so forcefully as it did now when he saw the two of them together in the

Esterhazys landau. This time he resolved not to come away from the encounter without a clearer explanation.

Ordinarily, Brett would not have wasted a second thought on it, but the very fact that each woman avoided the subject of the other one made him all the more curious as to why they did.

"Princess von Hohenbachern?" Brett executed what little bow he could, given the crowds of spectators pressing on all sides of the carriage.

The princess held out her hand, favoring him with a dazzling smile. "Major. Do let me make you known to the Prince and Princess Esterhazy. And I believe that you have told me that you have already made the acquaintance of Miss Devereux."

Brett watched fascinated as a delicate blush rose in Miss Devereux's cheeks. He would have been ready to swear that very little, if anything, could throw this redoubtable young woman, but now, suddenly, she looked as self-conscious as an awkward young miss just out of the schoolroom. And the glance she directed at the princess was decidedly odd—as though somehow she were looking to her for some sort of guidance. This hesitancy in a young woman who had carried herself with such confidence among the select crowd at the Princess von Furstenberg's salon seemed all the more strange because it was out of character, or at least out of the character, Brett had thought she had.

Just then a magnificently uniformed gentleman appeared to claim the attention of the Esterhazys, and Brett, deciding that there was no time like the present, seized the opportunity to elicit an explanation from both the princess and Miss Devereux.

He smiled at the two of them. "I am delighted to find the only two Englishwomen I know in Vienna—except, of course, for Lady Castlereagh—here together in the same carriage. I gather, since I have already encountered Miss Devereux in your library, Princess, that yours is a long-standing acquaintance. How fortunate that you have found one another for companionship in this foreign city."

Helena nodded in what she hoped was a noncommittal way. At this point she was more concerned with her own reactions to Major Lord Brett Stanford than his questions about her relationship to the princess. It had been disconcerting in the extreme to discover how quickly her eyes had found him among the vast crowd of spectators at the celebration. True, his broad-shouldered figure, taller than all the others by at least a head, dominated the scene, and despite the mass of people crowding around him on all sides, he moved with the natural grace and confidence of a man accustomed to dominating every situation in which he found himself. But even more disconcerting was the warm feeling of gratification that swept over her on hearing that he had mentioned her to her mother. Why should she even care that she had made a favorable impression on a man whom she had only met twice before, favorable enough so that he had introduced her into a conversation with her mother? It should not have mattered, but somehow Helena was inordinately pleased that he had noticed her enough to ask the Princess von Hohenbachern about her.

Brett's eyes narrowed. Surely the politely blank expression that Miss Devereux was so carefully maintaining was assumed?

The princess, however, flashed a charmingly conspiratorial smile. "Perhaps not so fortunate as you might think, for I asked Helena to accompany me here to Vienna. In fact, she will tell you that I gave her very little choice in the matter, for if she were left to her own devices she would have remained immured at home in our library at Hohenbachern. But I felt that we both needed a bit of society, and she is nothing if not a dutiful daughter."

"Daughter!"

"You are surprised, Major?" Even though by now she felt quite sure of his admiration, the princess took great pleasure in Brett's patent astonishment. "Well, I *was* barely out of the schoolroom when Helena's father and I were married. It is astounding now to think of it, two such children as we were setting up housekeeping and then a baby immediately. But I shall not bore you with the details, as I . . ."

The rest of her words were drowned out by a roll of drums as three orchestras, spaced strategically around

the altar, struck up *The Hymn of Peace,* and every
church bell in the city rang a peel in celebration of the
Allied victory and the peace that had at last come to
Europe. The crowd remained silent until the last strains
of the music and the bells had died away, and then
turned to welcome the troops being honored by the celebration as they marched toward tables laid out for
their feast.

Brett turned to the princess. "Would you care to stroll
with me to the pavilion? I believe that the emperor and
the rest of the allied sovereigns will be toasting the
troops before they begin their feast."

The princess surveyed the soldiers filing down the
alley, which was lined on both sides by thousands of
cheering citizens, and shuddered. "Thank you, Major."
She tilted her straw-colored silk parasol coquettishly.
"But the crowds and the dust . . . so fatiguing, do you
not think so?"

He nodded at her, admiring the exquisite picture she
made from the tip of her fashionable bonnet trimmed
with green ribbon to the sandals of green kid that just
peeped from under the deep lace flounces of her dress.
But it was a picture better left as it was. Her daughter,
on the other hand, appeared to be more than eager to
escape the confines of the carriage.

Brett grinned. He had been right in his first assess-
ment at the Princess von Furstenberg's salon, even if he
was having difficulty adjusting to the idea of the redoubtable Miss Devereux being the daughter of the exquisite
Princess von Hohenbachen. Clearly Miss Devereux was
a most energetic young woman who despised sitting
tamely on the side when something of interest was occurring. "Then perhaps Miss Devereux would like to
join me."

"Thank you, Major." Grateful for the opportunity to
stretch her cramped limbs, Helena took his outstretched
hand and allowed him to help her down before the other
occupants of the landau had time to demur. "It is such
a glorious day, and there is so much to see that it is
a pity not to take advantage of it all. I do appreciate
your offer."

Ordinarily accustomed to striding along by herself,

Helena acknowledged the advantage of being escorted by an impressive-looking man when the crowd parted respectfully in front of them and they made their way toward the pavilion. There was something extraordinarily pleasant, not to mention reassuring, about having a strong arm to hold onto as they negotiated the press of people surrounding them. "It is most kind of you to escort me. I am sorry that Mama did not wish to come, but . . ."

"But being a beauty takes a great deal of time and effort, and the effect can be ruined in an instant if one indulges in such disarranging activities as taking a long walk through a horde of people. I quite understand."

Helena stared at him. Most of her mother's gallants were so concerned with the impressions that they themselves were making they had little thought or attention to spare on anyone else. And certainly none of them had ever wasted a moment's thought or effort on her daughter. But there was something about the sympathetic twinkle in this man's eyes and the conspiratorial intimacy of his smile that made her feel instinctively as though she could trust him. His humorously indulgent attitude toward the princess made Helena realize that, unlike her mother's other admirers, this man was fundamentally a kind person who understood the princess' foibles and forgave them, just as he admired her good qualities.

"Yes, it does take a good deal of time and effort." Helena shook her head ruefully as she thought of the hours her mother spent closeted with hairdressers, dressmakers, and maids, not to mention the time spent shopping.

"Time that the serious Miss Devereux, who has far better things to do with it, considers wasted, no doubt."

Helena frowned thoughtfully. "Not wasted, precisely. At least not for Mama. Mama has always been very gay, or at least she was before my father died and before the war took my stepfather away from Hohenbachern and kept her from entertaining. But now the war is over and she can be gay again. And if one aspires to that sort of life, one must be beautiful, or, at the very least, fashionable."

Brett looked down at his companion. Did he detect just the slightest note of wistfulness in her voice? Surely it must have been difficult, no matter how intellectual Helena's own interests were, to be the daughter of a noted beauty. "Yes, I can see that society with its entertainments, the dancing, the music, the crowds, the laughter, are the very breath of life to the princess, er, your mother, and she gives the breath of life to them. And it is her zest for it all, her gaiety that I find particularly attractive. She enjoys life and it enjoys her."

Helena glanced curiously at him. He truly meant what he said, and he had a point. There *was* something infectious about her mother's frank appreciation of all the diversions that life had to offer. Even Helena, who had witnessed enough of the other side of it to vow never to depend on the society of others for her own happiness, had to admit that life was always more vibrant, more exuberant, even more fun, when her mother was around. "I suppose you are right, but one cannot always count on balls and *fêtes* to amuse oneself."

"That is undoubtedly true, but neither should one become so philosophical and serious that one forgets entirely one's capacity for enjoying oneself or, worse yet, loses it altogether."

There was an edge in his voice that told her this was no idle observation. "You speak from experience, perhaps, Major?" Helena could not think what possessed her to make such a very personal remark, but she was curious about this man who was such a study in contrasts—a gallant who flattered her mother, but a soldier who believed strongly in the cause he fought for, a charming man of the world, yet someone who obviously reflected a great deal on it all.

"Extensive. My entire family sees its duty so clearly that it is impossible for them to derive amusement from anything. We must always be devoting ourselves to our estates, our tenants, or our responsibilities as landowners, and there is no room for the enjoyment of any of it." There was no mistaking the bitterness in his voice now. "Even when my mother and sisters attend anything so frivolous as a ball, they do so mostly because it is expected of them, and not because they could possibly delight in wearing an elegant toilette, or appearing to their best advantage. They could not even take pleasure in listening to music or dancing to it. Do not mistake me, they are good, admirable people, but old before their time, not the least attractive to look at, and astoundingly dull as well. Your mother, on the other hand, enjoys being beautiful, makes the most of it, and therefore offers a delightful feast for the eyes. She will always retain a good deal of her beauty no matter how old, because she is so alive and she takes care always to look her best."

Helena did not know how to respond to this. Never had any of her mother's admirers honored her by speaking so frankly with her. And even the most admiring ones had failed to make her appreciate anything about her mother. But now she could see that there was a great deal of sense in what the major had to say. "You do make a strong case, Major, but pray do not repeat it to Mama. She already chastises me for being far too serious. But it is not so much that I am serious as it is that I simply do not enjoy what she enjoys."

"As long as you enjoy something, and I do know that you enjoy one thing at least—putting me at a disadvantage. In fact, you took far too much pleasure at my discomfiture when I learned that you were not your mother's maid. Furthermore, now that I think of it, I suspect that you did your very best to avoid any mention at all of the relationship between you and your mother."

Helena chuckled. "I did, rather. But it is so rare that I have anyone at a disadvantage that I must be pardoned for taking what pleasure I could from it."

"Miss Devereux, I feel certain that you have people at a disadvantage a good deal of the time."

"I? What advantage could I possibly have over other people that would make them feel that way?"

"A very fine mind." Brett watched the delicate shade of pink spread over her cheeks and decided that he liked to make her blush. It gave her a certain softness and vulnerability that was very attractive in someone so matter-of-fact and self-possessed.

"Really?" There was something infinitely touching in her genuine pleasure at such a small compliment and her eagerness to hear more. Then her face fell. "But Mama says that most people do not like cleverness, especially in a woman."

"Your mama is quite correct. Most people do not. I, however, do. I find it as intriguing as it is rare."

"But I thought you preferred to feast your eyes on beauty."

It was his turn to chuckle. There was a roguish twinkle in the big hazel eyes and a teasing smile tugging at the beautifully shaped lips that was utterly enchanting. "If I were allowed to do so in peace, yes. But most women insist on talking, which is often all that is required to make one forget their physical charms completely. Or they expect so many compliments that it becomes onerous rather than a pleasure. You have my word for it, it can rapidly become tedious, if not exhausting. You, on the other hand are quite unique. Your conversation is so interesting that one forgets all else."

"Really?" Helena found herself experiencing the oddest feeling in the pit of her stomach, as though a flock of butterflies had suddenly taken flight. There was something in the way he looked at her that made her feel he was absolutely sincere, in spite of the extravagance of his claim. The intentness of his expression, the light in his eyes told her that he truly did believe she was special. Still, she was not at all certain this was a compliment. After all, no woman wished to be thought of as an antidote, no matter how fine her mind.

"Yes. Really. I may be a novice when it comes to diplomatic affairs, but I know enough about people to know that no one at the Princess von Furstenberg's salon that evening was a casually invited guest. It was quite clear to me from the moment I entered the room that everyone there had been asked there for a purpose, and only those capable of advancing that purpose had been selected. No, do not argue with me. According to all that I have heard and all that I saw, Princess von Furstenberg is too dedicated to her cause to waste her time with anyone who cannot contribute effectively to it. She quite obviously considers you to be a valuable member of that group."

"No. She only invited me because I speak both English and German."

Brett shook his head slowly and emphatically.

"Oh." Helena was silent for a moment while she digested this intriguing idea. "I had not thought . . . I mean, I had rather hoped . . . Do you truly think so?"

Her eagerness for his reassurance was almost childlike. He was oddly touched by it, and it was all he could do not to clasp the hand resting on his arm, raise it to his lips, and assure her that she was a person of value and importance.

"But I am only a woman, and . . ."

"That does not matter. Why there are women . . ." He caught himself just in time. She might have been born in England, but she had spent most of her life in Europe, or at least most of her adult life, and her sympathies clearly lay with the smaller German states. There was no need for her to know Wellington's opinion that there were women in Vienna who had the power to affect the entire outcome of the Congress.

"Why, there are women. What women?"

"Er, all I mean, is that there are women who are intelligent enough to be as well-informed as any man," he concluded lamely.

The large hazel eyes regarded him thoughtfully. She knew that that was not what he had been about to say, but she would not press. She was too clever for that, far too clever. And she was more experienced at the diplomatic game than he was, Brett reminded himself grimly. "You must think it amazingly presumptuous for a rough soldier such as I, whose only experience in foreign relations has been with a pistol and saber, to comment on such things."

She smiled at that and cocked her head to one side. There was something completely disarming about the man's honesty, and something dangerously attractive in his refusal to indulge in even the ordinary self-delusions that most people practiced. "No. I realize that you may not have experience in European diplomatic affairs, but I believe your years in the Peninsula must have given you a very broad knowledge of people in general. Surely you must have been in many situations where your ability to judge a person was critical. Undoubtedly you became rather good at it over time, so I will allow myself to trust your judgement and say thank you, I think, for your positive opinion of me.''

"And thank you for trusting my judgment.''

The humorous twinkle in his eyes warmed her in a way she had rarely, if ever experienced. It made her feel extraordinarily close to a man she had only just met, a man she had not spoken to more than once or twice, a man she had been prepared to dislike on her well-established principle that any man who aspired to be one of her mother's admirers was shallow and superficial. Yet this man made her feel understood and appreciated in a way no one else had. "You are welcome, Major.''

Her smile transformed her face, he thought. By the strictest conventional standards, it was not a beautiful face, not like her mother's at any rate. The cheekbones were a little too prominent and the large hazel eyes with their thick dark lashes were almost too large for it, but it was a face that radiated intelligence and humor. Most men, and most women for that matter, did not necessarily find such a combination attractive, however, he found it oddly compelling. It was a face with character, a face that told even the most casual observer that a thoughtful and interesting mind lived behind it. But above all, it was the humor lurking in the ironic half smile, the twinkle in the eye that told anyone who cared to think about it that its owner, while she might be a serious person with serious interests, was under no illusions about herself in particular or life in general.

Chapter Nine

By now they had reached the pavilion where the troops that had marched down the alley were seating themselves at the enormously long tables arranged in the shape of a star. Sergeants from each regiment were distributing bowls of soup among their men as well as platters heaped high with pork, beef, and fritters, all accompanied with generous servings of wine.

Brett and Helena watched as the emperor and the tsar, standing together in the balcony looking out over the tables, raised their glasses in a toast to the thousands of men seated below.

It was an awe-inspiring moment, and Helena felt a lump rise in her throat. Her eyes misted over as she looked at the sea of men in front of her, veterans all of them from the wars with the French. Some had the grizzled faces of battle-hardened soldiers while some still had the fresh soft features of boys; but all bore the signs of war, whether it was in their grave expressions, the scar here, the empty sleeve there, or the crutches scattered throughout the crowd.

Seeing them brought the memories flooding back to her, memories of wounded stragglers she had tried to help back in Hohenbachern, of peasants watching as their larders were stripped bare, their livestock pilfered, and their crops burned by foraging armies. Friend or enemy, it had made no difference to the local villagers who had lost the fruits of their labor to hungry soldiers and faced the cruelty of winter without provisions.

"And I hope that this is truly the end of it all." Helena did not even realize she had spoken aloud until she saw Brett looking at her in some surprise.

"You do not think that it is? Surely we are all tired of war?"

"The soldiers, perhaps, but there are those to whom power is more important than peace, and, believe me, they are even now prepared to go back to war if they do not get what they want in this peace and if we can not convince them not to, which is why I spend my time reading political pamphlets and attending the Princess von Furstenberg's soirees. I am trying to help convince them not to, trying to keep them from fighting from all that terrible . . ." She could not go on.

"Are you all right, Miss Devereux?"

Helena blinked rapidly. "Yes . . . yes I am. It is just that I was remembering all those poor men I tried to help. We set up beds in one of the outbuildings of the schloss for the wounded and the sick, and we tried to care for them as best we could, but it is all such a waste—fine healthy young men destroyed in an instant, men who . . ."

She shook her head, swallowed hard, and continued. "If I were a man, I could do something to stop it all, but as a woman, I am forced to stay quietly at home and do nothing, nothing! And I hate it. I loathe being useless!"

"But you were not useless. You did something." The fierceness of her tone had made Brett see with a blinding clarity how frustrating it must be for a woman as passionate and energetic as Miss Devereux to be confined to the female role as a decorative fixture in men's lives. It even made him see why his mother and sisters clung to their duties as they did. Perhaps they were not so different from him as he had thought. They too wished to live productive lives, to make the world better, but their choices were far more limited than his. "Believe me, Miss Devereux, if you had ever been wounded, exhausted, hungry, and discouraged as I have, you would know that being given safety, shelter, food, and comfort is no small thing. It is everything, in fact. And it is the compassion of those like you who offer those things that bring back thoughts of home, thoughts that keep one alive, keep one fighting, that give us hope that we are better than savages or animals." Gently he covered the hand that lay on his arm with his own.

Helena looked up into blue eyes that were dark with sympathy, and a sadness that touched the very core of her being. Who would have thought that this man who possessed the charm to impress her mother, could understand so well the feelings of the daughter. She was silent for a long time, mesmerized by the look in his eyes and the comforting warmth of his hand on hers. She wanted to thank him, to tell him that his words had given meaning to her life, had reassured her that there was value in what she had tried to do, but nothing would come out.

A burst of applause broke the spell.

"Yes, Franz, I agree with you, they may celebrate peace now, but who knows how long it will last?"

The voice of the man next to Helena echoed her thoughts exactly. Glancing over her shoulder, she could just make out the angular features of the speaker, a young man of medium height and build and an aristocratic bearing who appeared to be scrutinizing the major intently.

"To my way of thinking, it all depends on the English," Franz replied. "It all depends on how strong they are. For if it were not for them, who knows that Napoleon would not still be the master of Europe."

The aristocratic young man moved slightly forward. "And what do you think of our celebrations, Major?" He bowed to Brett and addressed him in English, but with a heavy German accent. "It is a pity we could not honor our British warriors here today as well, but there are so few on this side of the Atlantic. One hears that all the heroes of the Peninsula have been shipped off to America to fight the colonials. In fact, I am surprised to see you here, Major . . ."

"Stanford. Lord Brett Stanford, at your service, sir. And you are correct, I was . . ."

"Ahem." A pointed cough and a squeeze on his arm reminded Brett that he was not alone. "Ah, do forgive me, this is Miss Devereux."

"Delighted." Clicking his heels punctiliously, the young man bowed to Helena. "Augustus von Stieglitz, also at your service. We are indeed fortunate to have an English young lady at our celebrations. I do hope that you are enjoying herself."

"Miss Devereux is here with her mother, who . . ."

"Is a great friend of Lady Castlereagh," Helena interjected quickly. "And I am enjoying the ceremonies immensely. They are indeed impressive, but I am afraid I find myself quite overcome with the noise, the heat . . ." Helena pressed her hand to her brow, and doing her very best to imitate her mother's charming die-away air, allowed herself to lean more heavily on Brett's arm. "I beg your indulgence, sir, and yours, Major, but I am very much afraid I must ask you to restore me to our carriage, if you would be so kind."

"But of course. It must be rather overwhelming for a delicate young lady." Augustus von Stieglitz turned and held out his arm to clear a path for them through the crowd.

"I do apologize, Miss Devereux. You should have told me sooner that you were not feeling quite the thing." Taken by surprise at this sudden sign of weakness, Brett glanced down at his companion.

"Oh, it is nothing, I . . ." Helena broke off as she tried unobtrusively to get a good look at the Franz, who had been talking to von Stieglitz and had remained behind when his companion stepped forward to converse with Brett. Taller than von Stieglitz, with a narrow bearded face and wearing clothes that were as common as his speech, he seemed an odd companion for the clearly aristocratic von Stieglitz. Yet his bearing had been the rigidly straight posture of a soldier. Helena frowned thoughtfully as she tried to make sense of the entire episode.

Even more puzzled by Helena's sudden fit of abstraction, Brett studied her closely. The sudden weakness had seemed most uncharacteristic in the redoubtable Miss Devereux, who now appeared to have recovered miraculously once they parted company with Augustus von Stieglitz. She was as sprightly and alert as ever, though preoccupied, and she no longer clung to his arm as she marched determinedly back to the carriage. "Why did you not mention your relationship with the von Hohenbacherns to von Stieglitz? I would have thought he would have been delighted to encounter someone with such an interest in and sympathy for German affairs."

"Saxon." Helena corrected him.

Brett stared at her blankly.

"The man is a Saxon," she reiterated fiercely. "I could tell by his accent when he spoke with the man behind us. After Napoleon embarked on his conquest of the German states, Saxony became one of his most loyal allies, and many of the Saxons, especially the younger generation, were his great admirers. In fact, they are still. Did you not think it odd that he asked you about the troops being sent to America, or that he was even aware of it?"

"No." Brett was more at sea than ever.

"The more troops Britain has in America, the fewer she can call on here should there be war in Europe. Not everyone is glad to have Napoleon beaten and the old monarchies restored. Some of the younger generation of Germans welcomed the democratic ideals that the revolution represented and that Napoleon brought to the conquered territories. They do not want life to return to the way it was."

"What? Surely you are not suggesting . . . why the man is miles away, on an island, cut off from the rest of Europe by ocean on all sides."

Helena shrugged. There was a dismissive tone in his voice that she found thoroughly annoying. "That may very well be true, but as you have already admitted, you have not the least knowledge of European politics."

"But it is absurd to think that Napoleon could possibly be a threat!" Finding her air of smug superiority to be equally annoying, Brett did not even bother to stifle his own irritation.

"Is it? You, after all, were on the Peninsula, where the troops you fought against were led almost entirely by Napoleon's marshals. I, on the other hand, have seen firsthand the soldiers led by Napoleon himself and have witnessed his troops' utter devotion to him. Even to the sick and the wounded he was both a hero and a god who could do no wrong. I have no doubt they would welcome him back in an instant and follow him any-where should he reappear." And with a triumphant nod of her head, Helena stalked off in the direction of the carriage without giving Brett a chance to reply.

Thoroughly taken aback, he stared after her. Then collecting his wits at last, he hurried to catch up. "But I thought you loathed the man."

"Of course I loathe the man! But I am not such a simpleton that I cannot appreciate what enormous feats he has accomplished in a very few years, especially for the ordinary Frenchmen who fought under him."

Brett ground his teeth at the scornful glint in her eyes. No man, and certainly no woman, had ever accused him of being a simpleton. True, she had not out and out stated it, certainly not directly, but the implication was clear enough. Simpleton he might be, stupid he was not, and he knew what she thought of him.

By this time they had reached the landau, where the princess, after one glance at their faces, sighed gently. "Oh, dear. I do hope Helena has not been too impatient with you, Major. She simply does not understand that not everyone possesses such a thorough knowledge and understanding of diplomatic affairs as she does, and she is inclined to express her opinions somewhat forcefully." The princess shook her head apologetically, as though her daughter's intense political debates and their subsequent disagreements were all too common an occurrence. "Well, never mind. Let us talk of something that is more amusing."

She glanced around her at the flags, the patriotic decorations, and the throngs of people. "In general, I would say that Vienna is inferior to London; however, the Prater is very pretty and compares quite favorably with Hyde Park. Do you not think so, Major? I admit that I infinitely prefer ballrooms to parks myself, a carriage ride now and then is all the nature I can take, but to Helena, the Prater is a godsend. She is quite a dedicated horsewoman, and people who know about these things tell me that she is most accomplished. And you too, Major, are someone accustomed to spending a great deal of time in the saddle. You must appreciate it for the same reasons she does."

The princess chattered gaily on, now smiling at Brett, now nodding to her daughter until she succeeded in drawing the two of them back into some semblance of friendly conversation. It was slow going at first, for the two of them truly had appeared to be at daggers drawn when they returned from their stroll, but the princess' charm was such that eventually they quite forgot their differences and found themselves chuckling at her wealth of amusing *on dits.*

And it was not until he was climbing the interminable flights of stairs to his room many hours later that Brett finally recalled the original point that had turned their discussion from amicable to acrimonious. Did Helena Devereux really think it possible that Napoleon Bonaparte could rally enough support to be a serious threat to the fragile peace now being painstakingly hammered out in Vienna's drawing rooms?

He racked his brain trying to remember von Stieglitz's every word and every gesture, if von Stieglitz was even the real name of the man who had accosted him in the Prater. But Brett could recall nothing that seemed to support Miss Devereux's suspicions that the man was a spy except for her claims about his Saxon accent and the Saxons' loyalties to Napoleon. Surely she was over-reacting? Surely von Stieglitz was just a congenial young man making pleasant conversation with one of the city's many foreign visitors. Undoubtedly if Brett had been Italian, he would have made some equally appropriate comment. It was Miss Devereux's total immersion in politics that made her so unusually sensitive to the possible implications of everything, even when there were none.

It would do her good to clear her head by taking more of that fresh air and exercise her mother had alluded to. It was bound to give her a better perspective on things.

Her mother! Brett chuckled to himself as he recalled the secret smile on the princess' face when she had introduced Helena as her daughter. She had known what Brett's reaction would be and had taken great pleasure in his astonishment when he had learned that the youthful, vivacious, beautiful, not to mention flirtatious, Princess von Hohenbachern was the mother of a young woman. And she was the mother of not just any young woman, but the serious, the studious, the passionately political Miss Devereux.

It was hard to believe that the intellectual Miss Devereux was related in any way to the pleasure-loving princess. How could two such very different women be mother and daughter? Intrigued by the paradox of it all, Brett paused on the top step of the landing in front of his chambers. Were they so different, or was there, under the daughter's reserved intellectual exterior, a creature as alive and vibrant as the mother? Certainly, during the conversations he had had with Miss Devereux, she had done her best to convince him that she despised the things that amused her mother as so much foolishness and considered them to be so frivolous as to be beneath her, but he wondered. Clearly Helena Devereux was a passionate creature, though in her case the passion was an intellectual one fired by political idealism. What if that passion were to be redirected to something less intellectual, something more sensual perhaps? It was an intriguing notion and Brett found himself, much against his better judgment, tempted to put it to the test.

Chapter Ten

It was only a few days later that Brett was presented with just such an opportunity as, taking advantage of the continued and unusual warm spell, he decided to extend his morning routine after the completion of their exercises in the Prater with a leisurely exploration of its many paths. It was a glorious day, and Rex, who had been accustomed to a much more demanding existence on the Peninsula, seemed as loathe to return to the British delegation as his master. The two of them trotted sedately along the alley under the chestnut trees, enjoying the fineness of the day and their escape from the narrow confines of the city.

Suddenly there was a pounding of hooves behind them, and an enormous bay shot past at tremendous speed. Rex, who had been as absorbed as his master in the soporific atmosphere of the beautiful autumn day, pricked up his ears and tugged at the reins. Brett's attention, captured first by the magnificent animal, quickly focused on the trim figure of the rider—a woman, and a very impressive woman indeed—who sat her horse with the grace and ease of one born to the saddle.

Thoroughly intrigued, he urged his own horse forward and they were off, thundering down the length of the alley. When Rex at last caught up with the horse and rider at the far end of the Prater, all the somnolence of the day had worn off. The horse and its mistress raced on as though the hounds of hell were after them; indeed, it almost seemed as though they would continue their headlong rush until they plunged into the Danube itself, but at the last possible minute they wheeled to gallop back toward the city. It was only then that horse and rider became aware of their pursuers.

The rider reined in her horse with a strength that was surprising for such a slender frame and waited for Brett and Rex to catch up with them.

As he approached, Brett could not help thinking that somehow the rider knew him. Perhaps it was the fact that she had halted instead of tearing back past him, or perhaps it was the tilt of the head under the high-crowned hat. Whatever it was, there was definitely a suggestion that, whoever she might be, she was very well aware of who he was.

"Good morning, Major." In spite of her furious pace and abrupt halt, Miss Devereux did not appear to be the least out of breath. She addressed him as coolly and calmly as if he had just been ushered into her library. Did nothing unsettle the woman?

Prompted by a devilish impulse he could not explain, Brett determined to try—anything to shake that air of composure. "I hope I am not disturbing you."

"Disturbing me? No. But why would you be disturbing me?"

At least he had succeeded in making her look faintly surprised. "Well, usually young ladies in this city do not come alone to the Prater at this hour unless they are indulging in a romantic assignation."

"A romantic assignation!" The delicate eyebrows rose in astonishment and then quickly lowered into a scornful scowl. "How dare you! I would no more indulge in such . . ." Thoroughly annoyed, she gathered the reins in her hands and prepared to urge her horse forward.

Brett chuckled. "No, please, Miss Devereux, do not go. Forgive me for teasing you. I could not help myself. Of course you are not here for an assignation."

Paradoxically enough, his swift apology did not appear to mollify her.

In fact, Helena herself could not explain this new spurt of indignation in response to his swift apology. *Of course you are not here for an assignation.* Naturally she did not wish to be thought of in the same terms as the Princess Bagration, the Duchess of Sagan, or even her own mother, as just another flirtatious woman taking advantage of the scores of powerful and attractive men gathered in the city. Still, she did not relish being written off so quickly, as though she were an antidote or an ape-leader, especially by the dashing Major Lord Brett Stanford. No, she did not want that at all. "And, pray tell, what makes you so sure that I am not here for a . . . for . . . an assignation."

He brought Rex close enough to her so that he could cup her chin with one gloved hand. A playful smile hovered around his lips as he turned her face toward him. "Because, my dear, you do not have the look of it."

"The look?"

"Believe me, Miss Devereux, I have, er *attended* many such meetings myself, and there is usually a look of eagerness about the eyes, a delicate flush on the cheeks"— he removed his glove to trace her lips with a gentle finger—"and a redness about the lips of young ladies about to meet someone. You, my dear young lady, exhibit none of these signs. Or, if you had already been with some handsome young diplomat, your eyes would be soft and dreamy instead of clear and bright. Your lips would be swollen from a lover's kiss, your breathing would be erratic. No, Miss Devereux, you show no signs of such weakness. You are alert, aware, and fully in command of yourself and the situation as always."

Helena was not at all sure she agreed with the accuracy of his statement. The warmth of his finger on her lips was in fact producing all the signs he identified as being absent. Her cheeks were hot, her lips tingled, her heart, usually a most reliable organ, was pounding in her chest, and even the simple act of breathing was impossibly difficult at the moment. She gulped and strove to regain her composure. "Of . . . of course I do not show signs of such weakness. One person in a family who indulges in such things is quite enough; there is no need for another."

Where had the bitterness come from? Ordinarily she was able to keep a healthy perspective on her mother's affairs. Could it be that she was at this moment just the tiniest bit jealous of someone who had not only enjoyed, but doubtless inspired many such romantic assignations?

"Oh, so it is like that, is it?" His tone was teasing, but there was a wealth of sympathy in the blue eyes, and the hand that had cupped her chin now closed over her own hand in a reassuring clasp. "Someone in the family had to have her wits about her while others were being, ah, *carried away*?"

The statement was so accurate that Helena could only stare at him and nod dumbly. At last she found her voice. "Well, yes. I mean, in a way, that is quite true. Mama has always been a far better judge of style than character. And since she always places her entire happiness on the man of the moment, this has led to a rather precarious existence. My real father was only the first of many. I never knew him, but according to Mama he was extremely dashing and romantic, but wild to a fault, and they moved with a very fast set. He would gamble on anything and everything. She would too." Helena stopped, appalled. What was she doing sharing such things with a near stranger, things she had not fully acknowledged even to herself?

"Come, let us walk and you shall tell me about it." Brett dismounted and came around to offer his hand to Helena, but, not to his surprise, she had already slid off her horse before he could help her down.

For reasons she could not fathom, Helena found herself pouring out the sordid details of her early existence. "They went through my father's inheritance at a great rate, so much so that when he died, she was left deep in debt. But she refused help from his family and hers because it would have meant being forced to live quietly and respectably in the country with the family. Instead, she looked to other admirers to help her out of her desperate financial straits, but all they did was make her try to forget her worries by seeking further amusement. Or, worse yet, they encouraged her to recoup her losses by gambling further. With each new admirer came the new hope that this one would solve her problems, but the men she was drawn to were not the men with enough substance to do such a thing. She fell deeper and deeper into debt, and the more desperate her circumstances, the

more her admirers—all bent on their own amusement—
drifted away until Papa appeared and offered her marriage. By this time her reputation was in ruins, as well
as her finances, so to avoid it all, she married him and
fled to the Continent. But he was forced to be away
from home so much that she soon became restless and
unhappy. She needs constant attention and admiration
to keep her happy."

"And you, having witnessed all this, have resolved not
to follow in her footsteps."

"Never! It is the height of absurdity to place one's
entire dependence for happiness on another person.
What does one do if that person is not there? Fall into
a decline? No." She shook her head vigorously. "We are
all responsible for our own happiness, to make of our
own lives what we will."

Lost in memories of the past, of watching the string
of admirers who came and went, raising her mother's
hopes and dashing them as they appeared and disappeared, Helena paused by a small ornamental pool and
sat down on the rock next to it. Unable to resist the lure
of the water, sparkling in the warm autumn sunshine,
she pulled off her glove and dipped her fingers in it.
Trailing them slowly back and forth, she recalled all the
men her mother had said were going to rescue them
from their dubious existence, men who had no sooner
appeared in their lives than they had disappeared.

Eventually one of them had rescued them. He had
given them a home and a family, but he had been unable
to rescue the princess from the crushing boredom that
came along with the security he offered. For Helena, the
peaceful bucolic existence had been a dream come true.
For her mother, it had been closer to a nightmare of
rustic isolation, the very thing she had been avoiding
when she refused to live with her family or the family
of her dead husband.

Brett watched in fascination as the slim white fingers
drew twinkling ripples in the water as though they were
caressing it. The simple sensuality of it quite took his
breath away, and he suddenly had a vision of her ca-
vorting naked in the water like Diana at her bath. Something in her dreamy expression—the half-closed eyes, the

gently parted lips—suggested to him that she was thinking the same thing he was, that she longed to pull off her clothes and plunge into the crystal-clear water.

He blinked and swallowed hard, desperately trying to wipe the distracting image from his mind, but he could not. It remained there, tantalizing him, challenging him with the sudden revelation that Helena, despite her severe and serious exterior, was perhaps as much a sensualist as her mother, but she just did not recognize it—or refused to recognize it. Prompted by her intimate knowledge of the pitfalls of her mother's existence, she must have rejected it entirely and stifled every dangerous impulse that might possibly send her down a similar path. But deep inside her was a creature that gloried in the physical, a woman who enjoyed racing a powerful horse on a golden autumn day, who tilted her head to enjoy the warmth of the sun on her face, who reveled in the silky caress of the water on her fingers. What would she be like if she were awakened to these feelings? What would it be like to be the man who made her aware of her own sensual impulses?

It was dizzying thought. A woman as passionate as the mother, but as thoughtful and intellectual as the daughter. It would take a special man, a very special man indeed to bring such a person to life. Idly he wondered if there were any man capable of such a thing as he mentally cataloged the participants at the Congress. No mere functionary or petty plenipotentiary would do. She had her pick of German princelings, Italian and Polish counts. Alexander? No, irresistible as the tsar might be to most women, he was too volatile. Metternich? No, the chancellor might be the soul of courtesy and diplomacy, but he was too rigid, too self-involved. Talleyrand? No, brilliant though he might be, Epicurean that he was, he was simply too old and too frail for someone as active as Helena.

Enough! Brett forced the dangerously tantalizing thoughts from his mind. "But a life shared is a life enriched. Do you not agree? Perhaps that is what your mother sought. Surely you do not intend to be alone the rest of your life?"

Again, the vehement shake of the head. "No. To depend on another for happiness is to delude oneself. In addition to that, it puts an enormous burden on that other person—to entertain, to comfort, to solve the problems of someone else's existence. That is not fair. It is far safer and wiser to learn to solve one's problems on one's own. Then one never need fear being left alone."

Brett was silent, considering. What she said made a great deal of sense. In fact, he had been operating on that principle for much of his own life, but now, hearing someone else describe it, it sounded like such a barren existence. He was about to protest when her next words addressed his very objections.

"I expect that that is putting it rather baldly. I do not mean that we should isolate ourselves from one another, just that we should look first to ourselves and not to others for support. And that is why I wish . . . well, at any rate, why I do not count on some man to look after me."

He could not help chuckling at her scornful dismissal of his entire sex. "I can see that in your opinion, Miss Devereux, we men do present a rather poor risk. But you were about to tell me what you intended to do instead."

She colored slightly. Lord, the man was observant. He did not miss a thing. "Nothing very startling or unusual. In fact, I believe that most women would go to any lengths to avoid being a governess, but I . . . well, the truth of it is, I should like to be. I mean, I should like to start a school for girls. I am a good teacher. At least my stepsisters, Sophia and Augusta, seem to think so. I enjoy introducing them to new things, explaining things to them in terms they can understand. And I want girls like Sophie and Gussie to grow into intelligent women who can look after themselves instead of becoming clinging bits of fluff. There." She drew her hand out of the water, shook it a few times, and wiped it on the skirt of her riding habit. "Now you know why Mama gets that disparaging tone in her voice every time she refers to me."

Brett reached in his pocket and drew out a clean linen handkerchief. Taking her hand in his, he proceeded to

dry it off gently and thoroughly. "It is not a disparaging
tone that I hear, but a reluctant pride."

"Pride? In me? Mama?" She snorted in a most
unladylike manner and shook her head, but she did not
draw her hand away. Nor did she try to hide the hopeful
gleam in her eyes.

"Yes. I can see that she does not know what to make
of you. After all, the two of you are very different in
many ways, but, yes, I do think she is proud of you for
your quick and clever mind. She just does not understand what use it will be to you."

Helena stood mesmerized by his words, the look in
his eyes, the sympathetic smile and the warmth of his
hand. Her heartbeat, which had at last returned to normal after he had touched her lips, became erratic once
more, her breathing irregular, and her knees, which were
usually so dependable that she never spared them a second thought, now threatened to give way under her.

The twinkle in his eyes grew more pronounced and
his smile went from sympathetic to impish as he read
the telltale signs. Yes, Miss Devereux could be affected
by such things after all, even if she did not know it yet.
His own breathing grew erratic as he thought, for one
breathless moment, what it would be like to introduce
her to all the delights that could be shared between a
man and a woman.

Ruthlessly, Brett squelched such a tantalizing notion.
"Come, it is time that we pay attention to our horses
before they become utterly disgusted with this tame excuse for a ride in the park and demand that we give
them the exercise they deserve."

Chapter Eleven

Unresisting, Helena allowed him to help her into the saddle. Ordinarily she took it as a point of pride to be able to get on Nimrod's back unaided, but she was too bemused by a riot of conflicting thoughts and emotions to do anything but meekly accept his assistance. As he lifted her up, it felt, for the tiniest instant, as though he were going to kiss her. And, even more alarming, it had felt for a far longer space of time that that was what she wanted.

Settling herself in the saddle, Helena could not help wondering if she had completely taken leave of her senses. Never in her wildest dreams, not even at the height of her fascination with Ursula's tales of heroic knights and mythical warriors, had she ever imagined one of those heroes kissing her. And now, here, with a perfectly ordinary man, cavalry officer though he might be, she was actually wondering what it would be like to be swept up in his arms, to feel his lips on hers, to be meeting him as though he were the lover he had teased her about meeting. What on earth was wrong with her? Even if she had indulged in such dreams as a foolish, impressionable girl, which she had *not*, Helena knew that such dreams were not for her, for she knew from her mother's abundant experience that they did not come true. And she certainly had no intention of repeating her mother's folly, especially with a man who was one of her mother's many admirers.

With an effort she diverted her thoughts from such dangerous ground and faced the present. "Major?"

"Yes." Settling into his own saddle, Brett looked at her curiously. It was not like Helena Devereux to sound anything except confident or knowledgeable, but at the moment she sounded neither. In fact, she almost sounded unsure, as though she found herself in a position that was unsettling or upsetting to her. It was a glorious day, no one else was around. There was nothing to cause her any distress, which left only Helena and himself as the source of her unease. Scrutinizing her carefully, he thought he detected just a hint of color highlighting her cheekbones, the faintest glisten of sweat on her upper lip, and a more rapid rise and fall of the tightly molded bodice of her gray riding habit.

Brett stifled a grin. So his insinuations had affected her after all. Good. He was glad she could be as affected by him as he was affected by her. Granted, it was he, and not she, who had conjured up his mental image of her lithe nude body swimming in the pool, but her actions had inspired it. Whoever had been ultimately responsible for it, however, did not matter; he knew that he would never view Helena Devereux with dispassionate complacency ever again, which was a prospect he found to be unnerving in the extreme.

"I was wondering if you could . . . I mean, would you be so kind as to demonstrate the figures I saw you and your horse performing in the park before?"

"What?" Whatever he had expected her to ask of him, it had certainly not been that. "Oh, you meant the *haute école* exercises that Rex and I have been working to perfect."

He hoped his disappointment did not show, that she did not know he was hoping she was going to ask some special favor of the man and not the horse. "It is nothing, really, merely an expansion of the basic elements of dressage with the rider helping to bring the balance to the rear and lightening the forehand so the horse's gait is shorter and raised without sacrificing extension and freedom of movement. I acquired Rex when he was quite young, so was able to teach him with the aid of a training rope, which allowed him to develop and perfect his gait at the outset. Naturally his cavalry training added to all that, but it was not until we arrived here in Vienna and I saw what was being done at the Spanish Riding School that we truly began our work. At the moment we are trying to perfect the *levade* so we can move on to the *courbette* and then the *capriole*. Rex is comfortable enough balancing on his hind legs for the *levade,* but going from that to the jump for the *courbette* is something that still makes him uneasy."

As he finished his explanation, the enormous horse rose in one fluid movement on its hind legs, drawing in its forelegs until it was perfectly balanced while the rider, seemingly expending no more effort than his mount, remained as calm and unruffled as he had been moments before when all four legs had been firmly planted on the ground.

Helena held her breath in awe as she watched. Animal and rider were so perfectly controlled, so in tune with one another's movements that it was impossible to tell where one left off and the other began. Indeed, each motion seemed to begin in one and end in the other just as the horse's balance flowed smoothly from its forelegs to its hind. Only an experienced equestrian could appreciate the effort and the skill involved, a skill built upon understanding, trust, and communication between man and animal, a trust that was so deep, so complete that it seemed more magic than anything else.

Slowly they returned to earth, transformed from a mythical figure to earthly horse and rider once again. "Magnificent, truly magnificent." Helena was not sure whether she had uttered the words or only thought them, so overwhelmed was she by the sheer power and beauty of the demonstration.

"Thank you." Brett patted Rex's shiny neck as he tried to sort out the welter of emotions her reaction inspired in him. The look of wonder in her eyes and the undisguised admiration in her voice were strangely moving, and he realized that while women of all types had cast admiring glances in his direction often enough, they had always seemed contrived, as though they were adopted for effect rather than an expression of any true emotion. Furthermore, anything that they had admired was purely superficial, his physical presence or his social connections. The look on Helena's face was an unaffected, unrehearsed tribute to his accomplishments, pure and simple. The fact that he knew her to be an accomplished horsewoman herself only added to the meaningfulness of her appreciation, for it meant she was able to appreciate the effort, patience, and skill that it took to perform such a feat, and he felt oddly grateful to her for recognizing it.

"I know you explained it all to me, but I still cannot fathom how one even begins to work up to such an accomplishment, though I would dearly love to try."

Brett grinned. The thought of Helena Devereux on a rearing horse was quite enough to take anyone's breath away, but from the little he had seen of the way she rode, he felt quite certain that if anyone were equal to the challenge, she was. "It is like anything else. One does these things slowly and in sequence. You walked your horse before you trotted; you trotted before you cantered or galloped. And I would say, judging from the looks of your horse, that he is itching for a gallop at this very moment. Shall we?" Leaning forward over Rex's neck, he urged his own mount forward.

By the time they had reached a gallop, he heard her thundering behind him. In no time at all, she had shot past him, a magnificent picture of power and speed as she sat the big bay with all the assurance and poise of an Amazon. Horse and rider were so perfectly molded that the animal's legs almost seemed an extension of hers, as though she herself were galloping at a breakneck pace, urged on by the pure joy of speed.

When Brett finally caught up to her, he was overwhelmed by the sheer exuberance of the moment. With her cheeks pink from exertion, her lips parted, and her eyes shining, Helena Devereux was a lovely woman indeed. Though not so classically beautiful as her mother, she radiated the same image of vitality and energy, and a love of life that was all her own.

And as their horses trotted shoulder to shoulder matching stride to stride, Brett felt as close to her as he had felt to any woman. There was something oddly intimate about it. He had only intended to catch up with her, but when he had discovered that he could not easily pass her, everything had changed. He had leaned forward over the neck of his horse and urged Rex to even greater speed, but the only result was that she too had done the same thing and they had remained neck and neck as though frozen in space and time. Gritting his teeth and throwing all his effort into it, Brett had again urged Rex forward, but to no avail.

In all his life he could not remember ever having competed against a woman; certainly not on such a physical level. In fact, there were few, if any men who had offered him such a challenge as Helena did. Competing against her was a heady feeling indeed. As every muscle had strained in the effort to beat her, he could sense hers straining as well, the very evenness of the match binding them together in a bond that was closer than any he had shared with anyone.

It had all been the impression of a moment, and then they were reining in at the end of the alley in front of the formal parterres of the Augarten. He glanced over at Helena as loosening her grip on the reins, she tried to catch her breath without appearing to do so. A slow grin spread over his face. "There is nothing you can do to convince me that you are not just as winded as I am."

She chuckled. "As if I have the strength left to do so. You ride very well, Major."

He snorted. "And so I should. But you, on the other hand, Miss Devereux, are something of a miracle." The grin faded and his eyes grew serious. "I have never been so tested as I was just now, nor have I ever enjoyed a challenge more."

"Why, thank you." The warmth of his approval and appreciation was like a kiss itself, leaving her as weak and breathless as if his lips had actually touched hers. She could not remember ever having shared a moment so precious or so intimate, with another human being. For an instant, the communication and the understanding between them was so complete that it felt as though they were one in the same person instead of two.

They remained fixed to the spot, smiling at one another until the pounding hooves of another horse intruded upon their solitude and broke the spell.

Helena looked up at the passing rider, flushing self-consciously. "I have tarried too long, and though Mama is accustomed to my morning rides, she will wonder at my tardiness. I must go." And with a flick of her heels, she was off, leaving Brett and Rex to stand there, like a statue as they watched her go.

A slow smile spread across Brett's face. Helena Devereux might scorn the notion of pinning her hopes for happiness on men, but she was certainly not immune to them. He had been with enough women over the years to know when one was attracted to him, consciously or not. The very abruptness of this one's departure gave him good reason to believe that this particular woman was beginning to be drawn to him just as he was to her. It was certainly not something he had wished for—quite the opposite in fact, for it complicated matters considerably. But the effect she was beginning to have on him was too tantalizing to ignore. He had never experienced such a tug of attraction to any woman, an attraction that was more mental than physical; though, after this morning, the physical attraction was beginning to be as disconcertingly real as the mental. Brett shook his head wryly at the thought as he headed slowly back to the British delegation.

Chapter Twelve

"Well, you must have had an enjoyable ride; you look positively invigorated." The Princess von Hohenbachern set down her cup of morning chocolate to examine her daughter's flushed face more closely. In fact, Helena looked more than invigorated, she looked radiant in a way that she had not since they had left the rolling hills of Hohenbachern and the schloss far behind. The princess' eyes narrowed speculatively. Now that she thought about it, she could never remember her daughter looking quite that way—vital and alive. Helena's eyes sparkled, her face glowed, and the customary serious expression was replaced by an air of happy expectancy as though she had been privy to some wonderful piece of news or a special secret.

If it were any other woman but her daughter, the princess would have said that she had been meeting a lover, but she was well enough acquainted with Helena's view on men and the women whose happiness revolved around them to know that something as farfetched as a romantic assignation was simply not possible.

"It was such a glorious day. Nimrod and I galloped the entire length of the Prater." *And enjoyed a most delightful interlude with an intriguingly attractive and charming gentleman,* an uncomfortably truthful voice inside her added.

"Ah. That was nice for you." The princess reached for the copy of *La Belle Assemblée* that she had been perusing. For the moment she would leave it at that, but her curiosity had been piqued and she was not about to accept a facile explanation of the fineness of the day. Almost every day that season had been exceptionally and uncharacteristically fine, but none of them had managed to kindle the glow in her daughter's face that this particular day had.

"What do you think of this? I am considering having something similar made up with a blue satin slip under Urling's net, though I shall wear my sapphire bandeau with it instead of a turban. Turbans may be all the rage, but I have yet to see one that does not add years to a woman, no matter how youthful her countenance. Perhaps you would like Madame Albert to make something up for you as well?"

"Mmm," Helena replied vaguely as she perused the pictures, wondering what the results would be if she were to put as much time and effort into her appearance as her mother did. Could she be as lovely as the Princess von Hohenbachern? Definitely not. Uninterested as she was on the subject of female beauty, as well as uninformed, Helena still knew enough to be aware that she lacked the requisite softly rounded lines and lush curves needed to be considered a true diamond as her mother was. But would more time and effort make her more attractive, at least to certain people? Quite possibly. She sighed and nodded slowly. "Yes, perhaps I would."

The princess stared at her daughter for the second time that morning. Something definitely had come over the girl. Ordinarily Helena vigorously resisted all attempts to embellish her wardrobe. It had been a fight to get the first ball gown made up before they left Hohenbachern, for she had insisted that someone who was not planning to attend any balls had no need for a ball gown. And even when it had become abundantly clear that there were functions where she needed such a gown, and more than one, she cheerfully maintained that her serviceable white lace gown over a white satin slip was perfectly suitable for any and every occasion if it were varied now and again by a change in trim or the addition of a shawl.

"Very well, I shall see that she comes this very afternoon." Not one to miss such an opportunity or to give her daughter time to think better of such a rash step, the princess rang for her maid and directed her to send a footman immediately to Madame Albert's fashionable establishment in the Kohlmarkt with the message that the Princess von Hohenbachern and her daughter were in urgent need of her services.

The instant she had spoken, Helena regretted it. What did she care if she was attractive—to anyone? And now, because of her imprudent tongue, she would be spending her afternoon being poked, prodded, twisted, turned, and subjected to hours of critical examination, when she could have been peacefully ensconced in the library perusing the newspapers and poring over the latest political tract. What madness had made her agree to such an uncomfortable program? The warmth of the blood rising in her cheeks gave her an answer that she did not want to know.

But a week later, as she gazed at her reflection in the looking glass, Helena was forced to agree with her mother that, while the sessions with the dressmaker and seamstress had been as interminable as they were uncomfortable, and as uncomfortable as she had feared, they had produced admirable results. The pale pink satin slip under a rich blond lace dress brought out the color in her cheeks and emphasized the fineness of her eyes.

"It is a lucky thing that we are in Vienna, where they are less nice about such things, and not in London, where you would be constrained to wear white," the princess had remarked critically as she had surveyed the finished product. "The styles of a young miss in her first Season would not become you so well as this. Madame Albert has done very well indeed. However, the true measure of any costume is its effect on others. We shall see how successful her creation is at the Hofburg tomorrow evening." Again, the princess awaited the usual cry of protest from her daughter, or at least a modest demur. Again she was intrigued to note that there was none.

And indeed, though she took herself severely to task for such frivolous preoccupation, Helena herself was curious to see if her finery produced any of the effect that her mother anticipated.

As she and the princess entered the brilliantly lit ballroom at the Hofburg that evening, Helena could not
help gazing across the richly dressed crowd gathered in
the vast imperial ballroom, but the sea of heads was of
a distressingly uniform height. There was no tall dark-
haired Englishman in a cavalry officer's uniform tower-
ing over the rest of the European delegates, and she was
beginning to ask herself why she had come, when suddenly she became acutely and uncomfortably aware of a
tall figure making its way through the press of the
ballroom.

Her heart began to pound. Telling herself that her
attack of breathlessness and the warm flush rising to her
cheeks were only the natural results of trying to make a
passage through the crush of people, Helena drew a
deep breath, exhaled slowly and deliberately, and sum-
moning up what she hoped was a calmly serene smile,
joined her mother in welcoming the major.

Brett was far too experienced an observer not to notice the pinkness of her cheeks or the rapid rise and fall
of the lace trimming on Helena's décolletage, and he
struggled to stifle a grin. It was sufficiently unusual to
discover the scornfully intellectual Miss Devereux at
such a large and purely social gathering in the first place,
but to discover her in a state that could almost be con-
strued as flustered was rare indeed.

What, Brett wondered, could be the reason behind it?
The grin widened as, giving in to the devilish impulse
that prompted him, he decided to test his theory. "Good
evening." He bowed to both ladies. "I expected to find
you, Princess, gracing such an illustrious assembly, but
you, Miss Devereux, are a most unexpected and welcome sight indeed. And from what I can see, it would
appear that you are *not,* as I would have predicted, here
under duress."

He watched with a great deal of satisfaction as Helena's pink cheeks grew pinker. He was glad he had this
effect on her, for he had been thinking far too much
about her since their ride in the Prater. When Brett had
entered the ballroom, he had been looking for the Princess von Hohenbachern, or at least that is what he had
told himself, but in reality, he had been more curious to

see if the princess' daughter were there with her than he had been in seeing the princess herself.

And now, having found them, he only had eyes for the daughter. Not only was Miss Devereux uncharacteristically flushed and breathless, she looked unusually fine. The glossy brown hair was not ruthlessly drawn back into its customary severe coiffure, but a few curls had been allowed to escape to frame and soften the delicate oval of her face. And the pink ball gown, cut lower and more provocatively than anything he had seen her wear, revealed a figure that was certainly as elegant, if not so voluptuous as her mother's. Even in his unwelcome visions of Helena swimming naked in the pool in the Prater, Brett had always pictured her as being slender to the point of boyishness, but her décolletage proved him wrong, very wrong indeed.

Swallowing hard, Brett forced himself to speak to her mother. "I do not know how you contrive to do so, Princess, but you always appear to greater advantage than anyone else at these affairs. Perhaps it is because you rely on your own natural charms to attract rather than a veritable treasure chest of jewels." He glanced significantly in the direction of a dumpy German countess whose masses of diamonds completely obscured the bodice of her gown. "One is left with the impression that these European ladies, and the men as well, are wearing their entire fortunes."

The princess laughed. "It is true that they favor more display than the English do. Madame Albert at least has brought her French sense of style to Vienna. There is nothing like one of her creations to show a woman off to her best advantage. Why, even Helena has been so impressed with her skill that I was able to convince her to order a new gown as well."

"A rare accomplishment indeed." Brett laughed as he asked himself why he should feel so enormously gratified at the self-conscious look in Helena's eyes. Why did he want so much to think that it was his remarks about her mother that caused the daughter to order a new and most becoming gown? Why did he hope that the unwilling attraction to her that he had struggled against in the Prater had also driven Helena to pay more attention to her appearance? Did she wish to prove to him that if she put her mind to it, she too could attract the admiring glances that were the very stuff of her mother's existence?

As he looked down at her, the dark fringed hazel eyes widened and he read the answer in their honest gaze. Yes! She was too open, too forthright to look away or indulge in the coquettish dissimulation designed to drive a man wild with uncertainty. But had she done it only for him? That was the question. "A rare accomplishment indeed," he repeated slowly, his eyes still fixed on Helena's, "but well worth the effort."

If Helena's cheeks had been hot before, they were positively burning now. Her tongue felt glued to the top of her mouth, and she could do nothing but goggle at the major like a simpleton. Just the sight of him had made her feel weak and dizzy, though she had told herself that it was simply in anticipation of his possible reaction to her presence and her unusually fashionable appearance. Deep down inside, however, she knew that it was the major himself who caused her knees to feel wobbly and her heart to beat so loudly that she could not even hear the buzz of conversation around her.

Now he was looking at her with a half-admiring, half-teasing glint in his eyes that told her he knew exactly what she was thinking. *Yes,* the look told her, *I know it was our conversation that prompted you to go to such lengths over your appearance, and, yes, those efforts have succeeded even beyond your expectations.*

She shivered. Something about the expression in his eyes sent a sensation akin to an electric shock tingling through all the nerves in her body. So this was what it felt like! This was the feeling that her mother and so many other women were constantly seeking. Helena was glad she had spent her life concentrating on other things, for she found it unnerving in the extreme to imagine what it would be like to feel those arms around her, to trace the line of his jaw with her fingers, to feel the warmth of his skin under her hands, to press herself against the strength and solidity of the broad chest instead of merely sensing it as she was now.

Helena's mother watched in fascination as the color

stained her daughter's cheeks. She had never thought to see the day when her own Helena responded to a compliment with anything but a politely dismissive smile and a scornfully raised eyebrow. Was she at last suddenly becoming aware of all the delightful possibilities that existed between men and women, or was it only this particular man delivering this particular compliment that was having such an effect on her? Certainly Major Lord Brett Stanford was one of the most charming men the princess had encountered, and one who was extremely skilled at making a woman feel irresistibly attractive. Of course, the fact that he was devilishly handsome added to his appeal, but chiefly it was the way he made a woman feel that set him apart from other men. If he had such an effect on her, Louisa von Hohenbachern, as wise in the ways of the world as any woman, then it was only natural that his effect would be doubly devastating to a young lady who had no experience in such things whatsoever and who tended to dismiss flirtation and all that it entailed as foolish, useless, and highly overrated.

In fact, the princess was so enthralled by the unexpectedness of the entire scene unfolding before her eyes that she quite forgot that it was her own particular admirer who was having this astounding effect on her daughter.

"That is very kind of you to say, Major." Helena at last found her tongue. "But I assure you that the only effort I put forth was to stand like a block for hours on end while the dressmaker worked her magic on me. Mama continues to insist that despite the hundreds of people who attend the balls at the Hofburg each week, I shall stand out if I appear in the same gown more than once. For myself, I do not care, but it would never do to have such a thing said about someone connected to the eternally elegant Princess von Hohenbachern."

"I am sure that the princess' reputation for exquisite taste, which is redoubled every time she appears, would remain supremely unaffected if she were accompanied by a dowd, which she is not." Brett's eyes drifted admiringly over the princess' own magnificent gown, but oddly enough, though her décolletage was far more daring than her daughter's, he barely noticed it. He found himself paying far more attention to the skillfully executed trimming of net lozenges ornamented by pearls than to the woman underneath it. There was no doubt that the princess was the picture of fashionable beauty, but lovely as she looked this evening, she did not have the effect on him that her daughter did. There was something about the half-shy, half-proud way that Helena carried herself which was more appealing to him than all the sophisticated charms of all the widely accredited beauties in the ballroom that evening. Her consciousness that she looked her best, coupled with her hesitancy as to what to do with it gave Helena an air of naturalness more provocative than the most revealing of gowns.

Brett found it nearly impossible to take his eyes off her. He longed to lead her to the dance floor, to move as one with her to the music, to feel her warmth under his hands, but he could not dance with the daughter without dancing with the mother, and he could hardly leave one woman alone as he led the other to the floor.

He was saved by the appearance of a gangly young officer who, bursting at last through the crowd of people around them hurried toward them, an eager smile lighting his large bony face. "Princess von Hohenbachern, Miss Devereux, at last I find you."

"Why, Wilhelm, what are you doing here? You have good news of my husband, I trust?"

"Oh yes. The prince enjoys excellent health and sends his warmest regards to both his ladies." The gangly young man beamed at both mother and daughter.

"Baron von Wölffling is aide to the Prince von Hohenbachern and an old family friend," the princess explained.

"And he was been sent to Vienna expressly by his commander to make sure that his ladies are enjoying themselves and to find out any news from the Congress. We hear rumor after rumor, but they all come and go so quickly and are so contradictory that I have come to get to the truth of the matter."

"Which changes from day to day," Helena informed him sardonically. "But tell me, how is Papa doing? Has he heard from Sophie and Augusta?"

The first strains of the Polonaise could be heard from the orchestra at the end of the room, and Brett, who was determined to share a waltz later with Helena, seized the opportunity to lead her mother to the floor.

Chapter Thirteen

As the line of dancers snaked its way around the floor, Brett smiled and went through the motions of the dance with the princess, but his eyes were all for her daughter, who was deep in conversation with her father's aide-de-camp. Head tilted to one side, her forehead wrinkled in concentration, occasionally emphasizing her remarks with a decisive sweep of one gloved hand, Helena stood out in a room filled with laughing, flirtatious women. Where they smirked and fluttered fans, she conversed seriously and intently, listening and speaking with an energy and a purpose that made those around her seem like so many flitting butterflies wafted here and there by the capricious breeze. What was she discussing with this old friend of the family? Surely he was only that and nothing more? She had never mentioned any suitors or admirers.

With an effort Brett forced himself to return his attention to his partner. What did he care after all if Helena Devereux was deep in conversation with another man? He was here to amuse himself with a beautiful woman who knew how to enjoy life without taking it seriously, not to involve himself with someone who invested everything she did with an intensity and concentration most people, if they exerted such effort at all, reserved for a few rare and critical moments in their lives. Not Miss Devereux. Whether it was riding or discussing politics, she threw herself headlong into the endeavor, immersing herself in it, while it lasted, to the exclusion of all else.

Brett ignored the uncomfortable little voice in him pointing out that it was not Miss Devereux's intensity that was bothering him, but her conversation with another young man, a young man she had quite possibly been friends with since she had arrived in Europe. Until now he had never thought of her as being at all connected with any man, and he was rather disconcerted to discover that he even cared, but he did. He had enjoyed his and Helena's moments alone together in the Prater sharing their thoughts and ideas, and he took great pleasure in thinking that it was his influence that was responsible for the new gown. He liked to think that he was the only man she was close enough to be influenced in such a way.

"What?" He started uncomfortably as he realized that his partner was addressing him. "Yes, I do see the Princess Bagration looking in our direction. Yes, I have made her acquaintance, but I am sure that she has very little interest in a simple English soldier. At any rate, she knows, as everyone else does, that I prefer the company of a lovely Englishwoman to that of a dangerous Russian beauty." He smiled down at his partner in a way that caused even the Princess von Hohenbachern's jaded heart to skip a beat.

"Flatterer." She shook her head dismissively, but was pleased, nonetheless, by his evident lack of interest in the beautiful Russian. "I have seen the way she smiles at you. I am more than seven, you know. I have lived in this world long enough to know when a woman is casting out lures."

The music stopped, and, just as Brett had hoped, couples were beginning to pair up for the waltz as he and the princess returned to Helena and the Baron von Wölffling. Conscience clear, now that he had danced with the princess, he turned to her. "I am sure that you have a great deal of news to catch up on with the baron, and I hope that he will accept my apologies for having snatched you away so precipitately, but I shall remedy that by asking Miss Devereux for the next dance and allow you time to speak with one another." Brett bowed to both the princess and the baron as he held out his hand to Helena.

"There is not the least need for you to . . . I mean, you must not feel that politeness requires that you ask me to dance simply because you asked Mama or to give her time to speak with the baron in private."

"And who says that it is politeness that is making me do so, Miss Devereux? Surely we have spoken together enough that you know me to be as stubbornly independent as you are. I do things because I choose to, not because politeness dictates that I do. And it pleases me to ask you to dance."

"Oh. Thank you." Not entirely convinced by this, she glanced at him warily.

"Besides, how do you know that it was not your mother whom I asked to dance for politeness' sake so that I then could dance with you?" He felt a surge of satisfaction as Helena, unable to sustain his gaze, dropped her eyes. So she had wanted him to ask her to dance. Good. He had been aching to hold her from the very moment he had entered the ballroom. It was an ache that had only grown in its intensity when he saw her conversing so animatedly with the Baron von Wölffling.

"I count myself as one of the fortunate to lure you onto the dance floor. In fact, I count myself doubly fortunate since I know that you avoid dancing.

"Oh?" Helena glanced up at him curiously. "Well, it is true that I rarely dance," she replied honestly, "but"— she lifted her chin daring him to say anything more—"I, like you, do as I choose. And if occasionally I am tempted to dance, why, then, I do. The music is exceptionally fine tonight."

"So it is and it is made even more fine by the fact that I am able to enjoy it with someone who dances as well as you."

"I?" She was both gratified and annoyed by his remarks, gratified that he wanted to dance with her and annoyed by his somewhat unflattering assumption that she danced so little. And now he was telling her that she danced well. It was all rather confusing, and not a little unnerving for someone who prided herself on remaining cool and unaffected by what other people said or did.

"You sound surprised. But it is only natural that you should be an excellent dancer, for you move with such grace. Also, you are a superb equestrienne, which only goes to prove that you are as well aware of other's movements as you are of your own and match yours to suit them."

The blue eyes were teasing now, but there was a light in them that made the breath catch in her throat and her heart pound. Yes, she was aware of others. And at the moment, she could think of nothing but the warmth of his hands and the strength of his arm as he guided her smoothly and expertly around the floor, or the way he carried himself with a self-assurance and a purpose that very few people possessed. Yes she was aware, aware of every movement he made, no matter how slight. She was even aware of the slightest change in his expression, the tightening of his jaw, the fractional lift of an eyebrow, the humorous quirk at the corner of his mouth. In fact, she could think of nothing else, but him, feel nothing else, but him. It was both exhilarating and frightening to feel so closely in tune with another human being. And for the moment, the two of them felt like one.

Helena knew that she was moving in a trance, but she was powerless to stop it or to break the spell. Her mind seemed to have abdicated control over her body, which had taken on a life of its own as they glided around the floor. The crowded ballroom receded into the distance, leaving the two of them alone with the music and one another, and it was not until some minutes after the music stopped that the spell was broken.

Helena was the first to speak. Forcing herself to focus on her surroundings once more, she drew a long shuddering breath as though she were surfacing at last after swimming a great distance under water. "Thank you, Major. You, too, are an excellent dancer." It was an absurdly inane remark, doubly so for a woman who ordinarily refused to resort to the exchange of social banalities, but she felt compelled to say something, anything to reestablish control over herself and the situation, to prove to herself that her mind continued to function, however poorly.

Brett grinned. "Why, thank you." He had experienced something akin to triumph as he had observed the dreamy look dawn in her eyes and felt the languor seep into her arms. He was right after all. She was a sensual creature who could give herself up to the pleasure of music and dancing with as much abandon as anyone. But she was a sensual creature with a mind that kept her sensuality under tight control, and now her obvious efforts to reassert that control only called attention to its earlier absence. He had witnessed the brief spark of alarm in her eyes when the music ended and she once more became alive to her surroundings, and he knew what it meant. Helena Devereux was not a woman who gave herself up to her senses easily, quite possibly, she had never done so until now, with him.

It was Brett's turn to gasp for air. Why should this particular woman have such an effect on him? Why should holding Helena Devereux in his arms make him forget everything—the Congress, all the other women in the room, his very reason for being there in the first place? He had sought out the safe, congenial, and unthreatening companionship of the Princess von Hohenbachern precisely so he could easily keep an eye on the more dangerous women at the Congress, and he had ended up by being rendered almost completely unconscious to it all in the company of her daughter. What was happening to him? He was a soldier, a man who routinely ignored danger, discomfort, and pain in order to accomplish his objectives, and now a simple waltz with a woman who avoided flirtatious interludes with men had made him oblivious to anything but her. The very fact that it was such a new experience for her made it a new and dangerously powerful experience to him as well.

Moving as slowly and deliberately as an automaton, Brett led Helena back to her mother who had fortunately been too distracted by her conversation with the young baron to pay much attention to her daughter's state of mind or to the state of mind of her daughter's partner.

Restored to her mother and Baron von Wölffling, Helena tried her best to join the discussion, but her mind refused to cooperate. She was too distracted even to listen, much less participate, and it all washed over her as though they were speaking some foreign language.

In fact for Helena, the rest of the evening passed in a confused blur of music, the buzz of conversation, the scent of candles and flowers, light gleaming on silks, satins, and jewels of every color and description, until she fell into bed exhausted as the moon sank below the hills to the west and a faint tinge of pink warmed the eastern sky.

Chapter Fourteen

The rising sun was not high enough, however, for its faint rays to penetrate the small attic room in the British delegation, where Brett was sitting at his desk struggling to focus his thoughts on the report he was writing. No matter how hard he tried to concentrate on the work in front of him, his thoughts kept drifting back to Helena. What was it that drew him to her so? Not since his childhood when he had idolized the young nursery maid for her merry brown eyes, smiling face, and infectious laugh, had he been so inexplicably attracted to a woman. From the moment he had outgrown his infantile crush on Lucy, he had always been able to retain enough command over himself to keep his perspective on any and every woman. He had been able to acknowledge that it was the beautiful face of one particular woman or the exquisite figure of another, or the lusty appetite of another that had attracted him to her. Not so with Helena. With her, all his cool analysis failed. He just knew that he wanted to be with her, and that was all there was to it.

The previous evening after dancing with her, he had forced himself to obey Wellington's instructions to him and had allowed the Princess Bagration to lure him into waltzing with her. But his thoughts had all been of Helena as he had gazed admiringly at the princess' décolletage and listened sympathetically to her chatter on about her adored Alexander and his noble ambitions for Europe, while she cast decidedly inviting glances at her partner and hinted more than once that he should call on her at the Palm Palace.

Brett had escaped from the Princess Bagration at last and then, giving into impulse with a weakness he had not thought possible, had again gone in search of Helena and her mother in the hopes that he could lure Helena into granting him just one more waltz.

As he had circled the room, he had struggled frantically to come up with some excuse to offer Helena's mother, for the princess was bound to take exception to being upstaged by her own daughter, even if it was only an extra waltz with the major. But in the end, it had been a useless exercise, for the Princess von Hohenbachern and her daughter were nowhere to be seen when he finally succeeded in making his way back to the spot where he had left them.

Undoubtedly it was better that way, but Brett had been unable to quell the stab of disappointment at discovering them gone, even as he acknowledged that it was more comfortable for all of them, and he headed back to his quarters, where he sought to distract his mind from the dangerous paths it seemed to be straying down by laboring over his reports.

However, he was so unsuccessful at putting Helena out of his mind that after finishing his reports he only dozed an hour or so before washing up, changing, and hurrying off to the Prater in the hopes of encountering the woman who rode like an Amazon and danced like an angel, thundering down the alley on her powerful bay horse.

The weather, which had at last turned cold, was keeping all but the most dedicated equestrians away, but Brett still rode the length and breadth of the park, scanning the paths eagerly hoping to catch sight of one particular horse and rider.

Again, he was doomed to disappointment, and taking himself severely to task for allowing a woman to dominate his thoughts to such an extent, he rode home disconsolately. He was determined to regain his perspective as well as some of his former nonchalance and to put all the disturbing and enticing images of Helena Devereux completely out of his mind.

He was almost relieved when, returning to the delegation, he was greeted with the news that Castlereagh wished to see him, for it meant further distraction. However, he was less pleased when he discovered what the foreign secretary wanted.

Castlereagh was pacing back and forth in front of his desk when Brett entered his office. His gaunt face lightened just a little when he saw Brett. "Ah, Stanford, there you are. I have a mission for you, something for you to do after all the writing and translating that has kept you confined to your desk. I know you military fellows are always desperate for action, and now you shall have the chance for it. The thing is I wish to send a message to the tsar, inviting him to discuss various delicate issues with me, but I do not want the entire world knowing that I have sent it to him. Naturally, since I do not write French, I shall need your help in transcribing it. I shall also need someone I can trust to deliver it to him in a way that will keep the entire communication confidential. I know that you are acquainted with that Bagration woman, and I have also heard that you have the reputation of being something of a devil with the ladies, so it would not appear at all unusual if you were to call on her. One hears that she has a veritable stream of handsome young men haunting her doorstep. It is also well-known that one of her most regular visitors is the tsar himself. He usually calls on her in the afternoons, so if you were also to call on her in the afternoon, you would very likely encounter him there. You would then be able to deliver my note to him personally, and no one would be the wiser. There are pen and paper. Be a good fellow and write down what I have to say."

It was a distraction all right, though not particularly the sort that Brett would have wished, but it was not distraction enough. Once he had completed the translation, he was free until the time he was to call on the Princess Bagration, and he again found his thoughts straying back to his waltz with Helena, of holding her in his arms as they moved to the music. Much against his better judgment, he soon found himself sauntering down the Herrengasse hoping against hope to catch a glimpse of her on some errand, though he knew very well that, unlike other members of her sex, Helena considered shopping to be excessively dull and a supreme waste of her valuable time. Still, his eagerness to see her kept hope alive, misplaced as it was.

Continuing to look for her, he suddenly found himself rounding the corner into the Bräunerstrasse. Miss Devereux might scorn such frivolous occupations as shopping, but she might possibly be setting out to call on some acquaintance such as the Princess von Furstenberg. He passed the ornately carved portals of the palace where the von Hohenbachern apartments were, and felt his pulses quicken like some lovesick schoolboy's.

"Damn and blast," he muttered to himself as he paused, and then, giving in to the inevitable, raised the knocker on the massive front door and let it fall.

"Miss, Dev . . . er, I mean, the Princess von Hohenbachern," he stammered, mentally cursing himself for a callow fool. But the grizzled butler either did not notice or preferred to ignore Brett's confusion as he led him to the princess' elegant gilt and peach-damask salon on the first floor.

"Ah, Major, how lovely to see you. The day has been decidedly dull thus far. I think it is the weather. This beautiful autumn lulled us into believing that winter would never come, but indeed it has. Do come sit here by the stove. It is one aspect of German culture we English would do well to adopt.

Brett glanced at the exquisitely painted porcelain stove in the corner. "Perhaps, but I find there is nothing so cheering as the sight of a good hearty blaze." He took his place in the chair indicated. "I trust that you and your daughter are thoroughly recovered after the festivities of the evening." *You and your daughter,* how transparent he sounded.

A mischievous smile tugged at the corner of the princess' mouth. "But of course. I have not lived in such complete rustication as to be exhausted by a mere ball. And Helena is never fatigued by anything. She is in the library now. Shall I send . . ."

But there was no need for the princess to summon her daughter, for at that moment the ornate gilt door opened and Helena herself appeared. "Mama I . . . oh, hello, Major." Helena executed what she hoped was a convincing, though utterly false, start of surprise, but she could feel the heat of a telltale flush rising in her cheeks. Blast!

It was quite true that she had been in the library, but she had not been able to concentrate at all. Try though she would to focus on the newspaper, thoughts of the ball and Major Lord Brett Stanford would keep intruding. Then she had heard the sound of the door below and footsteps on the stairs and, hoping against hope, had peeped out of the door just as Brett was being escorted to her mother's salon.

She had cursed herself earlier that morning for having missed her ride in the Prater and the chance to see the major, but contrary to her mother's assertion about her boundless energy, she had lain awake for hours after the ball and had therefore awoken late that morning, too late to ride. She had luxuriated uncharacteristically in bed, recalling certain special scenes from the evening before in endless detail, and she had even been so abandoned as to allow Hannechen to bring her chocolate as she lay propped up against the pillows dreaming of waltzing in the Hofburg with one particular partner.

". . . hope that this does not mean that the Prince von Hohenbachern . . ." the major's voice broke in on her thoughts.

"I beg your pardon, I er, was not attending." Helena's blush deepened as she became aware that the major had been addressing both her and her mother.

"Do forgive my daughter's abstraction, Major, her mind is often elsewhere." The princess chuckled. "Try as I will, I cannot instill a talent for simple conversation in her. She concentrates to such a degree on her newspapers and pamphlets that she inhabits a world of her own sometimes."

Observing the conscious look in Helena's eyes and her flushed cheeks, Brett was inclined to disagree with the princess. Political tracts and the news of the day, no matter how momentous or absorbing, would never cause the redoubtable Miss Devereux to look the way she did at this particular moment. No, she had been thinking about something far removed from politics, something—and he hoped he knew what it was—that made her heart pound and her breathing come in gasps just as his did.

Raising a quizzical eyebrow, he continued. "I was just inquiring as to whether the prince was in any danger of being called upon to fight against the Prussians in defense of Saxony, if it comes to that. You did say, I believe, that he was stationed near there."

Helena eyed Brett with dawning respect. "So you have been paying attention to European politics after all, Major."

He shrugged. "It is only what one hears on the tongues of everyone in Vienna." But he could not help feeling gratified by the approving smile in her eyes.

"Prussia take over Saxony? But what of Frederick Augustus? They cannot simply take away his lands. He is a king!" The princess was horrified.

"Kings have been losing their lands a great deal these past ten years or more, Mama," Helena responded dryly.

"I realize that, my dear, but that was when that dreadful Corsican was rampaging about Europe. Now that peace is restored, we can all behave like civilized human beings once more. Undoubtedly Metternich is unaware of this, for he would never tolerate such an appalling state of affairs."

Her daughter's eloquently raised eyebrows were ample testimony to the naïveté of such an opinion.

"Surely Clemens does not *condone* such a dreadful thing?"

"I am not in his confidence, Mama, but I suspect that he is well aware of it." Glancing at Brett, Helena was gratified to see that he too was having difficulty holding his amusement in check."

"But this is dreadful! Why, if the Prussians can just take Saxony away from Frederick Augustus, they can take anything away from anyone, even Hohenbachern!"

"Exactly so," her daughter responded acidly. "Which is precisely what I have been so concerned about and why I have been involving myself in all those *dull* discussions at the Princess von Furstenberg's salon." Helena struggled to keep a straight face.

"Then I shall just have to set Clemens straight. After all, he is a friend of Frederick's from their university days and used to visit him often in Hohenbachern. Kings cannot just lose their countries willy-nilly. He must put a stop to this nonsense."

"I am sure that if you were able to convince him to do such a thing, Mama, you would earn the undying gratitude of a great many people."

"All of Saxony, in fact," Brett murmured and, sneaking another glance at Helena, was rewarded by another look of surprised approval.

"At any rate, I shall speak to him about it at the very first opportunity." The princess spoke with all the assurance of one who was accustomed to having attractive males hurry to cater to her every whim.

"But enough of such talk." The princess turned to Brett with a conspiratorial smile. "You, Major, as a man of action must surely find all these politics as tedious as I do. We English are not accustomed to all this diplomatic wrangling. In fact, I have heard that one of the members of the delegation became so exhausted by it all that he was forced to leave. And I must say that Castlereagh does not look to be enjoying himself in the least either. The last time I saw him, he looked quite done in, poor man."

Brett shook his head slowly. "Castlereagh is doing well enough; however, he recently received a letter from Liverpool at home warning him that the Opposition Party in Parliament has become so strong, that he may be recalled in order to rally his own party."

"But who would take his place?" Helena broke in. "Not Charles Stewart, surely? Why, he is the laughing-stock of Vienna. In the streets they are calling him Lord Pumpernickel."

"I do not know, Miss Devereux. Wellington is an obvious choice, but according to his latest dispatch, the prime minister has plans for him as well. Liverpool wishes him to take command of our armies in America. It does make a good deal of sense, for many of the troops there now are his veterans from the Peninsula. On the other hand, there is no one who understands current European politics better than the duke, even Castlereagh."

"Wellington, here? How divine! I simply adore the man." The princess sighed ecstatically.

Brett frowned. "I cannot say that for certain, Princess. And certainly such speculations should not leave this room."

"Oooh. Secrets. How very intriguing." The princess' blue eyes widened with excitement. "I feel like *La Bagration*. But speaking of her, I saw you dancing with her last night. Surely even gentlemen, their tastes being what they are, could not approve of the décolletage she was wearing last night."

And for the rest of his visit, Brett was forced to confine his conversation to the latest scandals and *on dits* making the rounds of the Austrian capital. But at least, every once in awhile, he was able to exchange sympathetic glances with Helena, who made it plain to him that her interest in such titillating topics was just like his, which was to say, nonexistent.

Chapter Fifteen

The chiming of an elegant ormolu clock reminded Brett of the task awaiting him and, taking a reluctant leave of the ladies, he headed off to deliver his message to the tsar, hoping against hope that the entire mission could be accomplished quickly and easily, and with a minimum of interaction with the Princess Bagration. The entire undertaking filled him with distaste, for it smacked of duplicity and deception, which were anathema to a soldier accustomed to dealing with things openly and straightforwardly. But Castlereagh was right, at least he was doing something more exciting than transcribing and translating.

As the door closed behind Brett, the princess rose to go to her appointment with Madame Albert, leaving her daughter alone in the salon. Too distracted by the major's visit to go back to her reading, Helena strolled over to the window and gazed idly into the street, watching the passersby and smiling to herself as she caught sight of a tall, broad-shouldered figure striding purposefully along. The major was different from the other men around him. Not only was he taller and more powerfully built, but the very way he carried himself told even the most casual observer that he was someone who lived his life with energy and purpose, someone who scorned the pettiness that dominated so many people's existences.

Suddenly, out of the corner of her eye, Helena caught sight of two dark shapes detaching themselves from the shadow of a doorway and gliding swiftly along down opposite sides of the street from one another. Leaning forward so that her nose was almost pressing against the glass, she squinted hard in a vain attempt to make out their features or any other distinguishing characteristics.

Something about the way the men moved, looking straight ahead, never swerving from their line of sight, reminded her of hunting dogs closing in on their prey. A shiver ran down Helena's spine. She was as sure as if they had told her themselves that the prey these two were after was Major Lord Brett Stanford.

Without a second thought, she ran to her bedchamber, snatched up her wool cloak, and, throwing it over her shoulders, hurried down the stairs and along the Bräunerstrasse in the direction they had been heading.

At first there was no sign of the men, and certainly none of the major, but Helena hurried on, half running, half walking. Oblivious of the curious stares of passersby, she pulled the cloak more tightly around her and increased her pace until at last she caught sight of a figure hugging the walls of the building not fifty yards ahead of her. Quickly she glanced to the other side of the street and, sure enough, a few yards behind his accomplice, the other man was skulking along from doorway to doorway.

They continued moving rapidly, but furtively, until Helena, finally catching up to them, was able to make out the major just ahead of them. His head and shoulders rose above the crowd, making him easily distinguishable as he strode along ahead of them.

In this fashion the two men made their way past the Hofburg, hugging the sides of the square in front of the British delegation, and then plunging down a narrow side street until they suddenly came to a halt as if frozen in their tracks. Pausing to take refuge herself in a convenient doorway, Helena observed Brett standing under the stone balcony that jutted out over the doorway of the Palm Palace. He appeared to hesitate for the briefest of moments before ringing the bell and then disappearing inside.

Now what was she to do? Helena glanced up the street as one of Brett's trackers crossed over to join his companion. She had been so intent on following the men who were trailing Brett that she had not really stopped to consider what she would do if she were to catch up with them. Nor did she wish to examine the implications of Brett's presence at the Palm Palace. Obviously he was calling on either the Duchess of Sagan or the Princess Bagration, the implications of which, in either case, she did not wish to entertain now or later.

However, there was no turning back. Now that she had flung herself into the middle of it all, the least she could do was to try to discover more about the men who were following Brett.

Hugging the wall, Helena moved as unobtrusively as she could from doorway to doorway until she was able to get a good look at both of the men. Not to her surprise, she was just able to make out the long, angular face, dark hair, beard, and soldierly bearing of the man who had accompanied Augustus Von Stieglitz to the celebrations in the Prater.

What did these men want with Brett? And was Brett himself something more than the simple cavalry officer and translator that he claimed to be?

Helena crept close enough to distinguish voices conversing with the same Saxon accent she had heard that day in the Prater. Cautiously, ever so cautiously, she inched along, her cloak catching on the rough stucco as she tried to flatten herself against the building. Then at last she was close enough to distinguish phrases here and there, *fought under Wellington, regiments in America . . .*

She held her breath, so intent on focusing on every word that was said and guessing what it meant that she was not even aware they had paused in their conversation to look at her. But suddenly they were on either side of her, peering into her face and grinning lasciviously.

"Guten Tag, Fraulein." The first man reached forward to push Helena's hood back. "You are right, Franz." He turned to his companion. "We're in the devil's own luck. She is a cozy armful indeed. Just the thing to while away our time while we wait here. What do you say to a kiss, sweetheart?"

And before Helena could even think what he was

about, the man had grabbed her with one hand in a clumsy embrace while he struggled to undo the ties of her cloak with the other. "Come along, now, show us what you have got for us, sweetheart." He tugged harder. "Modest little thing, aren't you? Well, Hans will soon take care of that. I like a modest young lady I do." And just as Helena was recovering her breath to protest, he gave her a smacking wet kiss.

Revulsion washed over her, bringing her back to her senses, and she struggled to free herself from the crude assault. But both her captor's arms went around her now, pulling her into a crushing embrace so that she could neither scream nor fight very effectively. *Think, Helena, think!* She repeated desperately to herself. All her life she had prided herself on her intellect, on being able to solve any problem, deal with any situation. Where was that intellect now when she needed it?

Gathering all her strength, Helena forced herself to be calm, to review all the possibilities, to think herself out of her difficulties. Her arms were pinned beyond all hope of extricating them, but her feet were free. Putting all her energy behind it, she aimed as powerful a kick as she could muster at her attacker's shins.

"Verdammt!" He yelped in pain and loosened his grip just enough for her to twist her face away.

"Hilfe!" Helena yelled with every ounce of strength she had. *"Hilfe!"* She hoped desperately to catch the attention of passersby.

Suddenly she heard pounding footsteps and then a furious voice exclaiming, "What the devil?" as she felt her attacker being pulled roughly off her. "Miss Dev . . ."

"Danke, mein Herr, Danke." Reacting quickly, Helena yanked herself free from her assailant's grasp and flung herself into Brett's arms. *"Danke. Sie haben mich gerettet."* She continued to cling to him, repeating the words over and over as she listened to the sound of her attackers' retreating footsteps fade into the distance. Then, cautiously, she lifted her head to watch them disappear around a corner.

"Are you all right?" Utterly nonplussed by the entire episode, Brett struggled to gather his wits about him as he gazed down at her with some concern. "Miss Dever-

eux, it is I, Stanford." The poor girl was so undone by
the entire experience that she appeared completely unaware of her rescuer's identity.

Helena drew a steadying breath, but try as she would,
she could not seem to stop the trembling that threatened
to overwhelm her. Gratefully she clung to the strong
arms protecting her, supporting her. "I know," she
gasped. "I know it is you. Thank you."

"But, but . . ." Puzzled, he shook his head. "If you
knew who I was, why did you speak to me in German?"

"Because I did not want them to know who *I* was, or
that I knew who you were."

Thoroughly mystified, Brett stared down at her, but
she seemed perfectly sane, shaken perhaps, but clearly
in possession of all her faculties. "Come." Still keeping
a steadying arm around her shoulders, he led her gently
back in the direction of home. "I think you had better
explain. Either I am excessively dull-witted or I am missing something."

Drawing another steadying breath, Helena told him
about observing the men from the salon window as they
set off following him. At that he shook his head in mingled frustration and admiration as he listened to the tale
of her pursuit of Franz and his cohort through the streets
to the Palm Palace. "What ever were you thinking, risking yourself in such a way? You could have been hurt
or . . ."

"But I had to find out. I had to know if one of the
men was the other man we saw at the Prater."

Brett stared at her blankly.

"The man with whom Augustus von Stieglitz was
speaking before he spoke to you."

Again, Brett shook his head uncomprehendingly.

"But don't you see? They were spying on you then,
and they were spying on you now. Following them as
they followed you was the best way for me to discover
why they were spying on you. I thought that if I could
get close enough to them to hear, I might just be able
to discover what they hoped to find out from you, but
before I could really learn anything, they accosted me.
They thought I was a . . ." She broke off shuddering at

the memory of it, of the hot breath on her face, the look in the man's eyes. "It was awful!"

Brett's arms closed around her. "My poor girl. Hush now. Put it out of your mind. It is over."

She was silent for a moment, marveling at the wonderful sense of refuge and security a pair of comforting strong arms could give after brutal ones had made her feel so helpless, so hopeless, so threatened. She wanted to stay in Brett's arms forever, reveling in that circle of protection, in the feeling of being cared for, in knowing that there was someone who could save her even if she could not save herself. But no, that was madness. She did not want to be saved. She had been fighting against that all her life, struggling not to depend on anyone else to look after her. No, her independence and self-sufficiency had been too hard won to sacrifice it all now simply because one small incident had caused her to question herself. And she certainly did not want to be saved by a man who called on her mother one minute and was off to visit the Duchess of Sagan or the Princess Bagration the next!

Drawing in another deep breath, Helena straightened in his arms and carefully retied the fastenings of her cloak. "Thank you, Major, for coming to my rescue. It was stupid of me to let them catch sight of me that way. I appreciate your concern, but I am thoroughly recovered now."

And pulling her cloak more tightly around herself, she stepped out of his arms and marched off briskly down the street.

Chapter Sixteen

Once again, Brett was too caught off guard for a moment to react. One minute she had been clinging to him, grateful for his protection and support, and the next she was flinging off down the street as though she were trying to put as much distance between the two of them as she possibly could.

"Damn and blast!" He cursed himself for a fool, though he had not the slightest idea what had brought about the change in her. "Helena!" He hurried after her. "Miss Devereux, wait . . ." At last he caught up to her. "Please." Gently, he tucked her hand back under his arm. "It is I who should be thanking you. After all, it was your looking after my welfare that got you into tr . . . er caused the situation in which I just found you."

But she continued along, not slowing her pace in the least. What was wrong with the woman? He had apologized handsomely enough, acknowledged his debt to her even though it galled him to do so. He was a soldier, after all, a soldier, furthermore, who had been warned against the spies that permeated the city, and yet it had been a gently bred young woman, who just happened to glance out of a drawing room window and managed to follow his adversaries through the streets of Vienna. Did she not think it cost him something to admit that to her? Apparently not.

"Believe me, Miss Devereux, I am very much indebted to you, but it is rather difficult to take, you know."

That caught her attention. She stopped and looked up at him. *"Difficult to take?"*

"After all, *I* am supposed to be the veteran campaigner here. I have spent years successfully combating or avoiding dangers of all sorts in the Peninsula, in a far more hazardous environment than one of Europe's most cosmopolitan cities, yet here, not a few streets away from my own headquarters, I am rescued by a young woman who has spent the last several years enjoying the simple pleasures of the German countryside while I have spent them fighting the French all through Portugal and Spain. You must admit that such a thing could have a rather lowering effect on one's self-esteem. Small wonder that I am slow to acknowledge my indebtedness to that young woman."

She was no proof against the lopsided grin that accompanied this apology. There was something quite disarming about the self-deprecatory shrug of the shoulders and his grudging admission of her superiority. No other man she knew would have even acknowledged such a thing to himself, much less have admitted it to her.

"I suppose it might seem that way."

Brett had had no idea that he had been holding his breath until he saw her answering smile, heard the warmth creep back into her voice, and watched the twinkle creep back into her eyes. He let out a deep sigh. Why did he care so much about this young woman's opinion of him? Perhaps it was because he had such a high opinion of her. Not many men he knew, and certainly no young woman he had ever encountered, would have been as observant as she had been, and far fewer, if any, would have acted so quickly or courageously.

But there was something else too, something that ran deeper than mere respect, something that had struck him deep inside when he had discovered that the young woman struggling to free herself from her assailant's unwanted attentions was Helena.

Brett had been fortunate enough to arrive at the Palm Palace only a few minutes after the tsar and had been able to deliver his message before Alexander had been admitted to the princess' chambers. The entire mission had gone so smoothly that he had hardly been able to

believe his luck, and he had been congratulating himself
on the speedy conclusion of the distasteful errand as he
hastened to leave the palace as quickly as possible, before anything could happen or anyone appear to compli-
cate matters.

The moment the palace doors had closed behind him,
he had become aware of an altercation across the street
and hurried over to investigate. He would have been
quick to rescue any woman from any man's unwelcome
advances, but when he had recognized the face that
twisted way from her attacker's as Helena's, a blind fury
had washed over him. He had been filled with a rage he
had not thought he possessed, a rage more primal than
anything he had ever before experienced, even in the
heat of battle, and it had taken all his self-control not
to strangle the man then and there with his bare hands.

It was not only Helena's anguished expression and her
helplessness against a superior force that tore at him,
but it was the sudden realization that for some time now
he had longed to hold her in his arms and crush his lips
to hers just as this man was doing—but not as he was
doing. Not that way, not against her will, but drawn together by mutual passion.

And this revelation had been so shattering and so unwelcome, especially given the circumstances, that it had
left him shaken. Even now, the mental image of Helena
in another man's arms was profoundly disturbing and
left him feeling drained and confused.

In all his affairs with women, no matter how passionate they had been, Brett had always remained in control
of his emotions and in control of the situation. Not so
with Helena Devereux. From the moment he had met
her, she had seemed to have the advantage over him
and it never seemed to stop, no matter what the circumstances. Whether it was knowing his identity when he
had no clue as to hers, understanding complex political
situations in which he felt totally at sea, following spies
he had no notion were trailing him, or inspiring feelings
in him that he had not even known he possessed, she
always seemed to catch him off balance, and he always
seemed to be powerless to stop her.

Brett awoke from this unwelcome reverie to find her

regarding him curiously. What was it she had just said? *I suppose it might seem that way.* "Yes, it might. The one opportunity I have had to do anything actively since I left the Peninsula, and I am too blind to recognize it. Then to have it pointed out to me by a young woman, a most intelligent and capable young woman, but a young woman nevertheless, is daunting, you know."

It was Helena's turn to look somewhat self-conscious. "*A most intelligent and capable young woman* who was so blind herself that she did not stop to think what sort of person she would be taken for, loitering alone in a city street." Still, she could not help feeling absurdly pleased at being called *intelligent* and *capable* even though she had had to be rescued.

He gave a crack of laughter. "Most people would be appalled if you *had* realized what sort of person you might be taken for, yet you blame yourself, well-brought-up young woman that you are, for not stopping to consider it. You are a rare creature, indeed, Helena Devereux, and I consider it a pleasure and a privilege to have made your acquaintance." He clasped the gloved hand that was resting on his arm and raised it to his lips.

It took all of Helena's fast-ebbing strength to withstand the giddiness that overwhelmed her as she felt the seductive pressure of his fingers and the warmth of his lips through her glove. She struggled against the longing to feel his arms around her again, not comfortingly this time, but passionately. She wanted to feel the strength of him, the warmth of his lips on hers. She wanted . . . but then reason reasserted itself. She had only become acquainted with this man because he was an admirer of her mother's. And, if the events of the day were any indication, he was also an admirer of the Duchess of Sagan or the Princess Bagration, neither of whose reputations bore any looking into. Even Helena, dismissive as she was of gossip of any kind, was familiar with enough of it to know that both these ladies made a regular habit of collecting handsome, dashing young men— men like Major Lord Brett Stanford.

They had been walking as they were talking and to Helena's great relief, she realized that they were now back in the Bräunerstrasse and only a few steps from her door. Retrieving her hand from Brett's arm, she turned to face him. "Thank you for coming to my rescue, Major. I do not know . . ." she paused uncomfortably. She truly did not know what she would have done if he had not been there, but she did not wish to be beholden to any man, especially this one who already had a most disturbing effect on her even before he had saved her from the most unnerving, upsetting situation she had ever found herself in in her life.

"I consider it a privilege to have been of assistance to you, Miss Devereux." Again, he took her hand in his and looked deep into her eyes, eyes filled with confusion and a glimmer of what he hoped was recognition of something special that lay between them.

Helena's hand trembled in his as, mesmerized by the look in his eyes, she felt herself slowly dissolving, losing herself in the expression she saw there.

With a supreme effort she called herself back to the present, to reality. "And now I must go. Mama will be wondering what on earth has become of me. Good day, Major." It was a bald-faced lie. Undoubtedly the Princess von Hohenbachern was still closeted with Madame Albert and utterly oblivious to her daughter's existence, but Helena had to get inside, away from him and the spell he seemed to cast over her.

Mama! The Princess von Hohenbachern. Brett felt as though Helena had dashed a bucket of cold water over him. What was he thinking? He had begun his relationship with the princess because, beautiful and charming as she was, she posed no threat to his peace of mind. He knew he was in no danger of losing a moment's sleep over her. He was, however, dangerously close to losing not only sleep, but his heart and soul as well to the princess' daughter.

Brett straightened up and released Helena's hand. "Good day, Miss Devereux." And without a backward glance, he strode off down the street toward the British delegation, congratulating himself all the way on his narrow escape. He had recognized his danger before he had fallen deeper into it. Now, having recognized his danger, he would be able to avoid it.

Chapter Seventeen

Brett struggled to heed his own warning, but he was powerless to help himself, and in the ensuing days he fond himself riding religiously in the Prater every morning. Hoping that the increasing cold and the dusting of snow would not keep certain other riders from exercising their mounts, he never caught even so much as a glimpse of the powerful bay and its rider.

His own corroding sense of disappointment would have been softened somewhat if he had known what it cost Helena not to indulge in her early morning gallops. She tried to tell herself as she battled the crowds of carriages, horses and riders, and the more fashionable company to be found in the Prater in the afternoon that the warmer temperatures were far better for Nimrod. And she tried to blame her dissatisfaction with these rides on the press of people that made it impossible for them to get any real fresh air or exercise. But she knew that it was cowardice on her part, pure and simple, that kept her out of the Prater as morning was breaking over the city. She knew that he would be there then, and she knew what happened when she was alone in the Prater with Major Lord Brett Stanford. She knew, and she was afraid of it, afraid of the magnetism that drew her to him, of the bond of shared ideals and similar passions that made her feel closer to him than to any other human being.

But it cost her dearly, oh, how it cost her, not to jump

out of bed when she woke every morning feeling alive and excited, as though something wonderful were going to happen. It cost her not to pull on her riding habit, run to the stables, throw herself on Nimrod and gallop to the Prater, where she could give in to the pure joy of sharing her excitement with someone she knew felt the way she did.

Instead, coward that she was, she burrowed deeper into the books in the library, burying herself in treatises, pamphlets, and newspapers, trying to focus her energies on her studies, which had once seemed so all-encompassing and now seemed merely enervating and dull.

Day after day Brett rode in a virtually empty park until finally there was nothing to do but call on the Princess von Hohenbachern. He hated himself for it because he knew he was flying in the face of his own good advice. But he hated even more not seeing Helena. He missed their frank and easy conversations. He missed her insights and explanations. He missed the twinkle in her eyes, and he missed the way he felt with her, at ease, yet excited, comfortable with her, but at the same time longing for more.

And what of the princess? Brett tried to tell himself that, from what he had observed, she now seemed to be involving herself with more important men, men like Metternich and Talleyrand, men who were equally skilled at lovemaking and politics, men who could offer her far more than a lowly translator in the British delegation could. Yet he could not help feeling guilty about her. He genuinely enjoyed the princess' company, appreciated her beauty and her charm, and despite her worldliness and her sophistication, he worried that his growing interest in her daughter was a betrayal of her trust.

He did not like it, but he could not help himself.

So he found himself knocking on a particular door in the Bräunerstrasse at an hour that Helena, and possibly her mother, were most likely to be at home.

As always, the princess welcomed him graciously, but it seemed to him that she was preoccupied. Once she would have concentrated all her efforts on keeping him amused and enthralled; now she was simply conversational. Or was this all wishful thinking on his part?

The first two times Brett had called in the Bräunerstrasse, hoping against hope to see Helena, her mother had been alone, and somehow, the half an hour he had spent with her seemed endless. But the third time he called, while the princess was regaling him with descriptions of the way in which the various delegations were celebrating Christmas, Helena entered the room in search of ink.

"Ink? Here? But you are the one who uses it most, so I have instructed that it be kept in the library." Nonplussed, the princess opened her eyes wide in astonishment.

Helena flushed ever so slightly, but said nothing as she took a seat in a chair near the stove.

Comprehension dawned and the princess' delicately raised eyebrows settled back into their customary position. "I was just about to explain to the major here the German custom of the *Christbaum*."

"It is more a Prussian custom, than a German one actually." Helena wrinkled her nose in a way Brett found particularly endearing, though he had not the least idea why. "And the Prussians claim that it originated with them. They call it a *Weihbaum*, a— At any rate, Papa saw it when he was visiting relatives in Berlin, and now every year at the schloss we also have a Christmas tree. Sophie and Gussie adore it, though I do not suppose we will have one here." Her voice trailed off as she thought of the two girls back in Hohenbachern and how much she missed their company. "Every year we would go out and choose just the right fir tree from the woods near the schloss, chop it down and bring it home to decorate with garlands and candles. Then we hung presents on it. It was ever so pretty."

Something in her face, and the wistful note in her voice, filled Brett with an overwhelming urge to ride off into the forests covering the hills outside of the city and seek out just the perfect tree for her. But during his months in Vienna, he had learned that the Austrians had rules for everything, and undoubtedly they had rules about cutting trees. Besides which, the Austrian police

were everywhere. If he were even allowed to get near
the forest without polite but firm interference, it was
highly unlikely that he would be able to bring back a
tree.

He stifled the thought and began instead to describe
the Christmas customs at Stanford Hall, the visitors from
neighboring estates, the Yule log, the servants' party.
"But we do not celebrate much ourselves. It is chiefly
an opportunity for Mama and my sisters to demonstrate
their charity to those less fortunate and to insure the
continuing good service from the staff in the coming year
by entertaining them and presenting them with gifts on
Boxing Day."

He had not meant to sound bitter, in fact, he did not
even realize that he did sound bitter until he became
aware of Helena's eyes fixed on him sympathetically.

"I am afraid that Sophie and Gussie, and even
Mama"—Helena smiled indulgently at the princess—
"are far too excited over their own presents to think of
the misfortunes of others, but we too have a feast to
which everyone is invited."

They continued to talk in a desultory fashion of the
customs of the season, and Brett left an hour or so later
with an invitation from both women to call upon them
the next day.

From then on, he fell into a regular pattern of calling
on them, though the discussion began to focus less and
less on the purely social topics that were of consuming
interest to the princess and more and more on the politics of the moment or Brett's experiences in the Peninsula, which were endlessly fascinating to the princess'
daughter.

"How fortunate you are to be a man," Helena remarked one day after the recital of one particularly hair-
raising adventure. "I should love to be able to go places
and do things all on my own as you have done. To experience so many different situations and meet so many
different people must be very exciting."

"Though often most uncomfortable." Brett's eyes
twinkled. "Believe me, hearing someone tell about a
sudden summer snowstorm in the Pyrenees and living
through one are altogether different circumstances. Even

as I recount it to you, it seems less miserable than it actually was. But you have traveled here to Vienna from Hohenbachern and to Hohenbachern from London. You know how such journeys are always fraught with delays and discomforts."

"Pooh. If Helena had had her way, she would not even have journeyed so far as Vienna."

Helena gave a tiny start. She had been so involved in Brett's stories that she had quite forgotten her mother was even in the room. "It was not the journey I minded, Mama, it was leaving the girls. And it was not even that so much as having to come here where one is so confined and restricted, where the chief activity seems to be dancing." The words were barely out of her mouth, however, when the memory of one particular dance with one particular person came flooding back in full detail.

She glanced over at the major's well-shaped hands with their long lean fingers, remembering the way they felt clasping her hand and holding her waist while they glided about the floor as if they were the only two people in the world, and she felt the telltale pulse at the base of her throat beating faster. She had come a long way indeed from her original distaste for such things— so far, in fact, that she was hoping for a chance to be that way with him again.

The next opportunity, however, did not occur at a ball, but during one of Brett's regular calls several days later. The day was a fine one and the princess, remembering her resolve to talk some sense into the Austrian chancellor, had gone to pay a visit to Laure Metternich in the hopes that she would also encounter Laure's husband.

So when Potten came to inform Helena that the major was below in the salon, she was alone; With a dignified reserve she was far from feeling, she told the butler that she would receive him. Hastily checking herself in the looking glass, which she rarely did, Helena tried her best to stifle the guilty thought that now she would have the major all to herself. Nor would she allow herself to acknowledge the pleasure with which she looked forward to being alone with him.

He was standing at the window, watching the traffic thread its way through the narrow street below, and it was not until he turned to face her that Helena saw he was carrying an oddly shaped package.

"Good afternoon, Major. I regret to say that Mama is not here, but, please, sit down." Helena felt the color stain her cheeks at such a bold-faced lie. She did not regret the princess' absence at all. She, Helena Devereux, who had always prided herself on being honest to a fault, was telling a lie. And worse than that, she was actually glad her mother was away.

"Good. I mean, actually, what I have is more for you than it is for the princess, though, I am sure . . ." Brett's voice trailed off awkwardly as he thrust the package at her. Whatever was wrong with him? He had clasped diamond bracelets around graceful wrists, draped pearl necklaces around slender throats with more finesse than he handed the silly token to Helena.

With surprisingly shaky fingers, she struggled to remove the paper from a tiny fir tree decorated with garlands of brightly colored ribbon. "Oh." Tears stung her eyes, and for several minutes she could not trust herself to speak.

"How very . . . I mean it is ever so kind . . . Thank you." She gulped, blinking rapidly against the rising tide of tears. Her mother would have smiled enchantingly, uttered gracious words of thanks, disposed herself gracefully in a chair, and ordered refreshments for her visitor. All Helena could do was stand there, tears welling in her eyes like a watering pot, cursing herself for an idiot.

But it was her very awkwardness that moved Brett to the core of his being. He had hardly known what he was doing that morning when, putting Rex through his paces, he had spotted the tiny tree almost under his horse's hooves. He had quickly dismounted, pulled out his pocket knife, cut it, unbuttoned his tunic, bundled the tree tightly under his tunic, and re-buttoned it as tightly as he could before he was even fully aware of what he was doing.

As he rode back to the city trying to look as nonchalant as one could possibly look with needles scratching under one's clothes, Brett had been filled with a joyful anticipation he had not known since the morning he had gotten his first pony. That feeling had lasted as he purchased a few scraps of ribbon from a peddler in the Kohlmarkt and draped them as artistically as possible over the tiny branches.

Yet in spite of all the anticipation, he had been unprepared for the sudden onslaught of emotion as he watched Helena fight back her tears. He longed to pull her into his arms, to cover her mouth with kisses. He wanted to surround the little tree with fabulous and expensive trinkets even though he knew she would not want them. Even though he loved her for being the sort of person who preferred a tree to diamonds and gold, he still longed to give her things, to indulge her every whim, to make her dizzy with excitement and anticipation the way she must have been during those Christmases in Hohenbachern. In short, he wanted her to have joy in her life, and he wanted to be the one to give it to her.

"Thank you so very much. I am afraid that I cannot stay, however. Mama has gone visiting and I have just had a note from Princess von Furstenberg requesting that I call on her immediately. But thank you, thank you." Helena pressed his hand gratefully and then, succumbing to a cowardice she was too ashamed to acknowledge, and uttering her second barefaced lie for the day, she ran from the room, leaving him to gaze thoughtfully at the door she closed behind her.

But he was not seeing the ornate gilt scroll work that rioted madly over the door's cream-colored surface. He was seeing instead the light in her eyes and thinking he had never felt so gratified in his life as he did now knowing that he had made her happy.

Over the years Brett had weathered his share of tears and tantrums, and managed to remain impervious to them all, but there was something about Helena's struggle to hide her emotions that touched him more deeply than anything had in a long, long time. Her prosaic sniffs and rapid blinking lacked the drama and allure of all the tear-drenched lashes that had been fluttered at him over the years, but the very real emotion they betrayed, in spite of her best efforts to hide it, caught at his heart. She was such a serious thing, always trying so hard to follow the demanding code that she had created for herself, that he found himself wanting desperately to help her break out of the confines of her own expectations and enjoy all that the world had to offer. He wanted to help her give in to her emotions and take pleasure in them instead of fighting them or worrying about losing control over them.

He had brought pleasure to so many women, or at least there were many who claimed that he had; now it was time to do it for someone who could truly benefit from it. Nor could he ever remember wanting so desperately to make anyone else happy. Until now, his entire life had been centered around fulfilling himself, setting his own goals and striving to accomplish them, establishing his own ideals and doing his best to live up to them.

In fact, when the war had ended, he had been somewhat at a loss as to how to proceed because he had reached his goals and lived his ideals by fighting Napoleon's tyranny. They had won. The tyranny had been stopped, and Brett had been faced with the emptiness of *what next?* Working briefly under Wellington in Paris and then taking on his duties in Vienna had undoubtedly served as a distraction, but still, at the back of his mind, he had known he would have to face *what next?* someday.

Now *what next?* suddenly seemed so simple. He wanted to make Helena Devereux happy, and he wanted to share that happiness with her.

Chapter Eighteen

In the hectic days following Christmas, Brett was too overwhelmed with work to revisit this astounding revelation. In fact, he barely had the time to do anything except grab a hasty bite to eat in between reports. The political situation had grown even more tense as rumors poured in that the Prussian army was mobilizing in Saxony itself, and the Dutch were complaining about the ominous presence of Prussian troops at their own borders. The dispatch riders were kept busy scurrying back and forth with the reports being sent to Paris and then on to London in diplomatic pouches. In this atmosphere of heightened tension, the British agents were more active than ever, gathering information whenever and wherever they could find it. Much of the written information they obtained was in French, the language of the Congress, and Brett was kept occupied translating in addition to helping to write some of the reports being sent to London. Most of what he was given to put into English turned out to be nothing more than laundry lists or hotel bills, but the British were leaving no stone unturned.

Days of wrangling among the major powers wore on without a break until the night before the beginning of carnival when the delegates put aside their differences long enough to attend a lavish soiree at Count Razumovsky's magnificent new palace in the Landstrasse.

Brett pressed hard to finish his work that day in time

to attend the soiree, hoping that he would see Helena at the Russian ambassador's palace that evening, for he had not seen her since he had given her the little Christmas tree, had not spoken with her since he had realized how much his future happiness was bound up in hers. He wanted to know for sure if his revelations had been an emotional reaction to a poignant moment or if they were truly the answer to the ennui that had been troubling him since the end of the war. Only the sight of Helena would resolve this question for him.

And it was with this goal in mind that Brett joined the throng crowding into the tapestry-hung salons of Count Razumovsky's extravagant creation.

But crane his neck as he would, Brett could not catch a glimpse of Helena anywhere. The Princess von Hohenbachern was part of a merry group surrounding Metternich and Count Razumovsky, but her daughter was nowhere to be seen.

"Ah, Milord Brett Stanford, one hears that you are wearing yourself out these days laboring over your reports to England. It is good to see that you can take some time out at least to enjoy the gayer side of this Congress."

Brett turned to find himself staring into the mysterious depths of the Countess Edmond de Talleyrand-Périgord's dark brown eyes. She bent her long slender neck closer to him, whispering huskily, "And, L'oncle tells me that it is up to you to make your fellow countrymen understand the finer points of our language."

"Monsieur Talleyrand is far too kind, madame. I am but a simple translator and nothing more." Brett tried his best to picture the elegant elder statesman of France playing an avuncular role to the seductive countess, but failed entirely. Talleyrand might be many things to many people, but *L'oncle*? No, Brett simply could not see it.

"You are far too modest, milord." She slipped a dainty white hand through his elbow and leaned even closer. "But tell me, it is rumored that the oh-so-heroic Lord Wellington may be coming to Vienna to replace Lord Castlereagh. Is that true? On the other hand, I have also heard that he is being sent to command the troops in America and give those colonials a taste of the man who beat Bonaparte. What do you say, milord?"

Brett prayed that the countess did not notice his start of surprise. Where on earth could she have heard such a thing? It was certainly true that Talleyrand had a well-deserved reputation for omniscience, but not even he could have known that, for a little while at least, Wellington had been ready to assume command of the troops in America. "Madame, I am but a poor scribe. My only knowledge of important affairs is secondhand at best. For that sort of information, you must consult Lord Castlereagh himself."

The countess smiled slyly at him. "Very well, milord. I shall take your so excellent advice." And without further ado, she glided off, presumably in search of the British foreign secretary.

The evening had suddenly lost all its promise for Brett. The lights were too bright, the air stiflingly hot, and the guests seemed frenetic in their constant quest for diversion and amusement. Thoroughly disgusted with it all—the politics, the intrigue, the flirtations, he decided to walk back to the peace and quiet of his own quarters. A long walk in the cold crisp air was bound to clear his thoughts, or at least to tire him out enough that he wold fall asleep the moment he climbed into bed. And without further ado, he left the brilliantly lit palace and began walking back along the Landstrasse toward the British delegation. As he breathed in the frosty air and gazed up at the stars twinkling in the velvety blackness above him, he wished that Helena were with him. She would know how he felt, would sympathize with his disgust at the frivolity and vanity of it all, and she would revel in the clearness of the night, the purity of the fresh air, and the exercise after the stifling atmosphere of the crowded ballroom.

In fact, Helena had briefly considered attending the Razumovsky soiree, but the very feelings that had sent Brett in search of her at the Russian ambassador's palace had kept her at home.

She had not shown her mother the little fir tree, but had taken it directly to her bedchamber, where it held

pride of place on her dressing table. There she could
take delight in looking at it while treasuring the memory
of Brett's thoughtfulness. She did not know how she
would explain this uncharacteristic secretiveness to her
mother if Brett happened to mention his gift to the princess—she would think of something if she had to—but
in the meantime, she wanted to keep it to herself as long
as she could so that she could savor the moment when
Brett had presented it to her. No one had ever tried so
hard to find a gift that would truly please her. In fact,
no one had ever before paid enough attention to her
even to know what would please her.

But, a treacherous little voice inside her warned,
Major Lord Brett Stanford knew how to please every
woman—little wonder that he knew how to please her.
He had even known how to make her feel appreciated
when he had thought her a simple serving girl. Naturally,
now that he had become acquainted with her, it would
take no effort at all on his part to select a gift that would
appeal especially to her. Why, he was even successful in
catering to her mothers' sophisticated tastes and the
jaded ones of the Princess Bagration, so it must have
presented him with no challenge at all to win the heart
of an unsophisticated young woman from the country.

At the moment, however, Helena did not want to
think of it that way, the way her mind told her it truly
was. She preferred to follow her heart's interpretation,
that he too had felt the special bond between them and
had sought out the very present that would best express
that bond. And so, in order to keep that interpretation
alive just a little while longer, Helena declined her mother's invitation to accompany her to Count Razumovsky's
in favor of remaining at home, where, it was true, she
would not have the pleasure of waltzing with Brett, but
neither would she have to watch him waltz with her
mother, the Princess Bagration, the Duchess of Sagan,
or all the other beautiful, sophisticated women who
haunted the ballrooms of Vienna.

She ordered a simple supper in the library and tried
to focus her mind on her work, but it kept drifting back
to a pair of bright blue eyes in a tanned face smiling
into hers, and strong arms whirling her around the floor

until she finally gave up and gave in to her daydreams as she slowly dozed off in her favorite bergère chair.

Helena woke hours later to the clanging of church bells. Not fully awake and still half in and half out of her dreamworld, she struggled a moment to figure out where she was. It was still dark as night, and the candles were guttering in their sockets, but the sky off in the east was tinged by a faint orange glow. Was it dawn already? Had she spent the entire night in the library?

Then she heard shouting and the sounds of running feet. Hastily she opened the window. "Fire! Fire!" people in the street below called out as they hurried past, some carrying buckets of water as they ran.

She hurried downstairs where servants were clustered in the doorway watching the crowds surge past.

"Oh, Fraulein, it is an enormous fire somewhere in one of the suburbs," her maid Hannechen gasped.

"They say it is at Count Razumovsky's new palace," Potten added.

"Count Razumovsky's palace? Are you sure?"

The butler nodded. "That is what they are saying, miss."

"Mama! Has she returned home?"

They all shook their heads.

"I must go to her." Helena turned and raced back upstairs to her bedchamber to pull on a stout pair of half boots and grab her serviceable wool cloak.

"No, Fraulein, you cannot go out in this," Hannechen pleaded with her mistress as Helena returned to the little group in the doorway.

"But Mama was attending the soiree there. I must go and find her."

"You cannot go by yourself, miss. We must send someone with you." Potten glanced at the assembled group, but no one seemed particularly anxious to venture forth into the frosty night and the certain danger of a blazing building.

"It is best if I go alone. In all this crowd, we are only likely to be separated anyway."

"If you insist, miss."

It was a halfhearted protest, and Helena's decisive *I do* raised a collective sigh of relief from the onlookers.

Pulling her cloak more tightly around her, she started to head off in the direction of the glow.

"Miss, at least let me call you a carriage," Potten begged

"What, at this hour, in this crowd? No thank you. I shall be far swifter and far more efficient on my own two feet." And Helena hurried off into the darkness before anyone else could voice any more objections or, worse yet, screw up their courage and come with her. The last thing she needed was to worry about someone else's welfare.

But as she reached the Graben, doubts began to assail her. The crowd was growing. She knew that everyone who was anyone would have been at the count's. How was she to find her mother among the hordes of people, and what was she to do if she did not find her? What could she, a gently brought-up young female, no matter how independent, self-sufficient, or intelligent, do to help in a fire?

Before her mind could even frame the answer to that question, she found herself turning toward the British delegation. She might not be able to do anything herself, but she knew a man who had spent the better part of his life dealing with dangerous situations. Brett would know what to do.

As she hurried along she berated herself for giving in to weakness, and scolded herself for the way the vision of that determined jaw, angular face, and observant eyes flashed into her mind unbidden, but it was no use. She hated herself for turning to him with a problem she could not solve, and she truly hated herself for wondering unhappily if perhaps he was enjoying himself with her mother at this very moment. If he were, she comforted herself, then her mother was undoubtedly safe. But it was small consolation, for if they were together, it would mean that the closeness she herself had begun to feel with Brett was just a figment of her imagination and nothing more.

Had her mother mentioned him lately? Helena had begun to think that his name had come up less and less often in her mother's conversations, but perhaps that was just wishful thinking on her part.

And why did she care? Thoroughly annoyed with herself, Helena strode faster along the cobbled streets toward the British delegation. All that mattered at the moment was her mother's safety. The rest was nothing but pointless speculation.

She had been so intent on finding help, on seeking the reassurance of someone she instinctively felt would know just what to do that Helena was surprised to discover herself so quickly in front of the massive door of the Liechtenstein Palace, where the British delegation was housed.

Now what? She asked herself ironically. *Do you just march up to the porter and say, "I am in desperate need of a brave man to help me, so could I please speak to Major Lord Brett Stanford"?*

Chapter Nineteen

In the end, that was precisely what she did do. After a
few minutes spent pacing helplessly back and forth before the impressive statues standing guard on either side
of the door and fighting the last remnants of her pride,
Helena gave in and banged forcefully on the door until
at last the porter appeared.

"I have an urgent message for Major Lord Brett Stanford," she informed the goggling servant in a tone that
sounded far more authoritative than she felt. "It demands his immediate attention!" As the man nodded
and disappeared, she willed him to hurry in search of
Brett before someone else could appear to ask uncomfortable questions.

When the servant had vanished into the gloom of the
cavernous stairwell, she asked herself again if she had
gone completely mad, and more uncomfortably yet, if
she wanted to find Brett at home alone or if she wanted
him to be at the Razumovsky palace, where possibly he
would be watching out for her mother's safety.

It seemed ages before she heard footsteps echoing on
the stones of the stairway, and even longer before Brett
appeared, still shrugging himself into his coat, his dark
hair tousled. "Helena! Miss Devereux. Whatever is
amiss?"

"It is Mama." She rushed up to him like a helpless
ninny, cursing herself for feeling so reassured as he took
her hands in a warm comforting clasp.

"What about her? What has happened? I saw her not long ago at the Razumovsky palace talking with Metternich, and she looked as merry as a cricket."

Helena loathed herself for the wave of relief that washed over her at these words. So he had not been her mother's escort after all. He must have been at Count Razumovsky's alone then. Had he been looking for her there? Had he missed her? Helena shook her head angrily. How could she even wonder such things at a time like this? "That is just it. She has not returned from the count's, and now they say that the palace is ablaze." She pointed off to the east, where the orange glow had become a vivid red and sparks could be seen shooting into the sky.

Then, without warning, she was engulfed in tears. She had been so intent on assuring herself of her mother's whereabouts that she had not paused to consider the implications of it all until now. But now, knowing that she had someone who could truly help her, feeling his strength in her hands, trusting implicitly in his courage and resourcefulness, she could relax enough for the worries to overwhelm her. The sympathy and concern she read in his eyes was the final straw. She covered her face with her hands and wept.

"Helena, my poor girl." Strong arms pulled her to him, and she laid her head on his chest overcome with it all—the anxiety, the relief of having someone to share it with, and a host of other emotions that had been bottled up inside her since the day Major Lord Brett Stanford had walked into their lives. "Hush, now. Do not fret so. I shall find her."

At last Helena was able to establish some modicum of control over herself. She gulped and swiped angrily at her wet eyes with one gloved hand. "No. *We* will find her."

She straightened up and looked Brett squarely in the eye. "I may be a watering pot, Major, but I am not a coward."

A hint of a grin tugged at one corner of his mouth. "Very well, then. I shall just saddle Rex and . . ."

"But the fire, is it not better to walk? Horses . . ."

"Rex has seen far worse than fires, believe me. The

question is, will you be able to sit in front of me on him?"

She nodded and then began to pace restlessly while he went to get his horse.

In no time at all he was back and, tossing her into the saddle, he settled himself behind her as best he could.

Without a word they rode through the narrow streets, picking their way among the growing numbers of people pouring out of doorways and heading toward the Razumovsky palace. In fact the only words spoken at all were the quiet commands Brett gave to his horse as they slowly but inexorably forged a path through the crowds milling around them.

At last they reached the palace, where citizens of every description, from servants to monarchs, were gathered in silent fascination as the flames devoured the enormous structure. In the flickering firelight, Helena was able to make out the pale thin features of the emperor, still in his nightshirt and a sable cloak tossed over his shoulders. A little farther on, the sparks gleaming on his gold-embroidered tunic, stood the tsar watching the horrible spectacle in silent awe.

A sudden clanging of a bell behind them roused their attention, and a team of horses pulling water pumps and hoses galloped up to join the groups of civilians passing buckets of water from hand to hand while a corps of engineers cut down the rare shrubbery gracing the main entrance to provide the firefighters better access to the vast park surrounding the palace.

Mounted police were slowly pushing the horde of onlookers back away from the flames, but Helena and Brett, moving steadily through the confusion, were able to get close enough to see that servants inside were hastily tossing valuables of every description from the windows in a fruitless attempt to save the count's priceless collections. From the second story dozens of the count's coats, vests, and trousers rained down, while other windows gave up all manner of things—chandeliers, books, alabaster vases, silverware—all hurled to the ground below, which was rapidly turning into a dirty, sodden mess.

At last they reached the edge of the crowd gathered around the blazing palace. Before them was a sea of mud, soaked by snow and the water that was being sprayed in futile attempts to quell the blaze. Beyond that stood the palace, its copper roof glowing red as flames and smoke poured from most of its windows.

"Wait here." Brett dismounted and turned to help her down.

Helena opened her mouth to protest.

"I need someone to hold Rex and keep him calm while I search for your mother. I cannot be worrying about him and you while I look for her." He seized a spare saddle blanket he had had the forethought to bring along, grabbed a discarded bucket that was still half full of water and, dowsing the blanket as best he could, threw it over his shoulders and headed off.

What he had said made a great deal of sense. In fact, it was the only thing to do, but having asked his help, Helena now found it very difficult to accept it. Always, since she had been a little girl, she had been the sensible one, the competent one, the one who knew just what to do in every situation. Reassuring as it now was to be with someone who truly did know what to do, it was difficult to accept that fact and allow Brett to handle the situation. Helena had never had the beauty or charm that drew people to her the way they were drawn to other women, such as her mother, for instance. What she had had to offer instead was intelligence and good sense, and these had in some way made up for her lack of the rest. She had taken a good deal of comfort and satisfaction in being unique in possessing these qualities, and now she was having to acknowledge someone else's superiority in areas that heretofore had been solely her own. She was having to cede her authority to someone who had even more competence and more experience to offer in this situation than she did. And while it pleased her immensely to have her confidence in Brett borne out by his easy mastery of the situation, it still required a certain amount of adjustment on her part to acknowledge it.

"Do be careful." Her voice could not compete with

the roar of the fire, the clanging of the bells, and the shouts of the people. "Oh, do be careful," she whispered softly. "For my sake as well as for Mama's."

Helena gripped Rex's bridle even more tightly and, squinting against the glare of the flames shooting from what seemed to be every possible opening, stood on tip-toe trying to keep her eyes on the tall, blanketed figure making its way purposefully toward the inferno. How could anyone possibly remain alive in there now? Objects were no longer being tossed from the windows and the dark shapes of servants no longer appeared silhouetted against the flames. Anyone in there would surely have perished by now. Had she sent Brett to his death then for no purpose?

". . . is tragic, simply tragic," the voices exclaimed behind her.

"Poor Razumovsky. That magnificent palace. What a loss."

"And all his paintings. All the Titians, the Raphaels, the Reubens, and so little time to appreciate them all. He has been working too hard on the negotiations to get any sleep, much less enjoy his new palace and all its treasures."

Metternich? Talleyrand? Helena could not be sure, but it certainly sounded like the clipped speech of the Austrian chancellor and the more cultured tones of the French ambassador, but she was too anxious to turn around or even to care.

"Such a great pity. And such a lovely party as it was. How thankful I am that we left when we did. If we had not decided on the way home to stop in and call on you, Monsieur Talleyrand, who knows . . ."

"Mama?" This voice was definitely one that Helena recognized. She whirled around to see the princess standing there looking as elegant as if she were sitting in the French ambassador's sumptuous quarters in the Kaunitz Palace.

"My dear, what ever are you doing here? I had thought you retired ages ago." The princess' eyes traveled critically over her daughter's warm, but eminently serviceable-looking cloak and then down at her own sable-trimmed one. "Indeed, you look as though you just snatched anything to hand and rushed over here without thinking."

"I did," Helena replied bluntly. "Mama, I thought that you were in . . . But never mind, I must stop him! Here." And thrusting Rex's reins into the princess' hands, Helena hurried off before her astonished mother could open her mouth to protest.

Completely oblivious to endless lessons on the conduct becoming for a gently brought-up young lady, Helena pushed her way ruthlessly through the mass of onlookers, shoving aside anyone who got in her path— foreign dignitaries and humble citizens alike—until she reached the edge of the crowd that maintained a respectful distance from the burning building.

Parts of the roof, beams, and columns traced fiery trajectories as they plummeted to earth. Too desperate to care what anyone might think, Helena pushed forward calling Brett's name, but aside from a few curious glances, she received no reply. However, the noise of the fire was such that even a few paces away a person would not be able to hear her.

"A man," she gasped, clutching the arm of a knowing-looking gentleman clad in the sober garb of a civil servant, "did you see a man go into the building just now?"

"No I did not, Fraulein, but I have only just arrived."

"No," another onlooker chimed in, "there has been no one seen lately except those two chimney sweeps trapped on the roof—poor fellows."

"Look! There!" His companion pointed to the middle of the trampled ground that separated the crowd from the inferno. "Isn't that someone there?"

Helena could not make out anything against the black background of the sodden ground, but she struggled forward through the mud, hoping that when the figure, if it was a figure at all, got close enough to the building, it would be silhouetted against the blaze.

At last she caught sight of a bulky shape poised to enter the only doorway that was not completely engulfed in flames. It paused a moment to adjust its protective covering and then advanced slowly, steadily toward the blazing entrance.

"Brett! Brett!" she screamed stumbling through the

mire as best she could. The mud clung to her skirts, slowing her down and making her slip and slide with every step. He could not hear her. How ever was she going to reach him in time?

"Brett! Brett!" Sobbing with the effort she struggled on, but still he did not hear her.

He placed one foot on the first step.

Desperate, Helena hurled herself the last few feet, trying frantically to stop him without pushing him further into the conflagration. Fortunately for both of them, she slipped just before she flung her arms around his waist.

Bundled up as he was, Brett was able to catch her and steady her as he fought to maintain his balance and keep both of them from tumbling into the flames. "Helena, I must. There is still a chance . . ."

"No. No." Tears of relief made crooked white tracks through the soot covering her face. "Mama is safe."

"Safe? How did she . . ."

"She left hours ago and went to Talleyrand's. I just saw her now among the people watching."

"You are sure? You are not just . . ."

Helena drew herself up. "Of course I am sure. I may look a complete madwoman at the moment, and I was frantic with worry over you . . . er Mama, but I still am enough in command of my faculties to recognize my own mother."

And then she totally ruined the effect by bursting into tears for the second time that night.

Brett pulled her close, or as close as the wads of wet blanket would allow, and held her in an awkward embrace, gently stroking her hair until the worst of the sobs had subsided. "Hush, my girl. It is all right. Everyone is safe."

She could not understand why she had been so suddenly overcome or why she was helpless to stop the tears now, but it had something to do with the solid, comforting reality of him and the terrible fear she had suffered just moments ago when she had thought she had already lost him to the fire.

There was a resounding crash as the beams in the doorway he had been about to enter collapsed in a shower of sparks. "You might have been there. I might have sent you . . ."

"Hush." He laid a gentle finger on her lips. "It is over now. Everyone is safe. Now we must get you home." And slowly, comfortingly, he led her back through the crowd to the spot where he had left her holding Rex.

Chapter Twenty

The princess was still standing there, Rex's reins dangling from her hands as she gazed abstractedly at the spectacle, Talleyrand at her side. Metternich had left, but the little group had swelled by now to include Talleyrand's niece, the Countess Edmond de Talleyrand-Périgord and her escort.

"Helena, wherever . . . Good heavens, Major, where on earth have you been?" The princess gasped as her gaze took in Brett's bulky costume and the soot-blackened faces of both the major and her daughter.

"You see, mama . . . you were not home, so I thought you were . . ." Even now, Helena could not get the words out.

"Miss Devereux was concerned that you might still be at Count Razumovsky's."

Helena nodded dumbly. How was he able to explain it all so simply and so calmly, when she, who had been a mere spectator, was still too overcome to be coherent. A moment ago he had been ready to risk his life, yet now he was unwrapping himself from the blanket and folding it up with no more fuss than if he had just returned home from a ride in the Prater.

"You went to rescue . . . Oh, my!" The princess gazed at him with renewed respect. No other man she knew, except perhaps her husband, who also took a soldier's simple pragmatic view of emergencies, would have even contemplated such a mad endeavor.

"However, having now assured myself of your safety, I shall be happy to escort you and your daughter home."

The princess glanced dubiously at Rex. "That is very kind of you, Major, but there is no need to trouble yourself. Monsieur Talleyrand very kindly brought me here in his carriage."

"And we cannot simply just return home to our beds after such a dreadful event," the Countess Edmond de Talleyrand-Périgord chimed in. "Count Clam-Martinitz here has taken me to Paperl's more than once. They serve an excellent breakfast there with superb *marillen knödel*. And it is nearly time for breakfast now. Let us all go there."

There was a general murmur of agreement, but Brett, seeing that Helena was utterly worn out after her exhausting night, turned without a word and lifted her up into the saddle. He climbed up behind her, and turned Rex back toward the city. Then they began to make their way slowly, silently back home, each one too worn out by the emotions of the evening to do anything but let the horse carry them back through city streets that were now slowly coming to life as merchants swept their doorsteps and peddlers began to appear with their carts.

The door to the palace in the Bräunerstrasse swung open the instant they arrived as the princess' entire staff, agog with worry over the fate of their mistress and her daughter, huddled anxiously in the doorway. Even before she allowed Brett to help her down, Helena quickly reassured them that the princess was not only safe but in the best of company.

"Not only that, but we are all indebted to Major Lord Brett Stanford for helping me to find her," she added with a shy smile as she slid from the saddle into his waiting arms.

Now that she was safely at home, reassured that her mother was also alive and well, Helena felt all the tension drain from her only to be replaced by an exhaustion more overwhelming than she could even imagine. Yet, even though her feet felt like lead and she could hardly hold up her head, she was loath to say good-bye to him and to end the magical protective spell that had surrounded her from the moment she had seen Brett coming down the stairs toward her at the British delegation.

"Your coat!" As she clung to his arm, Helena suddenly became aware of the dampness seeping through her gloves. "It is soaked through. You must come inside and let me dry it out at least a little bit before you go home. Potten will see to it that your horse is taken care of and that the fire is lit in the library." Helena turned to the butler, who was struggling to appear impassive while he absorbed the astonishing spectacle of his young mistress in the arms of a man. While it was true that the major had only been helping Miss Helena to dismount, it was clear to even the most casual observer that it was more than simple assistance. Something special existed between Miss Helena and the major. To someone like Potten who had known the fiercely independent Miss Helena since childhood, this turn of events was nothing short of a miracle.

The butler could not remember many instances when she had accepted help from anyone, or recall a time when she had not insisted on doing it, whatever *it* was, by herself. Now she was gazing up at the gentleman as if her life depended on him. Not that the gentleman did not deserve such a look. From the very first time the major had called on the princess, Potten had thought that Major Lord Brett Stanford presented an impressive figure of a man, and that favorable impression had only grown over time. Not only did the gentleman make a fine figure of a man, but his manners were those of true quality. He knew how to recognize and appreciate everyone, from the princess to her servants. And most impressive of all was that he also apparently knew how to make Miss Helena glow with happiness.

Potten motioned to the stable boy, who had magically appeared, to take Brett's horse and then sent a hovering footman to make sure that a fire was laid. The butler had witnessed scores of handsome gentlemen calling at the princess' over the years, but none of them could begin to compare with this one, and none of them had ever evinced the least interest in Miss Helena, or she in them. What, he wondered as he led his mistress and the major to the library, was to become of all this? Whatever it was, it was bound to be interesting. Life with the princess had never been dull, but this was a first, even for her. Gently the butler closed the door behind Helena and Brett and hoped for the best.

"Here, let me help you out of that wet coat." It only made sense to offer assistance, and Helena had only offered it out of purely practical reasons, but her cheeks grew hot the moment the words were out of her mouth.

"Thank you." Brett grinned. Helena might not be fully aware of the color flooding her face or the reasons behind it, but he was. It had taken her a long time to become aware of such things, yet he felt sure that she would awaken to them eventually. He refused to admit the other part of that wish, which was that this revelation would occur in his company. He had always been proud of his ability to retain his aloofness where women were concerned, an aloofness that had made it possible for him to avoid messy entanglements. He had always cherished that aloofness and the invulnerability that it had conferred upon him, but lately he had found that aloofness slipping away as he discovered himself spending hours at a time thinking about Helena Devereux, wondering what she was doing, what she was thinking, and if she was happy. He told himself that he was certainly not about to give that invulnerability up now, especially for a self-reliant young woman who possessed more brains than beauty and was far too independent for comfort, but he looked down at her again, and he was lost.

The touch of shyness in her tentative smile, coupled with an ironically humorous twinkle in the hazel eyes made him both uncomfortably aware that she knew what he was thinking and also surprisingly pleased that she did. It was the oddest sensation. He had never felt so close to another person in all his life, had always scoffed at the very idea of kindred spirits; yet here she was standing right next to him.

He shrugged out of his coat and watched approvingly as she hung it up in a businesslike fashion, close enough to the fire to dry but not so close as to be singed by a stray spark. Usually his women were well versed in the ways between men and women, but totally unaware of life's more practical aspects. Helena, on the other hand, was quite the reverse, and he found it dangerously attractive. "You hang up a wet coat as though you were the veteran of a score of campaigns."

"I wish I were." She sighed. "I have seen so very little of the world beyond Hohenbachern except for the few dim memories of England, which, I suppose is more than most women my age, but . . ."

"But?" He took the seat opposite her, watching the way the firelight flickered on her face, emphasizing its wistful expression.

"But I should like to have been able to go more places and do more things instead of being confined to the few tame activities that are acceptable for a woman. I would like to have my life make a difference the way yours has."

Brett reached over to grasp one of the hands that was twisting with the other in her lap. "Believe me, you *are* making a difference. You study the issues, form your own opinions, and speak what you believe. You influence people."

"Oh, talk." Helena dismissed it with an angry shake of her head. "You have been in the Peninsula risking your life to improve the lives of thousands of others. All I can hope for at best is to change the minds of a few pompous windbags."

He chuckled. "I assure you, that it is the pompous windbags who control everything in this world. A few minutes' conversation with them can have more far-reaching effects on the fates of nations than whole battalions of men." The blue eyes darkened and the humorous twinkle disappeared. "I have not only risked my life, you know, but I have also taken them."

Her heart turned over at the sadness in his voice, the bleakness in the taut pale face. The horrors he must have witnessed and the privations he must have endured were unimaginable. "But you at least have lived."

It was a simple statement, quietly made, but he suddenly understood the frustration she must have been battling her entire life, heard the desperation of an active, intelligent, resourceful person forced to sit quietly on the sidelines while the world passed her by, while events of momentous historic importance took place all around her. And she could do nothing, or at least, she was expected to do nothing beyond learning all the feminine accomplishments that would win her a suitable husband.

What would he have done in her position? Gone mad very likely. After all it had been similar feelings of frustration and uselessness that had driven him to join the cavalry. But for Helena Devereux, there had been no cavalry.

He rose and, still holding her hand, pulled her up to face him. "You are living now."

The way the look in his eyes made her heart pound, the way his touch made her skin tingle all over and her face catch fire told her that this was absolutely true.

Brett's other hand slowly traced the curve of her cheek and then gently cupped her chin. "And you *are* making a difference, believe me." His lips touched hers gently, caressingly, then firmly as his arms slid around her waist and pulled her to him.

Her entire body seemed to burst into flame in his hands. She felt as hopelessly out of control as the blaze they had just witnessed and as totally consumed by it. Yet, as unnerving as it was, it was also more exhilarating than anything she had ever experienced. He was right, she was alive—at last.

As Brett tasted the lips parted under his and felt her body molding itself to his, he opened his eyes to look down at the flushed face and the long dark lashes that fluttered against her cheeks. Yes, she was her mother's daughter after all. The sensuality had merely lain dormant all these years, kept ruthlessly in check by the fear that it would overwhelm her and cause her to lose that dearly won independence and self-control.

Her mother's daughter! A cold sliver of guilt stabbed through him. What was he doing? Major Lord Brett Stanford might have always succeeded in evading entanglements of every kind, but he was not callous, and he certainly did not wish to hurt either one of these women—not the mother and especially not the daughter. He was not free to love her as she deserved to be loved. At the moment he had a duty to his government that demanded all his attention. He could not become involved with anyone, which was why he had sought out the Princess von Hohenbachern's company in the first place, as protection against the possibility of any entanglements, romantic or otherwise, occurring—unlikely as the possibility had appeared to be at the time.

What a hopeless tangle it was! And now he found himself wanting to forget everything except this new-found feeling of tenderness fueled by desire. It was a dangerous combination indeed, and one that was almost irresistible.

Mustering every ounce of willpower he possessed, Brett gently grasped Helena's arms and carefully set her away from him. "Forgive me. The strain of the evening . . . you must be exhausted." Though in all honesty he had to admit that she looked as alive and vibrant as he had ever seen her. He longed to plant kisses down the slim white column of her throat, undo the fastenings of the simple muslin gown, and . . . He caught his breath. This was taking him nowhere except to dangerous ground, very dangerous ground indeed. "I, er, mean that I still have work left to do on a draft of the treaty Castlereagh means to submit to the French and the Austrians that must be finished by morning. Well, it is morning now, but it must be completed by today."

She nodded slowly, but he could see that his words were making no impression on her at all. There was a soft, dreamy glow in her eyes, her lips were full and red, exactly as he had described to her that long ago day in the Prater. And he longed to keep them that way so that she never had to wake from that dream of passion and desire. Certainly, he had no wish to wake from it either, but he had to for both their sakes.

Brett reached over and lifted his jacket from the back of the chair. It was still slightly damp, but at least it was warm. He pulled it on and then took her again by the shoulders. "Thank you for drying my jacket. Sleep well, Helena." He pressed his lips gently to her forehead and was gone, hurrying down the stone staircase to the courtyard below and out through the massive wooden doors to the street before he could lose his resolve.

The pink sky was fading into blue, and the air was cold and crisp. He inhaled deeply, hoping to steady himself, hoping to quell the longing that made him wish to throw caution to the winds and return to the arms of the woman who was rapidly becoming an obsession with him.

It was not until Brett was halfway down the street that he realized he had left Rex behind. Shaking his head at his own preoccupation, he retraced his steps, roused the stable boy, and, too worn out by the events of the evening to ride, slowly led his horse back to his quarters.

Chapter Twenty-one

Fortunately for Brett, the ensuing days at the British delegation were so frantically busy that there was simply no time to think of anything else but work, and he was spared the unnerving reflections that had begun to plague him the moment he had left Helena. Castlereagh had indeed been recalled to resume his parliamentary duties, which meant there was a scramble to get all his affairs in order before his departure. But before the foreign secretary left Vienna, Wellington arrived to replace him, so therefore, in addition to the work, Brett had to attend numerous receptions in honor of Europe's hero. Between Castlereagh's secretarial requirements and Wellington's observational ones, Brett barely had time to sleep, a situation for which he was supremely grateful.

The few hours that he was able to lie down, he was too exhausted to be kept awake, plagued by disturbing visions of Helena, her eyes half closed, her lips parted for his kisses, or troubled by dreams of any sort.

For her part, Helena was also blessedly drawn into the political fray. Her mother, galvanized by the revelation that the Prussians intended to take Saxony away from its hereditary ruler saw all too clearly that what had happened to Saxony's king could very well happen to other German sovereigns, and she did her best to use her increasing intimacy with Metternich to make sure that such a thing did not occur. And these same German sovereigns who had once gathered at the Princess von

Furstenberg's, sensing the Princess von Hohenbachern's influence with Metternich, now began to call on her.

"It is not that I am unsympathetic to their cause," the princess complained to her daughter one day as she yawned and shook her head groggily after a particularly lengthy visit. "After all, your stepfather distrusts the Prussians as much as the rest of them do, dreadful and pushy as they are, and they simply have no idea of good *ton.* It is just that he prefers to settle things in a more direct manner at the head of the Hohenbachern troops. And I am not at all sure what good will come of *my* speaking to Clemens. What can I say to him that has not already been said? Besides, I find these petty rulers to be so very stiff and so very dull. At least Friedrich is a soldier—so much more dashing an occupation than sitting around a palace trying to rule people."

"They are simply hoping that you can convince the Austrians to take a firm stand against Prussian encroachment by using your influence with Metternich, Mama."

"I?" The princess laughed, but Helena could see that she was flattered by it all, nevertheless. "If only they were not so pompous, so boring, and so very unprepossessing. At least Friedrich is doing something out there with the army. And he does make a fine figure of a man. I have always thought so, from the moment the Prince Regent introduced us. But these men . . ." The princess dismissed them all with an airy wave of her hand. "They do nothing but talk endlessly. Even Clemens would rather hear himself speak than actually *do* anything."

At any other time, Helena would have been highly amused by her mother's disparaging description of the Austrian chancellor, but the references to the Prince von Hohenbachern had brought to mind another military man of their acquaintance, another man who preferred to act rather than talk. And just the thought of that particular man made her feel weak all over.

Helena had had no idea that a kiss could be overwhelming. It had not been the kiss precisely, but the look in his eyes and the warmth of his hands as he held her. It had felt as though he had wanted her and only her. When Brett talked to her, when he listened so intently, his eyes fixed steadily on her, he made her feel as though she were the only woman, the only other person in the world, that no one else existed except the two of them. Her mind told her that it was all an illusion, that he made all women—the Princess Bagration, even her own mother—feel that way, but her heart told something different. Her heart told her that they were soul mates, that they shared something beyond mutual physical attraction, something unique and precious, and that he was as alive to the treasure they shared as she was.

"Er, what did you say, Mama?"

"I was saying that of course I shall do whatever I can, but tonight is Princess Bagration's reception for Wellington, and it will be such a crush that there will be no chance for conversation at all, much less private conversation with Metternich." The princess quickly stifled a sly smile at Helena's momentary loss of attention. Her daughter had not been herself lately. She had been subject to unusual moments of abstraction and often sat lost in some world of her own, a dreamy expression on her face that was completely at variance with her usual alert and clear-eyed view of the world. There was no doubt in her mother's mind that Helena was in love, and the princess derived a considerable amount of gleeful satisfaction at witnessing this paragon of intelligence and rationality exhibiting the same erratic behavior as anyone else who was in the grip of this supreme emotion.

"Yes, of course, you are right," Helena responded vaguely, but her mind was elsewhere. *Wellington.* Again, the name evoked thoughts of one of Wellington's officers, an officer on whom she had not laid eyes in far too long.

At first, Helena had been relieved that Brett seemed to have vanished from sight, for she hardly knew how she was to face him after she had practically thrown herself into his arms the night of the fire. Or at least it had felt as though she had thrown herself at him. While it was true that *he* had begun by kissing *her*, her treacherous body's response had been so immediate and so strong that she feared she was no better than a brazen hussy.

However, no sooner had she told herself that Brett's absence was conducive to her peace of mind than she found herself looking for him at every possible gathering place.

Heavy snow had fallen and the cold forced all those who might have sought fresh air and exercise in the Prater to gather in the streets instead. But no matter how often she and Hannechen joined the throngs strolling here and there, or became part of the constant promenade along the Herrengasse, or stopped to admire the Englishmen demonstrating their skating prowess on the frozen branches of the Danube, she never caught sight of a tall, dark-haired figure.

After a number of listless days spent in this fruitless exercise, Helena was forced into accepting the unnerving conclusion that no matter how much Brett's presence might threaten her peace of mind and her self-control, his absence was a far greater threat to her happiness itself. But, fortunately, before she could fall into a demoralizing decline, he sought her out one morning as she was perusing the latest issue of the *Weiner Zeitung*.

"Major Lord Brett Stanford," Potten announced in a stentorian voice as he ushered Brett into the library; however, his wooden expression was belied by the twinkle in his eye as he watched his young mistress scramble up from her chair, scattering papers right and left. No one else had ever caused her to lose that calm air of self-possession, but this particular caller appeared to do so on a regular basis.

"Er, I am sorry to interrupt you, but . . ." Brett was no more composed than she was. In fact, he was supremely disconcerted to feel sweat prickling at the back of his neck like any callow youth casting sheep's eyes at his ladylove. "But I have come to ask your advice on a diplomatic matter."

Helena's heart plummeted. "I am flattered," she lied with a promptness that would have done justice to someone who told bold-faced untruths on a regular basis. Why had she hoped he had simply come to see her instead of to consult her political expertise?

"You see, it is a rather delicate matter involving the Prussians." He held up an admonitory hand. "Naturally I realize that you distrust them, but you will admit that it behooves the rest of us to keep an eye on them and even do what we can to remain on good terms with them. Now, here is my question. This evening, naturally everyone, or almost everyone, will be at the Princess Bagration's reception for Wellington. However, we have heard that the Prussians refuse to attend out of protest over the recent alliance among Britain, Austria, and France. Instead, it appears that many of them will be gathering at the Countess Bernstorff's, where, naturally, members of the British delegation, though not specifically invited, would certainly not be turned away if they were to appear. It seems to me that it would go a long way to mollifying the Prussians if one Englishman at least is present at this reception; therefore, I have volunteered to attend. What do you think?"

Helena struggled to conceal, even from herself, her chief reaction to his proposal, which was the gratifying conclusion that he appeared to have no interest in the Princess Bagration, much less her reception. She swallowed hard as she admonished herself for even paying attention to such things when so much else was at stake. "It strikes me as a most excellent plan." Lord, how awkward and stilted she sounded. Why, for once, could she not be more like her mother, who remained charmingly articulate no matter what the circumstance or how attractive the gentleman.

"Good." It was not until he let out an enormous sigh of relief that Brett realized how much her opinion meant to him.

Hearing that sigh, Helena felt some of her own tension slipping away. He was as awkward and ill at ease as she was. That was some consolation, at least, and it offered her some hope. Surely a man as worldly as Major Lord Brett Stanford would not be awkward with someone he considered to be just another one of his flirts, or simply a woman whose company he valued because she was well versed in European politics. Clearly, his behavior showed that she meant something more to him than that? "I do think that you are very clever to do it. Such a gesture of respect is sure to be appreciated by the Prussians. Much as you profess to dislike what you might call intrigue, Major, you appear to have become sensitive to the importance of it all."

Brett grinned. Funny how such a simple acknowledgment could bring him such pleasure. "But I do not have to like it or even approve of it, for that matter."

She smiled in return. "No, you do not, but at least you do not dismiss it as useless like so many of you British do."

They sat smiling at one another for several minutes, happy that the easy intimacy so precious to both of them had been restored. In fact, there was no telling how long they would have remained that way had not the sound of a carriage turning into the street below and halting at the entrance to the von Hohenbachern apartments recalled Brett to his duties.

He rose, already feeling guilty at the amount of time he had spent away from the paperwork piled high on his desk. "Thank you so much. You cannot know what it means to me to have your approval. But I must go now. What with Wellington here and Castlereagh departing, there is a great deal to do."

"I am sure there is." Helena rose as well. Her day was brighter already, and so was her frame of mind. He had not kissed her again or made even the slightest reference to that night, but she was reassured to see that the special look was still at the back of his eyes when he smiled at her.

And, if the truth were told, she was not at all sure that she did want him to kiss her again. It had been wonderful, but it had been frightening as well, and she was more than a little afraid of the powerful feelings he inspired in her.

To Brett too, striding back toward the British delegation, the atmosphere had lifted. The pile of work facing him on his desk seemed far less overwhelming than it had when he had first set out for the von Hohenbachern residence. Just seeing Helena again had reassured him that the closeness and the feelings of the night of the fire had not been the madness of a moment or an overreaction to the drama of the evening. It was still there, not so obvious perhaps, but still it was the same strong undercurrent that always drew him to her no matter where they were or what they were doing and . . . Damn and Blast! He had forgotten to discover whether or not she had been planning to attend the reception for Wellington at the Palm Palace. Frankly he was rather relieved not to be attending the reception, but he would regret not seeing Helena if she had been planning to attend the princess' reception.

Chapter Twenty-two

The Countess Bernstorff welcomed Brett enthusiastically. "I cannot tell you how delighted we are to see you, Major. So many of the events at the Congress are such crushes that one only has time to nod to one's acquaintances across the room. As far as establishing any sort of rapport with anyone new, why it is virtually impossible among all the noise and the crowd. Do come sit beside me and tell me about yourself." She patted the place next to her on the rich brocade sofa in a most friendly fashion.

In fact, the countess turned out to be far more lively and pleasant than he had expected. She created an air of informality that even made the rigidly ceremonious Prussians seem less stiff and more approachable than he ever remembered.

However, once the countess left him to pay attention to her other guests, Brett soon found himself becoming bored. The Prussians were amiable enough, and absurdly pleased at having lured one Englishman at least away from the Princess Bagration's reception, but their endless self-congratulation on the wisdom of their king and their ministers, and the orderliness of their government, their calm assumption of superiority in all civil, political, and financial affairs were as repetitious as they were infuriating. Therefore, it was not long before Brett felt that mask of flattering attentiveness he had assumed beginning to slip, and for the hundredth time he wondered how Castlereagh and the other diplomats stood it, and why.

So desperate was he after only an hour or so of stulti-fying conversation, mostly one-sided, that he was barely able to stifle a sigh of relief when he happened to look up and catch sight of the elegant figure of Prince Louis de Rohan. Normally Brett, who only knew the prince by sight and had no use for the opportunistic Frenchman, would not have paid the least attention to the man, but now he welcomed him as cordially as if he were a long-lost friend. At least they could share reminiscences of Paris and news of some of the people Brett had met during his brief sojourn at the British embassy in the French capital.

In fact, Brett was so delighted to be able to talk with someone who understood the art of conversation that it did not occur to him to wonder at the Frenchman's pres-ence among such a purely Teutonic crowd.

It was not until hours later, when Brett was at last able to free himself from the increasingly raucous com-pany and make his way to the Palm Palace, where the reception for Wellington was still underway, that it oc-curred to him to wonder what the prince had been doing at the countess' reception, where except for Brett, he had been the only non-Prussian there. In addition to that, it was even more odd to find the Frenchman among such a dully respectable crowd, for it was well-known that his tastes ran to far more exotic amusements. By the time Brett arrived at the Palm Palace, the crowd had thinned enough for him to scan the princess' brilliantly lit ballroom and assure himself within a matter of min-utes that Helena was not there.

Exhausted by the previous hours of enforced joviality and having no particular reason to remain now that he knew Helena was not present, Brett was turning to go when a gentle hand touched his arm and a low, musical voice interrupted him. "What, are you leaving so soon, Major? You have been working too hard lately not to enjoy yourself now."

Stifling a sigh of annoyance, he looked down into the large dark eyes of the Countess Edmond de Talleyrand-

Périgord. The countess' lips parted in her characteristically mysterious smile. "Surely Wellington will let you stay a little while. One always hears that he encourages his aides-de-camp to enjoy themselves, and you no longer will have Castlereagh to keep you laboring over the drafts of his treaties all hours of the day and night."

An uneasy pricking feeling spread along the back of Brett's neck. This was not the first time that the countess had been strangely privy to his affairs and movements. Where had she come by this information on an insignificant member of the British delegation, and why was she so interested?

The nagging feeling bothered him enough that he broached the subject the very next day to John King as they were both leaving the delegation.

The British agent laughed. "No, Stanford, you are not being singled out for special attention. It is just that everyone is watching everyone else all the time. Their agents are keeping an eye on everyone in our entourage as we are observing everyone in all the others. Their agents are spying on our agents, who are spying on their agents spying on our agents. There is no one who does not have someone watching him. But"—King's expression grew serious—"I will admit that for the first time there does seem to be a leak somewhere in our delegation, or at least they are more informed about some aspects of our operation than they were. They do not seem to have learned anything terribly important yet, so I do not think they have succeeded in establishing someone on the inside so far. But someone somewhere is watching us very closely, very closely indeed."

The image of the Prince de Rohan at the Countess Bernstorff's reception the previous evening flashed into Brett's mind. The man had known he would be there! There had been something about the way he had paused in the doorway and then approached Brett directly that now, on closer examination, seemed suspicious in the extreme. The man's expression had not registered the slightest hint of surprise, yet it had been as odd and unexpected for Brett to appear at the predominantly Prussian gathering as it had been for the Frenchman to

be there, especially when a far more important reception
honoring Brett's former commanding officer was being
held somewhere else.

The nagging prickle of unease became the cold chill
of doubt and then the icy certainty of suspicion. There
was only one place the French could have discovered
Brett's plan to attend the Countess Bernstorff's reception because he had only mentioned it once, just the way
he had only once mentioned the work on Castlereagh's
treaty and the possibility of Wellington's going to
America, which the Countess Edmond de Talleyrand-
Périgord had referred to—all of those topics had been
discussed only in the von Hohenbachern apartments.

But who was the spy? Was it the princess or her
daughter? Or was it both of them? In an agony of guilt
over his own stupidity and guilelessness, Brett examined
and reexamined every conversation he had had with either Helena or her mother in excruciating detail. Had
he been a complete dupe from the very beginning or
had he simply been careless in front of one or both
women, who had been quick to take advantage of the
situation?

And why had they done it? Whoever had done it. Had
it been done for political reasons or for personal ones?
Had it been to gain political influence, for financial gain,
or to capture the attention of someone more important
than Major Lord Brett Stanford? Was it for all of these
reasons or for reasons so complex and so bizarre that a
simple, honorable soldier had no hope of understanding?

"Stanford? Major? I say, Stanford, calm down man."
John King's voice sounded faintly through the red mist
of rage and despair that threatened to consume Brett.

"That is better." The British agent gripped his shoulder. "You had me worried there for a moment As I said
before, there has been no serious breach of our privacy.
Nothing critical has been learned. I have managed to,
er, *obtain,* the contents of several well-known agents'
own hauls, and none of the papers I have managed to
obtain has been in the least way connected with our
affairs. In fact, nothing I have been able to *retrieve* has
even been written in English, so we are safe thus far. It
merely behooves us to be on our guard, as always."

Calling up every ounce of the iron self-control he had established during the grueling years in the Peninsula, Brett managed to summon up a smile as he returned King's reassuring grasp on the shoulder. "And I thank you again for the warning, King. I shall watch my back even more carefully now." And nodding his thanks, Brett sauntered off down the Herrengasse looking as though he had nothing more serious on his mind than taking a glass of wine and some *wienerschnitzel* among the congenial company at Sperl's.

But he had gone no more than a few steps along the main thoroughfare before he quickly turned into the welcoming dimness of the Schottenkirche. There were few worshipers in the church at this hour, but from force of habit, he glanced over his shoulder to see if he had been followed and then chuckled bitterly. Oh yes, he had taken the warnings of Castlereagh and others seriously enough to make sure that he was not being followed. He had successfully evaded the seductive traps laid for him by the Princess Bagration and even avoided being caught in the enticing flirtations of the Duchess of Sagan only to be betrayed either by a woman who professed to have no interest in politics or by a woman who professed to have no interest in men. He cursed himself as he recalled how Helena had referred to him as *you British*. Could he have been a bigger fool? Brett kicked furiously at the base of an enormous stone pillar. He doubted it.

Had he been done in by his own foolish arrogance or by their fiendish cleverness? He slumped down onto the unforgiving seat of a wooden pew. And what did it matter, really? He was betrayed in either case, and at this moment, he hardly cared whether he had betrayed himself or if one or both of them had betrayed him.

He sat for hours in silent misery only vaguely aware of the low chanting of priests, the flicker of candles, and the faint smell of incense until the creeping chill of the stone numbed him through. Then at last, cramped and miserable, he rose slowly and made his way back to his desk high under the eaves.

Forcing himself to look at the stack of papers piled high on his desk, he fought to concentrate on the words in front of him until slowly, laboriously, he was able to put all thoughts of the Princess von Hohenbachern and her daughter from his mind—for the time being at least.

Several hours later, as the gloom of winter twilight threatened to envelope him, Biggs, his batman, came to light the candles and offer him a bottle of port. "And will you be wanting anything else, sir?" The batman glanced at Brett anxiously. This latest assignment was clearly wearing his master down something fierce. The major was a man of action, born to lead men into the thick of battle. He was blessed with a spirit that thrived on a life of adventure, and it was a crying shame to see him there tied to a desk day after day, night after night. No wonder he was looking so peaked. No. Biggs took a second, harder look, the master was looking downright miserable. There was more to this than a simple uncongenial tour of duty, especially since by all rights things should have looked up the moment the Iron Duke had arrived.

Biggs coughed delicately. "Er, would you like a bit to eat, sir, or would you be wanting . . ."

Brett whirled around, fixing the batman with an oddly penetrating stare. "Yes, Biggs, I would like something more. I would like you to bring me the truth."

Biggs's jaw dropped. "The truth, Major, but . . ."

Brett jumped up and began to pace furiously up and down the tiny attic room. "Yes, the truth. If I am to be spied upon, then, by God, I can spy with the best of them. Yes, Biggs, I shall get to the bottom of this if it kills me, and you are going to help."

Chapter Twenty-three

So it was that in the gray early morning hours of the very next day, a heavily muffled itinerant conjurer juggler slipped out of one of the side doors of the Liechtenstein Palace and, hugging the shadows of the walls and doorways, edged around the square in front of the British delegation, down the street, past the Hofburg, and made his way through the narrow streets to the Bräunerstrasse. There, while keeping a weather eye out for the Princess von Hohenbachern or her daughter, he strolled up and down, juggling a variety of objects—oranges, balls, or anything handed to him by interested spectators—as much to keep himself warm as to attract the attention of passersby. At last he saw what appeared to be the young lady of the establishment leaving with her maid.

Still juggling, Biggs followed them down the Bräunerstrasse and then on into the Kohlmarkt, pausing as they browsed in shopwindows, and hovering for some time outside a bookseller's while they disappeared into the shop.

All in all, he was forced to employ every piece of sleight of hand, every card trick, and every theatrical artifice he had picked up from servants, batmen, and conjurers up and down the Peninsula, but to no avail. During the entire morning he never saw a person approach the young lady or even smile at her. Nor did she appear to leave a note or message of any kind, or receive one in all of her peregrinations.

Toward the afternoon Miss Devereux headed back to the Bräunerstrasse and Biggs took up his position again strolling up and down the street. Soon the princess emerged and was escorted to the carriage by Metternich himself. "And then I knew I was out of my league, sir," the batman reported back to his master. "For what could I do? I could only retrieve the princess' dropped handkerchief once before she became suspicious, and I certainly could do nothing more than follow them to the Austrian chancellery, but as to following them inside, I could no more do that than I could fly. Nor could I tell you who followed them in. The people entering and leaving the chancellery could have been spies, or ministers, or rulers of minor states for all I know. There is no finding out there who your spy is."

Brett sighed. "I know, I know. Thank you for all you have done so far. There is little more I can suggest except to try again tomorrow in the hopes that someone or something will arouse your suspicions."

In the end, it was not Biggs whose suspicions were aroused, however. Helena, leaving their apartments the next day to call on the Princess von Furstenberg, was mildly surprised to see the same juggler that she had seen the day before. If it had been one of the omnipresent strolling musicians, someone to whom she had tossed a coin on previous days, it would not have attracted her attention, but the presence of a man who, as far as she could see, had received no recompense from any of the passersby made no sense.

So if he was not earning anything from his audience or pursuing them in the hopes of doing so, then what was he doing there? Ignoring the curious glances of those around her, she suddenly whirled around to face the man who had been keeping pace with them a few yards behind her and Hannechen the entire way, juggling all the time. Her eyes narrowed as she took in the military bearing, the sturdy shoulders and the unflinching gaze of the so-called juggler. Acting on instinct, she addressed him in English. "And why are you making it your business to follow me, sirrah?" she demanded, eyes flashing.

"I am not following you, miss, I am . . ." Too late, Biggs realized the enormity of his mistake.

"Exactly so. And how many jugglers in the streets of Vienna speak English with the accents of someone who was born in London. Now, if you know what is good for you, you will tell me who you are and who is your employer or I shall raise such an alarm that you will find yourself clapped in prison before you can say *God Save the King*. And, believe me, I know how to raise the alarm in German, so I shall be instantly understood by anyone and everyone around me."

"So I had no choice, but admit it all to the young lady," the batman admitted shamefacedly to his matser a few hours later.

But much to Biggs' surprise, Brett seemed to be more amused than angered by this revelation. "You did your best, but she is a most clever young lady, is she not, Biggs? A most clever young lady indeed."

"That she is, Sir. And quick as a cat too. Why she had walked by me and then turned around before I knew what I was about."

"Ah." Brett scratched his chin slowly. Even if Helena were the spy, he was thinking, which he very much doubted, given the direct nature of her confrontation, she offered him a challenge such as he had not enjoyed since he had left the Peninsula. "And did she say anything else?"

"Nothing at all, sir, except that you was to call on her at their apartments in the Bräunerstrasse tomorrow at ten o'clock sharp."

"Interesting." Brett took a turn around the room. "Most interesting. I shall certainly do so. That will be all. Thank you, Biggs."

True to his instructions, Brett presented himself in the Bräunerstrasse the next morning at the appointed hour and was ushered into the library, where he was left alone, as he had been several months before, to peruse the titles of the leather-bound volumes arranged with no particular attention to any of the variety of languages in which they were written.

The door opened and Helena entered. "Good day, Major." She closed the door with a businesslike snap. "Thank you for coming. Ordinarily I would not send you a message in such a peremptory manner, but you must admit that I was provoked. Also, I have some rather interesting news that I wish you to convey to your colleagues at the British delegation. Last evening I attended one of the Princess von Furstenberg's regular salons. The talk was all of the division of Saxony and the lands on the west bank of the Rhine that have been ceded to Prussia. Now, it is clear that a Prussian presence on the left bank of the Rhine makes the French extremely nervous, so what the German sovereigns propose . . ."

Much to Brett's astonishment, Helena stopped in midsentence, turned quickly around, wrenched the doorknob, and threw the door open. There was a gasp, a clatter, and before Brett had a moment to react, Helena had dashed out, only to reappear clutching the wrist of a neatly dressed, pretty, dark-eyed lady's maid.

"This is your spy, Major," she announced grimly. "And the maid you thought you were addressing when you first encountered me here in the library. Mama has always considered fashion to be more important than politics, which is why, despite the unhappy events of the past decade, she has always employed a French maid.

"Oh, do stop being such a watering pot, Marie. No one is going to do anything to you. If we imprisoned all the spies in Vienna, there would be no one left to go free. Besides, now that we know you are listening at keyholes, we shall be even more careful about what we say. From now on you are just as likely to get deliberately false information as you are to get true."

"But, but, mademoiselle, whatever shall I tell Madame la Princesse?"

"There is not the least need to upset Mama with this. In fact, the less said the better. Just tell me to whom did you give your information? Was it someone in Talleyrand's pay or Hager's?"

"I do not know, mademoiselle. I mean I only met Jean since I came to this city. He heard me speaking French one morning when I went to the Kohlmarkt to purchase something for Madame la Princesse. He was so kind and so handsome in his livery, a sort of plum . . ."

"It is Talleyrand." Helena grimaced wryly. "That is his livery, though why he would be so obvious, I . . . well, never mind. Now, go, Marie, and, if you can help it, do stop listening at keyholes."

"Yes, mademoiselle, of course, mademoiselle." Hardly able to believe that she was not to be immediately cast into one of Vienna's numerous underground cellars, the maid hurried off still dabbing at her eyes with her handkerchief.

Helena closed the door behind her and turned back to Brett. All traces of the ironic resignation she had exhibited with the maid were gone, and she faced him, her eyes blazing. "As for you, sir, you have no excuse. A poor girl may have her senses addled by promises of love or gold, or both, but you . . . you . . ." She was so angry she could not even frame the words.

"I know, I know, it was stupid of me . . ."

"Stupid! Stupid? You befriend both my mother and me, and then you think so little of either one of us that you accuse us of being spies, and you call that *stupid*? How could you? Have you no sense of honor?"

Brett flushed uncomfortably. "I did not accuse you or your mother. I merely . . ."

"Setting your batman to watch our movements does not amount to the same thing? Oh yes, I even found out his name; it is Biggs. And I hope for your sake that he is a better batman than he is spy. A more inept . . . well that is neither here nor there. The point is that I no longer wish to have anything to do with you. If I had my way, I should ban you from the house, but I do not wish to upset my mother. She would be too horrified. Even she, who has been exposed to the duplicitous, self-serving ways of the world far longer than she should have been, exposed to the point of being inured to them, would be devastated to learn that a man who could be so charming could also prove so false. So, I shall spare her the disappointment and the betrayal. However"— Helena had been pacing back and forth, but now she turned on him fiercely—"if you do anything to hurt her, by even so much as smiling at the Princess Bagration or flirting with the Duchess of Sagan or the Countess de Talleyrand-Périgord, I shall tell Mama everything. I, however, am not so fortunate, so all I can do is pray that I forget I ever met you, and the quickest way to do that is to remove myself from your presence."

And without another word, or a backward glance, she swept from the room, shoulders squared, head held high, and wearing a withering expression of disgust that made Brett feel like some despised and lowly subaltern guilty of a most heinous offense.

Left utterly and completely alone after this well-deserved tirade, he had no choice but to make his way slowly down the stairs and out onto the street.

Not wishing to encounter anyone he knew, he avoided returning to the British delegation, but stumbled blindly along the Bräunerstrasse without any clear idea of where he was going. He could not bear the thought of speaking to anyone, but longed for solitude where he could sort out the uncomfortable thoughts and unpleasant revelations of the last half hour without interruption.

The Prater was too far away, and the weather far too cold and snowy for such an extended walk, so he settled for seeking out the relative isolation of the Bastei. The old fortifications of the city were deserted in this weather, and he was able to stroll on them completely alone with only his self-recriminating thoughts for company, his soul as barren and cheerless as the snow-covered park surrounding the walls, now empty of pedestrians, or the bare branches of the trees lining its walks that rattled in the wind.

How could he have doubted her for a moment? How could anyone, having looked into those clear, hazel eyes, think her anything but honest and true, as true and honest as anyone he had ever yet encountered. Then why? Had he been afraid to believe in her? Had she seemed too good, too perfect, too much a kindred spirit to be real?

Looking deep into his heart, Brett now acknowledged to himself that he had set Biggs to following her in order to prove to himself that Helena *was* the woman he desperately wanted her to be—passionate, idealistic, motivated by her beliefs—to prove beyond a shadow of a doubt that she could not be the source of the leaks, damaging as the evidence against her appeared to be. How could he have borne it if he had been mistaken in his belief in her? And, how was he going to face it now that he had been proven right, but having been right, still managed to lose her anyway? What ever was he going to do?

Chapter Twenty-four

Long walks on the Bastei and sleepless nights brought no counsel to Brett. They only deepened the corroding sense of loss that had reduced his world to an empty gray shapeless fog, devoid of time, joy, or hope. He performed his duties like a sleepwalker, writing reports, translating documents and correspondence from French to English, or English to French, whatever the circumstances demanded.

At last he could bear it no longer. He had to see her, had to explain himself, or at least try to. She had to listen to him! He had to make her understand that he had trusted in her all along, but even his trust in her had not obscured the obvious fact that someone in the von Hohenbachern household had been passing information about him to the French as Helena herself had so efficiently proved.

But offering Helena Devereux an explanation was easier said than done. She had warned him that she would deny herself to him should he call on her in the Braünerstrasse, and, true to her predictions, Potten always reported that *Miss Devereux is not at home* every time Brett requested an audience with her. Potten's information, as far as it went, was completely correct, for more often than not his young mistress had been watching from one of the library windows that overlooked the Braünerstrasse and, forewarned of the major's impending arrival, had snatched up her cloak and bonnet, descended the back stairs through the kitchens and out into the tiny alleyway in the back. To the butler, it seemed that this was carrying honesty too far, for often her mother, without so much as stirring, would instruct her butler to tell unwelcome visitors that she was not at home. But then, Miss Helena had always been a stickler for the absolute truth.

Nor was Miss Devereux to be seen at any of the social events that had taken on a renewed glamour and excitement with the arrival of the Duke of Wellington. Brett had haunted them all, but she was nowhere to be seen, and even the princess, while she still appeared to take pleasure in the company of both Metternich and Talleyrand, was less to be seen than previously.

Brett even took to sauntering frequently down the Graben, hovering as long as possible near the entrance to the Princess von Furstenberg's apartments, but to no avail. It was as though Helena Devereux had vanished from the face of the earth.

In desperation, he set Biggs to watching the von Hohenbachern residence again. "But *this* time, for heaven's sake, keep well out of sight." He admonished the batman.

"Of course, sir. Certainly, sir. You can depend on me, sir." Determined to redeem himself, the batman spent many chilly hours hanging in the deepest shadows of various doorways until at last he was able to report that the only times the young mistress did seem to emerge was late in the afternoon when, despite the unpropitious weather, she appeared to be heading toward the Prater on her horse. In fact, Biggs added, she might at that moment be there as he had followed horse and rider as far as the river before, fearful of being detected once again, he had headed back to his quarters.

"Perfect." Brett scrambled to his feet, pulling on his boots as he hurried toward the door. "Thank you, Biggs, you have done well."

"And let us hope that you do too, sir," the batman muttered as the door slammed shut behind his master. "For if you do not make peace with the young lady soon, life will not be worth living for all of us."

Biggs had served his master in the most desperate of

circumstances, but he could never remember a time
when the major had been so listless, so lacking in energy
and vitality, so unlike himself. In fact, to call him de-
spondent was not putting too fine a point on it. And it
had all begun with the batman's first unsuccessful observation of the young lady. Therefore, it seemed reason-
able to assume that the black mood that had had his
master in its grip for the past weeks had everything to
do with the young woman that the major characterized
as being *a very clever young lady indeed.* And, following
this train of thought to its logical conclusion, it seemed
obvious that the sooner the major could succeed in
working things out with this young lady, the sooner life
would return to normal, or as normal as life had ever
been where Major Lord Brett Stanford was concerned.

Ordinarily the batman would have had the utmost
confidence in the successful resolution of this problem,
for there was no one like the major for talking a woman
around. Biggs had witnessed it time and again, from jealous Spanish condesas to infuriated French mademoi-
selles, to the most rapacious of opera dancers, but in
this case, it did not appear to be the major who was in
control. It was Biggs' humble opinion, from the little he
had seen of this redoubtable young woman, that Major
Lord Brett Stanford had met his match this time. And
as Biggs set to tidying their chambers with a thoughtful
look on his face, he decided that if the master were able
to retrieve his position with this young woman, he would
finally achieve the one thing that had been lacking in his
life—true companionship and, yes, love.

In all the years Biggs had been with the major, he had
never seen him so happy as he had been the last few
months in Vienna. True, he had chafed at the inactivity,
but there had been a certain contentment that the batman had never witnessed before. Of course, someone as
clever and daring as the major had been admired by his
troops and well liked by his fellow officers, but even in
the midst of those closest to him, at the most raucous
moments of camaraderie, the major had seemed to remain set apart by something—call it seriousness of purpose—but whatever it was, it kept him from being able
to lose himself in the fellowship of his comrades in arms.

Maybe it was because he had not yet met anyone who shared all the rare qualities that distinguished him— courage, self-reliance, resourcefulness, and intelligence, coupled with a thoughtfulness and reflectiveness that was rare among most people that Biggs had encountered. But somehow, Biggs sensed that this Miss Devereux possessed many of these same qualities. If only the master were able to make her see that.

Biggs' master was at this moment urging Rex across the bridge over the half frozen branch of the Danube that separated the city from the wide-open meadows of the Prater. There, at last, as he entered the Prater, off in the distance, framed by the bare branches of the chestnut trees that lined the alley, he saw a solitary horse and rider.

Even at that distance, when she was little more than a silhouette against the barren landscape and the leaden sky, he knew it was Helena. He had sought her so anxiously in the streets and the ballrooms of the city, had spent so many hours recalling every detail of her face and figure, every gesture, every lithe movement, that his heart recognized her even before his mind identified her.

But she too appeared to be as sensitive to his presence as he was to hers, for the instant he was close enough for her to catch the sound of approaching hooves, she took flight and was off like the wind.

Brett bent low over Rex's neck, urging the horse to its greatest speed. They thundered along the alley, gaining on the horse in front of them inch by inch until, at last, cornered at the end of the alley, she was forced either to turn around or plunge into the icy waters of the Danube.

She halted and turned to face him defiantly. "I told you, I have nothing to say to you ever again."

Completely ignoring this ultimatum, Brett swung down and strode over to take Nimrod's reins. Short of putting up an undignified scuffle, there was nothing Helena could do except allow him to help her dismount.

The moment his hands touched her waist, however, she knew she was lost. There was a purposeful set to his jaw, and a steely look in his eyes that warned her he was not going to allow her to avoid hearing what he had to say. Still, she kept her chin high, her shoulders back, and her lips clenched, the very picture of unyielding scorn.

"Helena, I mean, Miss Devereux, you *must* listen to me."

She gazed off into the distance, refusing to acknowledge his presence by even so much as the flicker of an eyelash, but her heart was pounding so hard she could barely hear his words. Unwillingly she acknowledged to herself that her joy at seeing him again was the cause of the weakness that washed over and through her, threatening to make her knees collapse under her. Never in her life had she fought so hard to maintain her composure, to remain as stolid and impassive as the bare chestnut trees behind her.

Undaunted, Brett continued, driven by a desperation he had never felt before. "You have no idea what it was like to discover that my movements were being reported to the French, that things I had said within the privacy of your apartments were common enough knowledge at the French embassy that they were repeated to the Countess Edmond de Talleyrand-Périgord. I had spoken those things in confidence, something I would only have said to someone I knew very well, someone I counted as my friend, someone I knew I could trust with my life." He had reached her at last through that frozen wall of reserve. It was just the tiniest flicker of recognition in those deep-set hazel eyes, but he knew he had touched a chord.

Taking advantage of this moment of recognition, he continued. "I knew you could not have done it, but who could have? I went over and over our conversations in my mind, but it always came back to the fact that we had been alone when they occurred. I kept asking myself if I had been wrong about you. Had I become so enamored of you that I was being willfully blind? Had I resisted the seductive wiles of beautiful women from Portugal to Austria only to be taken in by the single woman I had felt I could call my friend? Had I been so overwhelmed by your passion, your idealism, your intellect, and your energy that I was overlooking something obvious? Was there some political reason that overrode what I had begun to hope were your feelings toward me? No. I could not accept any of that. It could not be you who was passing information to the French, but what other explanation was there? I had to prove that you were all the honorable, idealistic things I had come to believe you were, so I set Biggs to watching you— not because I mistrusted you, but because the entire situation seemed so unreal that I had come to mistrust myself."

Helena's hands clenched and unclenched at her sides. She could hardly breathe enough to keep from fainting, but she had to speak. "And," she was able to croak at last, "*friend,* that you felt yourself to be, you could not simply come to me and ask me if I had engaged in such despicable behavior? You say that you believed in me, trusted me, but you could not trust me enough to confront me face-to-face? And if it was your friendship with me that made you doubt yourself, why was it that you had my mother followed, as you have admitted to doing? No, such fine words may succeed with your *beautiful women from Portugal to Austria,* women gullible enough to care about you, but they will not work with me." She reached for the reins and turned on her heel to throw herself into the saddle.

But Brett was too quick for her. Still holding Rex's reins, he grabbed her shoulders and turned her around to face him. "So you do care! You admit it. No, do not look away." One hand let go of her shoulder to tilt her chin so that she was forced to look up at him. "You could not be so angry with me if you did not feel as hurt and confused over this as I. Helena, I am not proud of the way I acted. As you say, I should have come to you, but I was too upset to think clearly. I did not know what to do. I had never been in love before."

He stopped dead. That was it. He was in love. That was why in the space of a few weeks he had gone from being happier than he had ever been in his entire life to suffering more misery and despair than he could ever have believed possible.

"You what?" She could hardly believe her ears. Here was the charming, self-assured Major Lord Brett Stanford, who knew how to make the heart of the lowliest servant girl beat faster, admitting that he did not know what he was doing now because he was in love? Had he taken leave of his senses? The man who had flirted with her mother, the Princess Bagration, and the Duchess of Sagan without becoming embroiled with any of them was now saying that he had unwittingly fallen in love with a young woman who had never flirted in her life? How stupid did he think she was? Yet, against all reason, the brief flicker of hope that his words had ignited, continued to flicker in spite of every evidence that any rational person would consider absolutely damning. But hope she did, that somehow his claims, extravagant as they were, were true.

No. She shook her head vigorously. She must be crazed even to think such a thing. Men like Major Lord Brett Stanford *never* allowed themselves to fall in love, and certainly not with a woman like her, a woman with more brains than beauty, more independence than charm. And yet, and yet, there was a light in those blue eyes that gazed so steadily down into hers that seemed to prove her wrong.

"I love you. I love you. I love you." He pulled her into his arms and brought his lips down on hers, not gently like the first time, but hard, demanding, persuasive, willing her to believe what he had only just admitted to himself: that they belonged together. That he could not exist without her, and she could not live without him.

Chapter Twenty-five

Helena felt all the passion of his newfound belief pouring into her, the warmth of his hands as they caressed the back of her neck, the insistence of his lips as they forced her to respond to him. Her pride and her common sense fought against it, struggled to keep her mind alert and unyielding, but the battle was already lost. Her treacherous emotions and her own heart betrayed her. She wanted to believe him too much. Even during the dark days after she had banished him from her presence, she had longed so much for the sight of him, the touch of him that she had been afraid to go out-of-doors, afraid that she might see him and lose all her resolve.

And now she had. She could no more resist him than she could fly. She had to believe that what he said was true, because if it were not, if she could not trust him and believe in him, then she could no longer trust and believe in herself. To her, he had come to represent all that she herself had tried to be, and she sensed that it was the same for him, the recognition of himself in her.

Sighing, she gave herself up to it, the hunger that had threatened to consume her, the hunger to belong, to be one with him, and she reveled in the sheer power of it all, the closeness, the joy of feeling loved and wanted.

But, being Helena, she could not totally abandon herself to pleasure. A tiny doubt still nagged at the corner of her mind.

Sensing it in the slightest of hesitation as she returned

his kiss, Brett lifted his head and looked anxiously into her eyes. "What is it, love?"

"Mama."

His eyes darkened and he reached up to lift off her riding hat and smooth away a tendril of hair that had escaped and was now curling wildly against her flushed cheek. "I know. I have been thinking of that too."

Tears pricked her eyes. This was why she loved him and why she could believe in him. For all his worldly ways, for all the confident charm he exuded with women of all types, he was kind. He understood that pleasure-seeking, sophisticated, and flirtatious as the Princess von Hohenbachern was, she could still be hurt, and he did not want to do that. Nor did he wish to shirk his responsibility.

Brett gathered Helena's hands into his. "Helena, believe me, I would never want to do anything that would cause your mother pain. I do not think that her heart was ever involved, which does not mean that I am not concerned for her happiness, but I do not believe that I could have fallen head over heels in love with her daughter if her own affections had truly been engaged. And, it was her very clear wish to enjoy herself without becoming involved that drew me to her in the first place. I think that that part of it has not changed. It seems, as I have observed her lately, that she has become a great deal more interested in Monsieur Talleyrand and Monsieur Metternich than she is in Major Lord Brett Stanford. I trust that I am not deceiving myself with wishful thinking, but what do you think?" His eyes, full of concern, never wavered from her face.

"It seems . . . I mean . . . I think so too," Helena answered slowly. "But then, I have been so involved with my own, ah, er, *thoughts* that I cannot be sure." The blush that stained her cheeks left Brett in no doubt as to what those thoughts were.

A tiny gust of wind rattled the branches of the chestnut trees above them, and she shivered. Brett pulled her close, resting his chin on her hair. "We shall work this out, you and I, but for now, all that matters is that at last I have you, a woman whose existence I had not thought possible, a woman I love with all my heart.

Now"—he gently replaced the hat on her head—"you are getting cold and the horses have been more than patient. It is time we returned you to the warmth of your own stove and me to my duties, which, I am afraid, have suffered from my inattention far too long."

Still too bemused by the thought that she could cause someone to love her, much less neglect his duties, Helena allowed him to lift her into the saddle without any protest, and she rode back to the Braünerstrasse in a glow of happiness that did not escape Potten's attention. Nor did it escape her mother, who was waiting for her in the salon to discuss the gown she had ordered for the theatrical performance the next evening at the Hofburg.

Helena, though never so involved in questions of fashion as her mother, was so patently uninterested in whether the princess should wear pearls or emeralds with the stiff white brocade that had been designed according to the latest drawings from Paris that it was abundantly clear her mind was elsewhere. This was not just the usual abstraction that Helena often exhibited when interrupted in her perusal of her newspapers or political pamphlets, but the total preoccupation of a woman in love.

The princess smiled to herself and resolved to keep a closer eye on her daughter. Lately Helena had suddenly seemed far more serious than usual and had begun to shun all the social events that she had so recently begun to take an interest in. Such fluctuations in her daughter's behavior were far from normal, for usually she could be counted on to be the most rational and dependable of individuals, and the princess had been forced to arrive at the unavoidable conclusion that Helena was definitely in love. "And what do you plan to wear tomorrow, my dear," her mother asked, watching her daughter's expression closely for telltale signs.

"What? Oh, the pink satin, perhaps, or maybe the Venetian crepe."

It was a characteristically vague reply, but at least it indicated that she planned to attend, a major concession, given the studied reclusiveness of the past week or so.

"They are certainly equally becoming." The princess kept her tone carefully neutral. Helena might take any sign of interest on her mother's part as an excuse to forego the theatrical performance altogether and thus deprive the princess of the opportunity to discover which gentleman in the Austrian capital had been clever enough not only to pique her daughter's interest, but to occupy her thoughts to such an extent that lately she did not even hear the questions her mother put to her.

At one time the princess had thought that Helena was falling victim to the considerable charms of Major Lord Brett Stanford, but the princess herself had barely set eyes on that gentleman since Wellington's arrival in Vienna, and she very much doubted that Helena had either, which gave her cause to doubt the accuracy of that hypothesis.

In any case, all thoughts of love or intrigue were wiped from everyone's minds the next evening almost from the moment the guests had taken their places in front of the temporary stage surrounded by fragrant boxed orange trees in full bloom that had been erected in the ballroom of the palace. As the candles in the torchères were extinguished and the velvet curtains pulled back, one of the tsar's aides-de-camp hurried up to whisper something into his master's ear. Alexander immediately rose and followed him out, while the Austrian emperor murmured a few words of apology to the countess on his left. The countess turned to the baroness on her left, who whispered to the person sitting next to her.

And so, the news of Napoleon's escape, known only to a few people earlier that morning, was within the space of a few minutes, made common knowledge throughout the ballroom.

The days that followed were a blur of rumors and counter rumors. Napoleon had landed in Italy. He was on his way to Switzerland and then to Vienna. No, he was on his way to France. It was not until several days later that a weary messenger arrived from the King of Sardinia with the definitive news that Napoleon had landed in Cannes.

Helena had seen next to nothing of Brett after their encounter in the Prater. He had stopped only for a moment at their apartments the day after Napoleon's escape was announced to tell her that he was riding to Pressburg with Wellington, Talleyrand, and Metternich to meet the King of Saxony, who had just been released from captivity at the Schloss Friedrichsfelde, but that he expected to return to Vienna the following day. "My time is not my own, however," Brett explained, "and as soon as we learn where Napoleon is headed, I expect that I shall be kept busy while the Allies decide what to do with him."

Desperate for information of unfolding events, Helena, and even the princess, eagerly devoured every issue of the *Weiner Zeitung* and the *Oesterreich Beobachter* or any other paper they could lay their hands on, but the news only went from bad to worse. Regiments sent to Grenoble to arrest the former Emperor of the French had joined forces with him instead, and only a few days after that, the people in Vienna had digested the astonishing piece of news that Napoleon had marched triumphantly into Paris.

"The problem now," Brett admitted late one evening during a hurried call on Helena and her mother, "is to amass an army large enough to march against Napoleon and beat him for once and for all. You were right, Miss Devereux, we are now in desperate need here of our gallant fellows who fought on the Peninsula, but most of them were sent to America, and there is no chance of getting them back in time to fight the French. We are forced to rely heavily on what the various German states can supply. And now"—he turned to Helena with a smile that made her feel as though they were the only two people in the world—"now is the moment that I am truly in need of your assistance. The Prussians are assembling a force, and I expect that the Prince von Hohenbachern"—he nodded to the princess—"and other German forces will be joining them as well. However, we could use all the men we can gather from the unattached German states. If you two could use what I know to be your considerable influence with their leaders, we should be most grateful." He included the mother in his plea, but it was clear that it was really the daughter whose aid he hoped to enlist.

Helena smiled back, warmed by his confidence in her.

"I shall do my best, though, mind you, I cannot promise you anything."

"I will take whatever I can get and be most grateful for it." He bowed to both of them and was gone.

"Do you really think you can win some regiments over for him?" The princess regarded her daughter with dawning respect.

"I shall try, Mama. Believe me, I shall try."

But events moved too fast for any of them, and the very next day, Helena received a note from Brett begging her to meet him alone in the Prater that afternoon.

Mystified, she had Nimrod saddled and brought around. In a most reflective mood she trotted past the Gothic spires and multicolored roof of St. Stephen's cathedral, across the river, which, swelled with water from melting snows, was threatening to burst its banks, and into the Prater, where he was waiting for her at the top of the alley.

"Helena." Brett urged Rex forward until the two horses were nose to nose. He dismounted and turned to help her down. "There is no time. I leave tomorrow."

"Tomorrow? But I have not had a chance to . . ."

"Ssh." He put a finger to her lips. "I know. I know what I asked you to do for me, but there is no time for that now. At the moment, however, I care nothing for that. What I want to be sure of is that you know I love you. That whatever happens, no matter how much the world changes in the next few months, you know that I have never loved anyone the way I love you."

"But the troops. How will you . . ."

"Hush, my love. Just kiss me and tell me that you believe me when I say I love you."

He gathered her into his arms and her heart turned over at the sadness in his eyes. Could it be that they both had spent their lives never believing they could find a soul mate until now, just as the world was about to fall apart around them?

Her eyes filled with tears, but she would not let them fall. "I believe you," she whispered. "And I love you too."

"Never forget that." He pressed his lips to hers and

held her close, begging her, willing her to feel about him the way he did about her.

"And now, my love, there is no more time. I must go." Tenderly, he lifted her back into her saddle, threw himself onto Rex's back, and they rode silently back to the city, too full of their own worries for the future to say anything more.

Chapter Twenty-six

He was gone the next day, and Wellington soon after. Talleyrand, Metternich, and the major foreign sovereigns remained in Vienna, but there were no more grand gatherings at the Hofburg or any of the palaces. Everyone knew that, despite the continuing discussions and minor territorial disputes, the major scene of action had shifted northward and east to Belgium.

Even the Princess von Hohenbachern, apolitical sybarite that she was, complained of the dullness of the Austrian capital once the British ambassador had left to take command of the Allied armies in Belgium.

"But, Mama, Lord Clancarty and Sir Charles Stewart are still here, and Clancarty is head of the British delegation . . ."

"It is not the same, Helena, and you know it," her mother replied more forcefully than usual.

"How can you say that, Mama? Monsieur de Talleyrand is still here busily working, as is Metternich and most of the foreign dignitaries."

"Talleyrand, Metternich, bah!" The princess waved her hand dismissively. "Wordsmiths, all of them. They would rather discuss European affairs forever than settle them, talk rather than act. It is soldiers that we need now, not statesmen. Real men who will take the future of Europe into their own hands. Men of passion, men who know how to do something, how to live and how

to fight. By the way, you have not had any letters from
Friedrich recently have you?"

"Papa? No. Not since before Napoleon escaped. But
he must be very busy now marching with his troops to
join Blücher, I expect, if they are not already together."

"I expect so too. Which means that sooner or later,
he too will be arriving in Brussels. We must be there to
meet him. I shall gave orders to Potten to pack up our
things, and then I shall send some of the servants back
to Hohenbachern, as I do not expect we shall be living
on such a grand scale in Belgium. The rest I shall send
on ahead with Potten to find us suitable lodgings in
Brussels. We should be able to manage with our maids
and a few footmen in addition to the grooms and the
coachmen."

It said volumes for Helena's state of mind that it did
not occur to her to demur, not even now, when the fate
of the very German states that had previously preoccupied her hung in the balance.

Baron von Gagern, taking advantage of the Allies'
desperate need for troops, had formed the Association
of Princes and Free Cities and stood ready to offer up
the support of something between thirty-five thousand
and one hundred thousand men, provided that each state
was allowed to sign a separate treaty of accession.

"Our hour has come," the Princess von Furstenberg
informed Helena and her mother one afternoon as they
sat drinking tea in the princess' elegant salon overlooking the Graben. "It is only a matter of time before the
Allies realize how critical we are to the success of their
campaign against Napoleon. Naturally, Louisa, I understand and sympathize with your desire to join your husband, but Helena is more than welcome to remain here
with me to help see through to the end the noble work
to which she has dedicated so much of her time and
interest."

"Thank you, Elizabeth." The Princess von Hohenbachern directed a grateful smile at her hostess. "That
is most kind of you, and I am sure that Helena is most
appreciative, but I am afraid that I, poor creature that I
am, have my own selfish claims on my daughter, for I

really cannot contemplate such a journey all on my own." By now Helena's mother had gathered a pretty fair picture of the way things stood between her daughter and a certain handsome major attached to the recently appointed commander of the Allied forces in Belgium, and she directed a conspiratorial wink in her daughter's direction.

"Yes, Mama. Whatever you say, Mama," Helena agreed meekly as she silently blessed her mother for being so wise in the ways of the world.

And so it was that less than a week after this conversation took place, the von Hohenbachern entourage, consisting of several traveling carriages and an impressive number of outriders, quitted the city through the huge wooden customs gate on the Schönbruner Weg and headed first for Linz and then the road to Brussels.

Having made up her mind to leave Vienna, the princess left it with all the speedy dispatch in which she had arrived, traveling day and night over the rough German roads, not stopping to rest until they reached the relatively cosmopolitan atmosphere and more hygienic inns of Nuremberg. "For say what you will about the discomforts of a carriage, they are infinitely preferable to the filth and the primitive accommodations to be found in most of the hostelries in Germany," the princess remarked as they settled back against the velvet cushions of their luxuriously appointed berlin. "I, for one, agree with Madame de Staël, the Countess Bernstorff, and others who are accustomed to traveling in this part of the world. The roads are disastrous and the inns worse. Far preferable to have one's bones shaken to pieces at night in one's own carriage than risk heaven knows what dangers at some local lodging."

They spent a comfortable enough night at a well-appointed inn in Nuremberg, but beyond that, and one other night in Koblenz, they passed their nights in the carriage, fortifying themselves from the plentiful hampers the princess had had packed to the brims with delicacies before they set off.

After the traumatic events of the past two weeks, Helena was actually glad of the enforced captivity as she watched the German countryside, alive with the vibrant greens of spring, roll by. The warm weather they had lately been enjoying in Vienna quickly vanished to be replaced by the endless rain that had plagued the rest of Europe while the Austrian capital had basked in a very local freak of meteorological good fortune. But the gloomy weather exactly suited Helena's mood, which was reflective almost to the point of melancholy.

At least she had discovered love and passion, the zest and magic of life that had heretofore always seemed to elude her, only to lose it as soon as she had found it. For years she had thought that those delightful but unruly forces were a part of other people's lives, not hers. And she had both envied those other people for the joys they experienced and pitied them for the frustration and disappointment they inevitably seemed to suffer. But now she, too, was subject to those same joys and the same sorrows, for the instant she had acknowledged her attraction to Brett, she had also resolved to conquer it both for her mother's sake and for her own.

The princess, however, despite her daughter's reservations, seemed hardly to think of her former admirer at all. Her talk was all of Talleyrand and Metternich and now, increasingly, her husband. "I wrote to Friedrich that we were departing for Brussels. I do hope that my letter reached him, before he went to join Blücher and his troops—if he has gone to join Blücher and if Blücher has indeed gone to Belgium."

"Brett, er, the major, told me that once Blücher was given command of the Prussian forces, they would immediately march toward Belgium, so perhaps . . ."

"Brett?" The princess fixed her daughter with a quizzical look.

"Major Lord Brett Stanford. At any rate, he seems to think that Blücher will be coordinating with Wellington and that since Wellington's headquarters is in Brussels, in all probability they will be facing the French together somewhere near there, which means that perhaps Papa must already be there or on his way."

"Ah." For the moment, the princess was far less interested in the possibility of her husband's appearance in Brussels than she was intrigued by the self-conscious blush that stained her daughter's cheeks. So, Helena truly was taken by the charming major. A tiny wrinkle furrowed the princess' ordinarily smooth white brow, and she leaned over to cover her daughter's hand with her one lemon kid gloved one.

"My dear, are you sure you know what you are about?" She looked at her daughter searchingly. "The major is a very charming man indeed and excessively handsome, but you are a rather serious creature."

"I know, Mama." Helena did not pretend not to understand what her mother meant.

"It is just that the major is the sort of man who, er, finds *all* women charming, and you . . . well, you have always been a loyal little soul, and I think you need someone who would devote himself solely to you."

"I know, Mama." Helena gazed miserably out the window at the rolling hills.

"He would not willingly hurt you, for he is by nature a kind person, but he is not the sort to have his interest, ah, remain fixed forever. Not that he would not care about you in his own way, but he is just the sort of man who has, shall we say, *broad interests,* which you do not. And that sort of thing can be very upsetting to a woman, no matter how worldly and sophisticated she is. We women are sensitive creatures whose entire world is centered around those we love, while men have many interests to distract and amuse them, so they are not so affected by such things."

"Thank you for the warning, Mama." Helena, warmed by the look in her eyes and the concern in her voice, squeezed her mother's hand in return. The princess had always done her best to appear gay and carefree, for that was what drew people to her, her unadulterated pleasure in life, but Helena was only now beginning to understand what it might have cost her. True, she had vowed, after watching her mother's lovers come and go, never to pin her hopes for happiness or support on any man, and she was still resolved to rely solely on herself as far as her own future was concerned, but even if one were totally self-reliant, it did not mean that one could not be hurt, or powerfully affected by one man in particular.

What a dreadful coil she had gotten herself into in

spite of her clever mind and all her well-thought-out resolutions. Thank goodness Bonaparte had escaped when he had, for now, with entire armies converging on Brussels, it was highly unlikely that she would run into one particular major among all the officers swarming the Belgian capital—if he were even in Brussels, that was. It was far more likely that by now he would have returned to join his regiment, which, in all probability, would be deployed to defenses somewhere outside the city, and that would surely mean that the possibility of their paths crossing was extremely remote.

All her life, Helena had been proud of her own self-discipline, her ability to decide upon a course of action and then pursue it wholeheartedly. Where others had given in to momentary impulse or faintheartedness, she had not, and she had always been able to rely on herself to carry things through. Now she was not so sure. Her much prized self-control had vanished in a moment, it seemed—the moment Major Lord Brett Stanford had entered their lives.

She was not at all sure that she could count on herself to resist him in person, and was therefore forced to rely on his absence to give her the time to build up her resolve to remain indifferent to that crooked knowing smile, the twinkle in his eyes, and the understanding that ran so deep between them that she barely needed to voice her thoughts on a subject to know that he shared them. Yes, for all their sakes, she hoped he was stationed at the farthest reaches of the British defenses, far away from Brussels.

The increasing crowd of people choking the roads from Aachen to Liège and Liège to Brussels relieved Helena's mind somewhat. Surely among the hordes of refugees, soldiers, and émigrés pouring into the capital, the chances of running into any one person were slim to none.

When they finally made their way through the crush of traffic in the Rue de la Madeleine to pull up at last in front of the Hotel D'Angleterre, Helena was convinced that she could spend months in the city without ever seeing the same person twice, crowded as it was by people of all nations.

True to his instructions, Potten was waiting for them in a suite of rooms he had managed to engage for them at the hotel until they had recovered enough from their journey to move into their more permanent quarters overlooking the park.

"Thank you, Potten. You have done excellently, as always." The princess bestowed a tired smile on her butler as she allowed a subdued Marie to help her out of her pelisse, and sank gratefully into a chair. "I believe that we shall rest here for tonight and tomorrow, and then move into the apartments you have secured for us. The sooner we are settled at a permanent address where people can find us, the better."

Chapter Twenty-seven

They were quickly ensconced in their quarters in the Rue Montagne du Parc not far from Wellington's headquarters, and the princess, who soon discovered that a good many acquaintances from England had also gravitated to the city that now commanded the attention of the world, lost no time in establishing contact with them.

Thirteen years' absence and marriage to a German prince now leading troops along with Wellington's trusted ally Blücher served to erase all memories of the former Lady Devereux's questionable past and the profligate existence she had led as the wife and widow of that ne'er-do-well and embarrassment to his own family, Francis, Lord Devereux. All was forgotten. Even the starchiest matrons were delighted to welcome the Princess von Hohenbachern and her daughter to Brussels. In short order they were on easy terms with Lady Conyngham, Lady Charlotte Greville, and many others who were daily flocking to join husbands, brothers, and sons now attached to the regiments stationed in and around the city.

Indeed, their social life, which had seemed entirely filled with events in Vienna, was no less filled with them in Brussels, though now there was the constant undercurrent of tension caused by the certain knowledge that war was coming in the not too distant future, and that the soldiers now escorting wives, daughters and sweet-

hearts to the cafés, museums, and churches of the city would soon be called to battle.

The visitors to the von Hohenbachern apartments in the Rue Montagne du Parc were not all female, however. Helena and the princess returned one morning, after making calls on Lady Conyngham and others, to the information that a male visitor awaited them.

"I have put him in the salon, madame, as I thought for certain you would wish to see him," Potten reported, his blue eyes twinkling.

Helena's heart began to pound rapidly. How had he known they were coming? He had left Vienna several weeks before they had. Had her mother written to him? Her mouth was dry, her palms clammy as they entered the salon to discover a tall distinguished gray-haired man in the dark green uniform of the Hohenbachern regiments seated on one of the delicate gilt and damask chairs.

"Friedrich!"

"Papa!"

Both women spoke at once as they hurried forward to greet the Prince von Hohenbachern.

"Meine Lieben." He rose to meet them, his face beaming. "Ah, my dear, you are lovelier than ever. Vienna offered you a setting worthy of your charms, I believe." He lifted his wife's hand to his lips and then turned to his stepdaughter. "But you, my girl, found all the gaiety to be rather tiring, I think?"

"A little, Papa." Trying desperately to deny her disappointment in the identity of the visitor, Helena flushed under her stepfather's fond scrutiny.

"Well, then, it is a good thing I have arrived in time to escort your mama to the ball the Duke of Wellington is giving to welcome Blücher so that you can rest at home with a clear conscience."

"Thank you, Papa." But oddly enough, Helena felt let down rather than grateful for the opportunity to remain at home. Surely someone who had worked so closely with the duke in Vienna would be present at such a ball, no matter how far outside the city he was stationed.

No, Helena, she admonished herself firmly. *That is madness. For your own peace of mind, you cannot see*

him again. For your own peace of mind, you must *see him again,* another treacherous voice replied.

Sometime later, still wavering between the conflicting voices, Helena sought to clear her mind by taking a vigorous walk in the park. For an hour or more she and her mother had regaled the prince with the high points of their sojourn in Vienna and the tedium of their journey to Brussels until Helena, with a newly gained awareness to such things, could see that her mother would be just as happy to be left alone with her husband and, seizing upon her stepfather's earlier remarks, she excused herself ostensibly to get some rest. But her mind was in too much turmoil to do anything of the kind. Hastening to her bedchamber, she snatched up her pelisse, gloves, and bonnet and, calling upon Hannechen to come with her, hurried out to the park.

The rain that had plagued them for days had finally stopped, and the park was thronged with people, young and old, enjoying the sun and the fresh air. But Helena was oblivious to them all as she strode along in a most unladylike manner, trying to resolve the confusion of her thoughts. The warmth in her mother's smile as she welcomed her husband had told Helena all that she needed to know, which was that Major Lord Brett Stanford was quite forgotten as far as the Princess von Hohenbachern was concerned, and her relationship to him was no longer an issue. What was an issue, however, was that her daughter—still unwilling to place all her hopes for happiness on another person, especially a man with a reputation for enjoying beautiful women—fervently hoped that her own feelings for Major Lord Brett Stanford would simply disappear over time.

However, it was not a hope that was destined to be realized. The air had grown chilly as the sun sank lower in the sky, and the crowds in the park had thinned considerably by the time Helena slowed her vigorous pace and headed reluctantly back toward the Rue Montagne du Parc, when a voice behind her exclaimed, "Helena, I mean, Miss Devereux!"

Her face grew hot and then cold, and she was forced to clasp her hands in front of her to keep them from trembling as she turned around. "Major."

It was all she could manage. The rest of the dignified greeting she had rehearsed again and again in preparation for such an occurrence died in her throat. He was more handsome than she had remembered. The face looked thinner, the lines of fatigue were more pronounced, but the eyes, as brilliantly blue as ever, looked down into hers with the same intensity, the same special smile she remembered.

"This is wonderful! I had no idea you were planning to leave Vienna, much less come here!" *And how did you happen to choose Brussels,* his eyes asked her.

"Mama," she managed to gasp. And then, seeing the light slowly fade, his eyes darken, she hastened to add, "was worried about Papa. She knew that Blücher had been ordered to Brussels and surmised that Papa had been too. There was no time to write, so we just came. And Papa has arrived. In fact he is with Mama right now, and she appears most delighted to see him."

"Is she now?" Some of the glow came back into his eyes, and the anxious frown disappeared. "And you. How are you? Are you well? You look sadly pulled. The trip was somewhat tiring, I gather."

"The trip? I am not such a poor creature as to be worn down by a few days in a carriage." *But missing you, thinking of you was exhausting,* her heart added. And now she knew for certain. The dullness, the ennui that had plagued her for the past month was not the result of frenzied packing or a grueling journey, but because she had missed him—missed his smile, his touch, the look in his eyes that told her she was special, that he cared.

Once he had left Vienna, she no longer awakened every morning looking forward to the day. Because he was no longer there, one day was just like another, empty and without particular interest, in spite of her best efforts to keep herself amused and her mind occupied. Life without him had been dull indeed. It had been dull before she met him, she now admitted to herself, and it was after he had left. Yes, it was safe, but it was also dull.

Brett had been observing her carefully as these realizations struck her. He watched the consciousness creep

into her eyes and the flush stain her cheeks, and he reached down to raise one gloved hand to his lips. "I missed you too. Life here has been frantically busy, as you may imagine, but not a moment has gone by that I have not thought of you, wondered how you were doing, whether you were helping the German sovereigns negotiate their demands from a position that is now no doubt a great deal stronger in light of recent events."

"That is true." Helena marveled that someone so caught up in the preparations for war could keep track of such a thing, or even think of her at such a time. "And Princess von Furstenberg asked me to stay to help, but . . ." Her voice trailed off as she realized that she was on dangerous ground.

"And why did you not? Surely that was the opportunity you had all been hoping for?"

"Well, Mama was set on coming to Brussels, and I could not allow her to make such a journey alone."

Her response was logical enough, but her averted eyes told him that this was not the real reason she had come to Brussels. At least he hoped it was not the only reason she had appeared magically before his eyes not fifty feet away from Wellington's headquarters, appeared as if in response to his own longing to see her. For he had been absolutely, excruciatingly honest when he had admitted to thinking of her constantly.

When Brett's carriage had rolled through the Schönbrunner Weg on the morning he had left Vienna in the company of several other officers on their way to Brussels, he had been glad to leave the Machiavellian atmosphere of the Congress far behind him, had been glad to be doing something at last. But that sense of satisfaction had soon worn off to be replaced by regret at not having anyone to share it with. Naturally he had passed the time during the journey discussing the recent turn of events with his companions, speculating as to what Napoleon would do, how it would affect all that the Congress had worked to accomplish. But no one's responses had come close to those that Helena would have offered. None of his fellow travelers had the perspective or the intelligence to place the events as part of the larger political picture or analyze the possible outcomes the way

she would have. And no one could have sympathized with his own feelings as he prepared to face once again the enemy he had been fighting against most of his life.

Yes, he had missed her. And now he wanted nothing more than to sweep her into his arms, hold her close, feel her heart beating against his, and to cover her face with kisses. Instead, he had to content himself with holding her hand, feeling its warmth and reassurance, its delicacy and strength, just as he felt the warmth of her smile and read the understanding in her eyes.

"Ah, Stanford, I see that you are not with your regiment. Are you still attached to the duke, then?" An officer wearing the uniform of the Household Brigade came up behind them and clapped Brett on the shoulder.

"Why, hello, Thorney. Yes. The duke has kept me on as an aide-de-camp, so I am stationed here, but you, Thorney, what about you?"

"Oh, we are bivouacked out toward Enghien, but I am sent to headquarters with reports. However, I shall also take the opportunity to treat myself to a decent meal." The officer cast a respectful but quizzical glance in Helena's direction.

"Ah, forgive me. Miss Devereux, this is Thorney, Captain William Thornton, another one of our veterans from the Peninsula."

"How do you do, Captain Thornton." Helena summoned up a polite smile, telling herself all the while that she was actually grateful for the interruption. "I can see that both of you have important business to attend to. I must not keep you." And nodding to both men, she turned and hurried off down the path to the Rue Montagne du Parc toward their apartments and the solitude of her own bedchamber.

The very thing she had feared had happened. She had seen him again and she knew that she was powerless to forget or ignore him. She had known the instant that all the joy and energy so lacking her life those past few weeks had surged back into her at the very sight of him that she had been right to fear the effect he had on her, the power he held over her heart and her mind. The question was, having confirmed her worst fears, what was she to do now?

Chapter Twenty-eight

Brett, on the other hand, suffered from no such indecision. He had spent the better part of a month assisting the duke, as best he could, form a fighting force worthy of taking on Napoleon and his armies. His knowledge of French had been invaluable in helping the allied command pull together a formidable Anglo Dutch Belgian force by dividing and mixing the troops so that every division was a blend of nationalities rather than one composed of individual national regiments governed by their individual loyalties and a dubious commitment to the duke or the allied cause.

But the endless negotiating, the endless training, the tiring rides with messages from commanding officers of one regiment to commanding officers of another had only served to convince Brett that he had at last found the one fixed point in his universe, the woman with whom he wished to spend the rest of his life, the woman who offered him at one and the same time a place of refuge and a continual source of challenge and inspiration. All that remained was to convince her of that.

When he had caught sight of Helena in the park, it had at first seemed such a heaven-sent opportunity that for a moment he was afraid that she was a mirage. But then she had turned around, and he knew it was the living breathing embodiment of his own dreams.

Brett had sensed the hesitation in her in spite of the eager light in her eyes and the shy welcome in her smile

when she recognized him, and he was determined to get to the bottom of it, to erase any possible barriers between them. He had admitted to Helena that he was concerned about the princess' feelings, but since he had left Vienna, no word had reached him from the Princess von Hohenbachern though Wellington and others were receiving communications from the Austrian capital almost daily. This had made him more certain than ever that his attractions, at least in the princess' eyes, had been eclipsed by those of other, more powerful men such as Talleyrand and Metternich.

However, in order to reassure himself, he made inquiries as to the direction of the von Hohenbachern household and presented himself in the Rue Montagne du Parc the very next day. The princess, who was alone, welcomed him cordially enough, but her manner, though charming as always, utterly lacked the flirtatious intimacy that had characterized it in Vienna.

"I am sorry that Helena is not here, for I am sure she would be delighted to see you, however, she has just stepped out." The princess smiled at him in the friendliest of fashions, but all the while she was watching him like a hawk for any reaction he might have to the mention of her daughter, and she was instantly rewarded by his look of disappointment.

He recovered almost immediately, but not before she was able to ascertain that it was her daughter, and her daughter only, who was the object of his call. "I am sorry to miss her. I hope you will convey my best wishes to her. In the meantime, I am delighted to see that you arrived safely and that, judging from your customary exquisite appearance, the journey was less arduous than one might have expected."

"You are too kind, Major. But stay awhile. I expect Helena back quite soon. In the meantime, do let me offer you some refreshment."

It was no difficult task to convince him to stay, eager as he was to see Helena, and in no short order, fortified by a glass of port, he was soon explaining to her Wellington's plans for the defense of the city.

Not a quarter of an hour later, steps were heard in the front hall and voices conversing eagerly in German.

A few minutes later, Helena and a distinguished-looking officer entered the room, arm in arm exchanging looks in a manner that showed them to be on the best of terms.

The princess cast one glance at the rigid expression on the major's face and nearly burst into laughter. So, the dashing Major Lord Brett Stanford had fallen in love with her daughter, had he? The debonair officer who not so many months ago had told her that jealousy was too fatiguing an emotion to waste a moment's thought on was now fairly bristling with it himself. The princess wanted to hug herself with delight. Would wonders never cease? "Major," she rose, smiling graciously, "may I present you to my husband, Prince von Hohenbachern, general of the von Hohenbachern regiments attached to Blücher's forces, now stationed here in Belgium." She nearly laughed out loud at the idiotic smile of relief that spread over the major's angular features.

"It is *my* pleasure, Major." The prince bowed. "A great pleasure to meet the man who so gallantly escorted both my ladies in Vienna." The prince too was arriving at his own interesting conclusions as he watched the delicate color tinge his stepdaughter's face and the sparkle come back into her eyes. It was not exhaustion after all, but love that had left her looking so wan and pale. Good. It was time she found a man worthy of her, a man who could make her happy, and this fine-looking English major certainly appeared to be an upstanding young man, provided he survived the next few weeks, provided they all survived the next few weeks. But fate would decide that.

The prince smiled warmly at Brett. "I wish I were able to further our acquaintance, Major, but at the moment I fear that Blücher expects me back at headquarters. I only stopped in to say hello to my wife after being out with Helena, and to assure myself that the carriage and horses are all in good order should they be required to go on a sudden journey. My dears, I shall see you again tomorrow, I hope, for I shall be back in town to discuss further troop dispositions with the rest of the Allied staff." The prince kissed his wife and stepdaughter, bowed to the major, and was gone before anyone could say anything.

"Well, Major, I do hope that you will not be equally precipitate in your departure. Oh, these dreadful times." The princess twisted the delicate handkerchief she was holding with uncharacteristic anxiety.

Brett's face grew grave. "I fear that I too must leave shortly. I only stopped by to inform you both that the French have crossed the Sambre, and to beg a moment alone with your daughter." He saw the princess' look of alarm. "Have no fear, Princess, the duke assures me that you will all be quite safe here. He has even urged the Duchess of Richmond to carry on with her plans for the ball, but it does mean that my services are needed elsewhere for a time, and so I came to say good-bye."

There was no mistaking the look in his eyes. Interpreting it correctly, the princess rose and held out her hand. "Good-bye, then, Major. Godspeed, and please return to us soon."

"I shall do my very best." He bowed over her hand, then straightened and nodded almost imperceptibly to the encouraging look he saw in her eyes.

The door closed softly behind her, and Brett turned to face Helena, who appeared to be somewhat bemused by the rapid pace of events and the sudden disappearance of both her stepfather and her mother.

"Helena," Brett gathered both her hands in his. "I know you are a woman of a most independent nature who entertains the greatest dislike for people who have the temerity or the arrogance to interfere with her life. Believe me, I had hoped not to have to do it this way, but events are such that . . . in short, will you do me the very great honor, and bring me great joy by saying you will be my wife?"

"Your what?" She gasped and stared at him as though she could not believe her ears. In fact, she looked so utterly dumbfounded that he could not help chuckling at her expression.

"Surely you must see how much we think alike, how many opinions and ideals we share. I, for one, can think of nothing better than spending my life sharing them all, and so much more with you."

"But . . . but . . ." Helena's mind was in such a turmoil that she did not know what to think. She had spent night

after night dreaming of his kiss, the strength and comfort of his arms around her, the warmth of his lips on hers, the passion in her that responded to his slightest touch. She had even longed for more, but in all her wildest dreams, she had never thought of this! "But, but, Mama says that you are the sort of man who needs a great many women," was all she could manage to gasp.

Brett smiled grimly. "In many instances your mother knows a great deal about the world, but not in this one. Do you think she would have left you alone with me even for a moment if she had not known what was on my mind, had not known that I love you? No, I think that your mother understood, maybe even before I at last realized it, that I went from one woman to the next in the hopes that I could find someone I could truly love. But it had been so long, and I had known so many women over the years that I had begun to think it was futile, to think that what I was looking for in fact did not exist. I even began to doubt that love itself existed—until I met you. Then I knew. It was not that I did not believe in love or that I ignored it, I had just never met the woman that I could love. Now that I have found her, I want nothing more than to spend my life with her.

Helena pressed her fingers to her temples and sank into a chair. It was all happening too fast. She did not know what to think. He spoke of love, and when she looked into his eyes and saw the light in them shining just for her, she believed him. She loved him in return, deeply, agonizingly, with her entire being. But so had her mother been in love—time and time again. And her mother had been hurt time and time again, until at last she had met someone who had never claimed to love her, but promised to take care of her because he needed her to take care of his infant daughters. And that bargain, made without love on either side, had lasted longer and brought more stability into all their lives than all the passionate affairs her mother had flung herself into headlong.

She believed him and yet she doubted him. At the moment she knew that what he said was quite possibly true, and that he believed it wholeheartedly himself. But he could not know that he would always feel that way.

Helena's eyes filled with tears. Her mind told her that such happiness could not last, but at the same time, her heart wanted desperately to believe that it could.

Brett felt the uncertainty tormenting her. He wanted to say something, do something that would convince her, as he himself was now convinced that it was absolutely the right thing to do, but he could not. He could not *make* her see anything, *make* her do anything. He knew her too well. She was too independent, too accustomed to relying on her own intelligence for him to make up her mind for her.

Gently he pulled her to her feet cupping her face in his hands. "Do not fret, my love. I should have never rushed you into thinking of such things except that I shall be rather busy for a while. But I want you to know that I am yours . . . forever. That is all. You do not need to worry about the rest." Softly, he kissed her on the forehead and then headed toward the door.

He had not gotten more than a few steps when she whispered, "Brett?"

He turned around and she flung herself into his arms. They closed around her and he kissed her until she was breathless, until she wrapped her own arms around his neck, until her lips clung to his as though her life depended on it.

"Brett." She pulled away at last to look up at him, her eyes bright with unshed tears. "Do be careful."

He grinned. "Of course I will. I always am, else you would never have met me. I love you."

"And I love you too."

He held her close, savoring every detail, storing it in his mind forever, the soft touch of her hair on his cheek, the faint scent of rose water, the beating of her heart, the tenderness of her hands caressing his face, the intelligence and understanding in her eyes, and the sweet curve of her lips. At last he sighed and set her away from him. "And that is all that matters. Remember always that I love you."

Then he was gone. And she was left alone to stare blindly after him out of the window, watching as the tall figure strode down the Rue Montagne du Parc toward headquarters.

Chapter Twenty-nine

The princess found her daughter some time later sitting alone in the salon. Helena was still staring out of the window as though her soul had just taken flight and escaped through it.

Her mother sighed gently and went to fetch a cashmere shawl, which she draped around her daughter's shoulders. Whatever had passed between her daughter and Major Lord Brett Stanford, there was nothing left to do now, nothing left but wait and pray.

And wait they did, for every scrap of news they could glean. Fortunately for them, their neighbor, the Marquis of Juarenais seemed always to be a fount of information and the first to know the latest news. It was he who told them that the Prussians had been driven out of Charleroi by the French and explained that the distant sound of cannonading they had heard the next day came from the battle at Quatre Bras, where the Duke of Brunswick had been slain.

The princess had turned pale at the news, but Helena had hastened to reassure her. "I am sure that if anything had happened to papa, you would be the first to know."

"Perhaps." The princess sank back down into the chair she had risen from when the marquis had first entered their salon full of the news. "And what do they say of the rest of the forces, monsieur?"

The marquis shook his head slowly. He departed, only to return the next day with the information that Blücher

had been soundly beaten by Bonaparte and was in full retreat. The marquis urged them to pack their belongings and join the crowd of refugees fleeing toward Antwerp and the boats that could take them to England. "You know that is what your husband would wish you to do," he encouraged the princess.

The marquis' wife seconded her husband's opinion. "You told me yourself, madame, that the Prince von Hohenbachern made sure that the horses and carriage were all in order, in case of just such an emergency, and believe me, this is an emergency."

But the princess shook her head. "No, I must be here when he returns, whatever happens. And I am sure that Helena feels the same."

Helena swallowed hard and nodded, her throat too tight to speak. She had spent two sleepless nights worrying about Brett as she listened to the sounds of marching feet, the rumble of baggage wagons, and the steady clop of hooves as the troops moved out of the city toward the approaching French. And she had listened with her heart in her mouth to the distant cannonading, cursing herself for being a fool. How could she have sent Brett off the way she had? Why had she been so afraid to say that she would spend the rest of her life with him? What if there were no life to spend, and she had sent him off with nothing more than *I love you*?

The reports slowly filtered in, but they were so conflicting as to be useless. Still, the troops, baggage, and horses kept moving away from the city, making their way down the Rue Namur, which was choked with traffic, far into that night and the following one. Horses were bivouacked all around the park, and that night it became clear that there was to be a battle fought the next day that would be so desperate it would make the other engagements they had heard about appear like the merest skirmishes.

Helena stayed at the salon windows most of the night, watching the troops move slowly by, hoping to catch a glimpse of one particular horseman, though in the press of troops she knew it was a vain hope.

It did not seem as though she slept at all, but somehow, she found herself uncomfortably awakened by the

pale light of dawn, having fallen asleep in a chair by the window. She rose and went to her bedchamber to splash cold water on her face; however, she could not touch the rolls Hannechen had brought her for breakfast.

"Please, mademoiselle. Your mother says you must eat something," the maid insisted.

"Very well." Too worried and preoccupied to argue, Helena drank a cup of chocolate before returning to her seat by the window where her mother soon joined her.

"There continues to be a great deal of movement in the streets, but I still cannot be sure what is happening." The princess peered off in the distance, but saw nothing that helped answer her question.

They both sat tense and quiet for what seemed like hours, until finally the booming of cannon could be heard off in the direction that the troops had been moving, beyond the Porte Namur.

And soon the trickle of wounded began to return to the city. The trickle became a stream and then a veritable tide. Helena rose to her feet. "I cannot bear this any longer. I cannot just sit here wondering what has happened, if he is hurt or . . . I must *do* something. I am going to see what I can do to help these poor fellows just as I hope someone would help Brett . . . or Papa."

She went off to find Hannechen, and for the next few hours they gathered up all the lint in the house, searched out and tore up every available scrap of material that could be used for bandages. Then they headed out to offer any assistance needed, Helena carrying the bandages and her maid following her with buckets of water.

They did not have far to go. Wounded and exhausted soldiers straggled through the streets, collapsing in doorways and leaning up against any sheltering wall they could find.

The rest of the interminable day passed in a blur as Helena and Hannechen cleaned and dressed wounds as best they could, poured water into parched throats and distributed foods to those who had the strength to eat. As she bandaged wounds and gently wiped brows furrowed with exhaustion and pain, Helena tried to push all thoughts of another soldier from her mind. Was he lying hurt somewhere on the field, or, worse yet, dead?

And if he were dead, what use would her life be without him? Now she marveled at herself, marveled that she had tried to protect herself from hurt by denying how much she loved him, how much he meant to her. How silly that denial seemed now. What did it matter if she were hurt in the end? At least she would have been happy, felt that her life was full for a little while. Without him, her life was no life anyway, whether he were killed or whether she sent him away to protect her precious independence. If he survived and came back to her, she resolved to be with him, despite her fears of being left alone in the long run. Any time with him at all was precious. She would take anything she could get even if by doing so she was courting the possibility of being hurt in the end.

Day faded into evening and still the wounded kept coming. Helena was practically fainting with exhaustion herself when a wounded officer of the guards staggered to their very doorstep. She and Hannechen led him into the kitchen, where they began to bandage the saber cut on his head and another wound on his arm where the flesh had been torn by a spent bullet.

"Thank you, ladies," he gasped as he swallowed the cup of brandy Hannechen held to his lips. "Thank God they are at last in retreat, for I have never seen a fiercer fighting in all my days."

"They are in retreat you say?"

The soldier mustered a weary smile at the eager note in Helena's voice. "I should think so, my lady. It was about half past four when the duke himself was in our square, and he asked one of his aides what time it was. On being told it was nearly half past four, he responded, *The battle is mine: and if the Prussians arrive soon, there will be an end to the war.*" It was not long after that, around five o'clock, I think, that we were given the order to charge. We were up against the Imperial Guards themselves, but we ran down the slope at them and soon had them in full retreat. It was then that I got this." He pointed ruefully to the saber cut. "And I thank you for fixing me up right and tight. I shall just have another swig of brandy if you can spare it, and then I shall be off." He took another long drink from the cup and then,

before either Helena or Hannechen could stop him, headed back toward the Porte Namur.

It was at that point Helena laid down the bowl of water and bandages. "Here, Hannechen. Do what you can for them. I am going to saddle up Nimrod, and then I am going myself to see . . . to see." Tears clouded her eyes and the lump in her throat made it impossible to say more, but the maid understood. She had watched her mistress tending the wounded tirelessly all day, and she knew that to her mistress, every man she bandaged, every man to whom she gave a drink was one in the same. They were all Major Lord Brett Stanford.

"But, Helena, you cannot go. A young lady wandering about the battlefield all alone in the middle of the night." The princess was horrified to discover her daughter donning her riding habit a few minutes later.

"It is not the middle of the night, Mama, and besides, there are wives, mothers, daughters, sweethearts, and family members of every description going out there to look for their loved ones. Do not worry, I shall take Hans with me. I am also taking Nimrod with me in case he is wounded. The road is far too crowded for any hope of a carriage being able to get through, otherwise I would take that."

"I understand, my dear, believe me I do." The princess' voice broke as she laid a hand on her daughter's shoulder. "But you do not even know where to look."

"I *will* find him, Mama." Helena gave her mother a brief swift hug and then she was off, accompanied by the burly footman, to join the crowd making its way toward the Porte Namur.

She stopped first at headquarters to see if she could learn anything at all about Brett's whereabouts, but beyond the vague intelligence that he had been assigned to carry dispatches between General Maitland and the duke and the general disposition of Maitland's troops on the battlefield, she could learn nothing further. "Then that will have to do." Helena remounted Nimrod and they headed off, keeping to the side of the road, for the road itself was so crowded with wagons, carts, and carriages full of wounded as to be impassable.

Every half a mile or so she would stop and inquire of

a wagonload of wounded the spot where General Maitland
and his troops had last been seen until she had almost
arrived at Mont St. Jean itself. Clouds of acrid smoke from
the guns still hung in the air and through it, she could just
barely make out the forms of other searchers silhouetted
against the glow of the campfires that were being lit here
and there. The moans of the wounded and the heaps of
bodies—horses and men—were almost more than she
could bear, but she kept on steadily, asking whomever she
could if they had seen an aide-de-camp wearing the uniform of a major in the First Hussars carrying dispatches
between Maitland and his commander in chief.

She was almost at the place that the injured soldier
back in Brussels had described as being the site of the
final charge, and feeling herself nearly overwhelmed by
the vastness of the scene before her, the hopelessness of
it all, and the futility of her own quest, she was beginning
to doubt that she would find Brett when Nimrod snorted
and pricked up his ears. Helena looked up to see a horse
approaching, its rider slumped forward over its neck.

There was something about the arch of the animal's
neck and its powerful hindquarters that looked faintly
familiar. "Rex!" She was barely conscious of having said
anything, but the approaching horse flicked its own ears
and snorted in return.

"Rex. Oh, Rex." She urged Nimrod forward until she
could see for certain that it was indeed Rex. But could
the poor limp body draped across his back belong to
Brett? Surely not.

Helena jumped down, thrust the reins at Hans, and
hurried over to Rex's side. There was blood running
down the soldier's face from a cut in his temple and a
dark stain around a ragged hole in his shoulder, but it
was indeed Brett. She grabbed his hand, feeling frantically for a pulse. At least it was still warm, but either
the pulse was too weak or she was too distraught to
detect it. "Brett, Brett, my love, please do not die now.
Please. I love you."

She reached up gently to touch his face, desperately
searching for any sign of life. She held her hand in front
of his lips, surely there was breath coming from them.

Then as her fingertips touched his lips, his eyelids fluttered.

"Brett, Brett, please tell me that you are alive."

The eyelids opened and the lips formed themselves into a tired smile. "Helena." It was more a statement than a question.

Slowly through the fog of pain and exhaustion, he had heard someone speaking his name. At first he had thought it was his own disordered mind telling him what he wanted to hear, but the voice grew more insistent. He forced himself to focus on the direction it was coming from and, with his last ounce of energy, opened his eyes to find, against all odds, Helena looking up at him.

He had survived the hell of smoke and heat, the thunder of massive charges, the thud of cannon balls raining down from overhead, the whistle of shots around him, but only barely. And toward the end, when he had been almost too tired to hold the reins, faint with exhaustion and light-headed from thirst, the only thing that had kept him going had been the thought of her. It was the hope of living out the rest of his days with the woman he loved that had kept him alive, kept him focused enough to duck his head as stray shots whizzed over it, gave him the strength to carry his messages back and forth as one after another of Wellington's other aides were killed or carried off the field. It was only at the very end, when he had allowed himself to be distracted for a moment that he had felt the dull thud in his shoulder which slowly blossomed into a pain that threatened to overwhelm his entire body.

"Go on, man, you have been hit," one of Maitland's aides had exclaimed. "The battle is almost won; get off the field before you get yourself killed."

Brett had been about to protest when the troops had suddenly massed and charged, leaving him far behind as blackness overtook him.

When he had come to, the battle had moved far beyond him. The light was fading and he knew his usefulness had ended. And, not wishing to trouble the overworked surgeons in the field hospitals, he had turned Rex toward Brussels and headed back to head-

quarters in the hopes of at least finding a bed to collapse in.

But as he rode, the loss of blood made him grow more and more faint, and the reality of the battlefield had faded into dreams of her—her smile, her laugh, her touch—until suddenly, there she was smiling and kissing him, and telling him she loved him.

It was the shock of pain that woke him fully to reality. "Damn and blast." Brett at last shook his head, grabbed Rex's reins, and struggled upright. If he did not fight off the unconsciousness that kept threatening to overwhelm him, he would never make it to Brussels, malingerer that he was.

"You must dismount so that I can look at it."

Brett looked down in astonishment. "Helena! It really is you."

"Yes, it is. I thought you knew it was. Now, Brett, you must let me bind your wound before you lose any more blood. Hans will help you down."

"Damn Hans." He slid off Rex's back and, wincing fiercely, put his arms around her. "It *is* you. I love you so."

"And I love you." She was smiling through the tears that were pouring down her cheeks. "But I will love you more if you allow me to tie this up, take you home, and see that you are properly taken care of."

"Take me home—a dream come true." He leaned his head on Rex's shoulder and gratefully took a swig of brandy from the flask she handed him while she bound his shoulder as best she could and wrapped a bandage around his head.

Mounting again, however, was an altogether different story, and as Hans shoved him back up into the saddle, he fainted from the pain and exertion of it all. But revived somewhat by the brandy, he soon made it back to a semiconscious state, in which he was just enough awake to cling to Rex as they made their way slowly back to the city.

Chapter Thirty

The faintest shade of gray was softening the eastern sky as they finally made their weary way down the Rue Montagne du Parc to the von Hohenbachern apartments, where the candlelight could still be seen through the windows and the princess was eagerly awaiting them in the salon.

"You found him!" She exclaimed hugging her daughter to her. "I knew you would. Potten has seen to it that all is in readiness. The spare bedchamber has been prepared and Cook awaits instructions."

Helena's eyes filled with tears for the hundredth time that evening. In the end, her mother had had more faith than she had. The princess had given orders for preparations to welcome the major home when her daughter would not even trust herself to hope that she would find him alive.

The wounded man, worn out by the effort of clinging to his horse, had collapsed completely, and he did not even stir as Hans and the coachman carried him to bed.

The princess gave her daughter's arm a reassuring squeeze. "He is worn out from the exhaustion more than anything. Trust me, I was married to a man who sat at the gaming tables for days on end before coming home to collapse, I know the signs. His color is good, his breathing is steady. Give him a full day of sleep and mark my words, in spite of his wound, he will be wanting to be back on duty. You, my dear, should do the same

and get some rest. It would never do to have him wake at last only to find you looking so hagged." She read the stubbornness in her daughter's face. "Very well. But at least allow Hannechen to help you on with a fresh gown. Take it from me, no matter how much a man loves a woman, he is always put in a more cheerful frame of mind when she is pleasant to look upon, and he will not wake up anytime soon, I assure you." She shook her head at the unyielding set of her daughter's jaw. "I promise you, I shall watch over him until you return. And mind you, wash your face," she added in after-thought, but Helena had already left the room.

The princess was correct; Brett did sleep all the next day and the following night, oblivious to the sound of visitors who called in the Rue Montagne du Parc full of news of the battle or to the pounding on the door by the courier who came with a message for the princess that her husband was safe. Having fought with Blücher, he had been present when the general met up with Wellington at La Belle Alliance, and then he had joined the Prussians in their pursuit of Bonaparte, but he had first taken time out to scribble a note to his wife and step-daughter, assuring them of his safety.

During all this, Helena was content simply to sit at the major's bedside and watch him sleep. The Marquis of Juarenais had managed to convince the surgeon who had been at the Juarenais' apartments examining General Sir Charles Alten to take a look at Brett. The surgeon quickly seconded the princess' opinion that what the major needed most was sleep.

"You have cleaned the wound thoroughly, and he is a fine healthy man who did not suffer from the exposure to the elements or the fetid air of the field hospitals as so many have," the surgeon reassured them. "He should heal nicely if he is kept warm and allowed to get the rest he needs and"—his fierce dark eyes twinkled at Helena from under craggy brows—"when he awakes to see you at his side, he will recover even faster."

Brett woke at last on the evening of the second day after she had brought him home. Hearing the rustle of the sheet, Helena bent over him as he turned his head

toward her. Opening his eyes, he smiled. "Not a dream," he whispered, reached for her hand, and fell promptly asleep again.

She sat for hours holding his hand in her lap, not daring to move a muscle for fear of waking him. Who would have thought that holding a man's hand would be the sum of all her hopes and dreams? But she thanked Providence for having seen him safely through it all so that she could.

In her darkest hour, Helena had admitted to herself that life without him was no life at all, and now, just knowing that he was alive and safe brought her more happiness than she had ever thought possible. And she too fell asleep at last holding his hand.

When next she woke, daylight was streaming into the room and he lay there, propped up on his pillows, watching her, a curiously reverent expression lighting up the deep blue eyes. "I suppose it is never too late to believe in angels." He smiled at her. "Only an angel would have risked her life to find me."

"The battle was over. There was little danger." Helena found it oddly difficult to accept his gratitude.

"There was danger all around, and you know it. How can a woman risk her life to come find me, yet not have the courage to risk becoming my wife?"

Helena flushed uncomfortably. "It is not a matter of courage. It is just that . . ."

"Just that what?"

"I, I have always had other plans, plans that did not require a man to bring them about."

"I know. The school where you will teach young women to take care of themselves so that they will have no need for men. But what if there are men who happen to love them, men they happen to love in return? Is it not possible, that even if they do not require these men to make their plans happen, they could include the men in these plans?"

Helena twisted the ribbons of her jonquil sarcenet morning dress in her hands. "I do not know. I mean, I had not thought."

He raised a quizzical eyebrow. "And what if these

women wish to have daughters of their own who can follow the splendid examples of their mothers to grow into independent young women themselves?"

Brett reached over to clasp her hand in his. "Did it never occur to you, Helena, that as a man who is madly in love with a highly intelligent and self-reliant woman, that I might someday hope to have daughters who are equally as intelligent and self-reliant as their mother? And," he delivered his final shot, "one can be both a schoolmistress and a wife, you know, even a schoolmistress, a wife, and a mother."

Tears rose in her eyes. It all sounded too perfect, too good to be true. Love could lead people into harboring the most unrealistic hopes and dreams that only brought hurt and disappointment when they faded away into reality. Why her own mother . . .

"Helena." As if reading her daughter's thoughts, the princess spoke up from the doorway, where she had been standing watching her daughter.

"Yes, Mama?"

"I know that what you have seen of my life has had a great effect on yours. You resolved never to be like me, never to suffer from the illusions that continually brought me unhappiness. You were going to avoid all that, to look to yourself to fulfill your every need. But I have learned a great deal over the years. And what I have learned is that there can be no greater happiness than being married to a good man who loves you." She turned to smile at the prince, who stood behind her. "Do not lose that chance for happiness, my dear."

"I won't, Mama, I pro . . ." but Helena was allowed to say no more as one strong arm pulled her down toward him, and Brett's lips claimed hers in a way that drove all doubts from her mind.

She loved him. He loved her. And in the end, that was all that mattered, all that had ever mattered.